MEN

Lara Santiago

EROTIC ROMANCE

Siren Publishing, Inc.
www.SirenPublishing.com

A SIREN PUBLISHING BOOK
IMPRINT: Erotic Romance

MENAGERIE
Copyright © 2008 by Lara Santiago

ISBN-10: 1-60601-188-X
ISBN-13: 978-1-60601-188-1

First Printing: August 2008

Cover design by Jinger Heaston
All cover art and logo copyright © 2008 by Siren Publishing, Inc.

Printed in the U.S.A.

PUBLISHER
Siren Publishing, Inc.
www.SirenPublishing.com

DEDICATION

I'd like to dedicate this book to all the important boys in my life. You know who you are.

Lara Santiago

MENAGERIE

Lara Santiago
Copyright © 2008

Prologue

Valerie Thornhill despised jogging. She loathed exercise in absolutely any form. Most of all, she hated the fact that she truly needed to do it.

The pain she experienced while working out started with the first jarring step. Today's effort was no different as she stepped on the gravel pathway entering the local park.

Shooting spasms of agony crawled from her running shoe-clad feet to her legs to her chest and married up with the other ache lodged around her heart.

The steady pain in Valerie's chest grew to epic proportions of constriction with each step she took along the park's trail in an effort to get in shape. It was as if some invisible force with a large hand had a firm grip on her heart and squeezed it mercilessly in its steely grasp.

The apprehension strangling her insides was easily explained, and not all of it had to do with exercise, but it hurt all the same. She ignored the discomfort and pressed on in a vain pursuit of health.

Anxiety. That's all it was. Her mother was coming for a visit next month and Valerie knew her destiny in those two weeks would be fraught with repeated lectures of disappointment because Valerie hadn't snagged a husband yet.

Her mother was ever hopeful, but unfortunately, Valerie hadn't found any man that made her heart race with a single glance. She'd spent her time with toad after blind-date toad and honestly, not one had seemed worth the effort of compromising the single attribute that Valerie insisted upon. She wanted attraction. Inescapable, heart-pounding, immediate attraction. She wanted her socks knocked off with a single glance. *What was wrong with that?*

Her mother insisted that she was too picky. Whatever. Perhaps her mother was right. It wasn't like Valerie's unyielding search for a perfect, compelling mate was keeping her warm at night.

Valerie knew that whatever perfect man she one day found to love wouldn't care how she looked nearly as much as her mother did. Instead of this vigorous activity, she'd rather be taking a nap. Her job as a corporate accountant was stressful enough throughout the work week. Valerie enjoyed her time off on the weekend. Sunday afternoon would definitely be better spent wrapped in a comforter watching fragments of television shows in between naps instead of this run.

Today's jog in the park was solely because of guilt and fate. Guilt because in two weeks her mother would remind her that she needed to lose twenty-five pounds to attract a suitable man, and fate because she was destined not to lose an ounce before her mother's arrival unless she got moving.

Picking up the pace, Valerie jogged along in her gray sweat suit, and considered the looming visit from her parents. Her dad wasn't any problem, but her mother. She closed her eyes momentarily. The crushing sensation in her chest increased to the point where it became almost unbearable. *Happy thoughts.* The very air around her thickened as she drew in a heaving breath. The tang of flavor she tasted suggested it was about to rain.

Lifting her head in hope, she searched the endlessly clear blue skies for a reprieve to this abhorrent exercise. A sudden rain shower would force her inside. Not a single cloud graced the skies to end her torture, but a tingle ran across her skin and another deep breath brought the same thick ozone flavor into her lungs.

Was something about to happen?

Something...shocking?

Valerie brushed a strand of hair away from her face, tucking it behind one ear, and endeavored to calm her fanciful mind. The wind picked up and blew a piece of paper across her path, where it plastered flat against an outdoor wire trash can.

The paper had a picture of a buff, half-naked man on it with the partially hidden caption revealing only *escort service* and below that was part of a phone number. She imagined the covered part started with the numbers one dash nine hundred.

Hmm. Now there was an idea she could toy with for the rest of her reviled exercise period. She'd hire a delectable man as potential matrimonial arm candy for the duration of her mother's visit and then not only would she not need to diet or exercise, she could make a visit with her mother go by faster and much more pleasantly.

How much did two weeks worth of suitable marrying-man arm candy cost in today's market, she wondered, a smile creeping up.

Probably every dime she had in her savings, checking account and retirement IRAs. The right man would likely be worth every cent.

Valerie trudged along thinking that the fantasy was way too expensive for her meager budget, but still fun to contemplate.

One plodding, slow step at a time on the park's seemingly endless trail, she approached her least favorite section. There was a small hill just ahead. It was a steeper, more difficult climb for someone as out of shape as she was and besides, it ran parallel to the four-lane highway for about a hundred feet down an embankment. Traffic noise aside, she also hated the smell of diesel fumes that wafted across this part of the path.

Convinced that breathing it in would be harmful to her health, she always held her breath for as long as possible when she ran alongside the road.

At least until she felt faint, which was probably only seconds. As always, she ended up sucking in gobs of nasty road smell, without a doubt enough to put her on the ground from lack of oxygen.

Valerie's steps slowed as she hiked up the incline and when she got within steps of seeing the road, she heard what she thought sounded like...gunfire. A car wouldn't backfire that fast and so many times, would it?

Like a looky-loo at an accident site, Valerie couldn't keep from turning towards the road to identify the sound. Expecting to see a drive-by shooting in progress, she was surprised to see two motorcycles approaching. One was black. One was silver.

The silver rider, driving one-handed and located approximately a car length behind the black rider, held what looked like a small black oversized pistol. She's never held a gun of any kind in her life, but it looked like a fancy weapon from one of the action movies she'd been forced to endure on those blind date-toad fests of her past..

Visible plumes of carbon monoxide floated up from the road as Valerie watched the silver rider raise his gun arm and spray the black motorcycle with gunfire from the weapon. The black rider bobbled his motorcycle onto the paved shoulder of road, lost his balance and slid sideways with a screech of metal on asphalt into the foliage covering the embankment parallel to where Valerie had slowed to watch.

The silver rider continued firing and the arc of his weapon headed in her direction. Valerie realized, with dreadful insight, that she was about to be mowed down as an innocent bystander in a drive-by shooting.

Valerie also realized that she still held her breath. The curtain of black crowded her vision from lack of oxygen. She went down hard on her knees before flattening out on the pea gravel face down. Dusty air was quickly sucked into her lungs. She didn't even have the strength to cough.

Her last rational thought before unconsciousness was that her mother was going to be totally pissed if Valerie kicked the bucket while flat on her face, in the dirt, wearing a drab gray jogging suit, and still unmarried.

* * * *

"How many humans were brought aboard during this passage by Earth?" Golden asked.

Blue checked a digital flat board even though he undoubtedly knew the answer from memory. "The total for the eighty-one-day period in orbit is nine-hundred and sixteen."

Golden sighed. "That's more than twice what we had during the last trip."

"Yes, sir. The humans have reproduced at a higher rate than predicted from our last notation. Plus, the target area is more concentrated with human activity."

"With the newly installed living chamber, there is at least enough room for all of them this time. Has the ratio of males to females altered?"

Again, Blue checked his statistics and responded without looking him directly in the eyes., "Yes. With the current displacement equation, men outnumber women by a five-to-one ratio."

Golden closed his eyes, "That's worse. How do you account for this anomaly?"

"The humans have advanced to a greater technological state than previously anticipated. Plus, their lives are inherently more complex than before as a result. It was to be expected."

"Undoubtedly. However, we'll have to adjust the orientation content to explain."

Blue looked horrified. "Do we have the time for that, sir?"

"Make time. Otherwise, it'll be a long three years of unparalleled chaos."

"It likely will be anyway," Blue murmured under his breath.

Golden agreed and mentally prepared for the pandemonium that was about to begin with the new crop of accidental human passengers.

Chapter 1

"...is why the men here need sex." An unrecognized voice echoed in Valerie's sluggish brain.

Join the club, she thought, rousing further. She opened her eyes and realized she was sitting in a very uncomfortable chair.

"Therefore, after the gauntlet arena selection, you will be required to have sex with each one of the men in your selected group at least once every two months so that they won't die a painful death," the blue alien standing before her said in a stern tone.

Valerie was no longer face down in the dirt. She was no longer outdoors. Lifting her head slowly, she quickly realized she was also no longer alone. Half slumped in a hard metal chair, she straightened and stretched the kinks out of her back. After several satisfying pops, she resisted the urge to yawn.

Where am I?

Looking first to her right, she noticed fifteen or so other shell-shocked-looking women in various stages of dress. To her left was much the same view. There was one poor soul wearing only a bra and panties. But another was in a full fledged business suit complete with patterned pantyhose and stilettos. The others in the room looked like they'd been pulled from backstage at a play between acts.

Valerie looked down at her boring gray sweats. At least she wasn't in her underwear like half the women in the room.

The blue alien looked like a body builder that had been dipped in cerulean paint. He cleared his throat and all the women in the room sent their gaze forward. No one in the room spoke.

The grimace forming on his face wasn't attractive and bordered on hostile. He stared as if he was waiting for something from them. Valerie had no idea what it could be and resisted the urge to yawn, certain it wasn't the response he searched for. She wished she hadn't missed the first part of what he'd said.

"Don't any of you have questions?" he asked. "I usually get a lot of questions."

Valerie raised her hand. The blue alien man's expression softened. He pointed at her and gestured that she stand.

She sighed deeply and stood. Over a sea of heads seated in the several rows of chairs in front of her, Valerie fixed her gaze on the strange blue man waiting with eyebrows lifted for her question.

"What was your name again?"

He stiffened. "You may call me, Blue. What is your question? Or was that it?"

Valerie paused at his name. His skin was blue and his name was Blue? *Whatever.*

"We haven't got all day," he remarked and glanced at his clipboard thing.

"You want me to do what with a group of strange men?"

He sent a piercing stare through her, crossed his substantial arms over his chest and the hostile expression returned. "Haven't you been listening?"

Blue, the alien with the Smurf-blue skin, looked like he'd fallen into a vat of sapphire dye and soaked for awhile. Maybe that's why he was so grumpy. His hair was dark brown along with his thick eyebrows and his eyes were also brown. He wore snug pants and no shirt.

"Well, sure, to part of it, but..." she trailed off and sat back down.

Was she dreaming? If so, wouldn't she be the one in her underwear being called to task in the classroom?

"Have *any* of you been listening?" he railed and sent another stern gaze drilling to several of the other women.

No one else said a word. Perhaps they were all as confused as she was.

Valerie decided that this was the single most vivid dream she'd ever had, and the strangest. She felt like she'd come into the middle of a movie. Only she didn't remember how she got here or where she'd been before being seated at the back of the class. Someone else must have put her here, because if she'd seated herself, she would have been in the front row. Definitely a dream.

She sent her gaze forward again. Blue's expression hadn't changed from annoyance. A couple of phrases brushed her memory. *Gauntlet arena with groups of men* and *have sex with each of them*. If she'd remembered correctly.

Yeah. Like that would really happen. She barely knew what to do with one man let alone a group of them. The rest of the women seated around her seemed even less enthusiastic.

"Don't any of you have anything to say?"

No one responded.

The few women standing along the edges of the room, possibly due to the inadequate seating, seemed equally shocked into speechlessness by Blue's words. Perhaps it was a group dream.

Blue sighed deeply, as if he were dealing with children who were too ignorant to comprehend his words. "Don't you understand? There are never enough women to go around when you are brought here, so the men have to share. They suffer if they have to go without sex for that long in this environment. Do you want them to suffer?" He looked around the room, making eye contact with several of the attendees. "Well, do you?"

Like sheep afraid to stand up for themselves, they all began to shake their heads. Valerie didn't respond. She didn't particularly care about the suffering of strange horny men. It was a stupid dream, and therefore no participation was required.

"Now, we haven't much time, as we are running behind schedule. I don't have time to repeat myself. Therefore, we'll take you through orientation quickly and then bring you right to the beginner's gauntlet arena. It's a little quieter than the advanced one. Hopefully you can learn what you need to know along the way."

A woman to Valerie's right, who'd obviously been in the middle of putting make-up on and dressed completely in beige, raised her hand. "How many men are in a group?"

Blue nodded and the frown disappeared as if he'd finally heard a worthy question. "It varies. Never more than seven and no less than four. The average is five."

Valerie looked down at her gray jogging suit, wishing she'd managed to conjure up a nicer outfit for this dream. If she were about to meet men, a sweat suit wasn't exactly the most flattering clothing she could have worn.

Blue was talking again, but Valerie missed it due to her perusal of the unusual fashion statements being made around her. What did her clothing say about her? Was she an exercise geek? She sincerely hoped not.

The nebulous feeling in her brain wouldn't allow her to remember specifics of her life. She guessed it wasn't really important in the dream world.

"...come along now to the next station and all the important facts will be explained in greater detail. You can make your decision then. Stay together. Don't wander off."

Blue headed towards the only door in the room and the other women followed, one after the other, until the room emptied.

Valerie ended up at the end of the line with one of the business-suited ladies directly ahead of her. She followed along down a narrow white hallway, looking all around for a clue as to where she might be. The walls seemed to be constructed of white panels with lights hidden inside. Didn't you usually dream about places that were familiar? Apparently not, because this place was totally alien.

Up ahead on the right, a panel had dislodged as if the wall had been hastily constructed. Through the gap, Valerie could see another hallway and she slowed to peek through. She lost sight of the business suit she was following to wrestle the panel open further.

After a little effort she was through the narrow space and into a much wider hallway. The color of the lights in this hall were varying hues of aqua. She liked this hallway much better. The color was more soothing.

Valerie chose to walk to the left because the hall was longer in that direction, and seemed to go farther. After walking for several minutes, she heard voices. She rounded a corner and plowed into someone.

A tall, male someone.

"I'm sorry. I didn't see you," said a totally luscious, deep male voice over her head. There was another man standing next to him, but Valerie couldn't tear herself away to get a look. The man she'd run into felt too good.

"I don't mind." Valerie grabbed his arms and laid her forehead on his chest. He smelled delicious. Taking a deep breath, she tilted her head up to check out his face. Wide shoulders led to a square jaw and he had a cleft in his chin, too. Focusing in on his vivid, saltwater-blue eyes last of all, she noted that he was completely gorgeous.

Valerie had read somewhere that dreams were thought to be the brain's way of cataloging information gathered during each day of the dreamer's life. She must have seen this hunk at the park or something and filed him away for later dreaming. He'd been worth the wait. Now in this dream, she could do anything that she wanted to with him.

Plus, she had the benefit of a better personality. In dreams she was always funnier, smarter and definitely prettier.

A bemused smile greeted her as she stared. He gripped her shoulders, squeezing gently. "Are you on your way to the gauntlet arena?"

Valerie scrunched her eyebrows. Hadn't that blue alien guy said something about an arena and a gauntlet?

"Is that where you're going?" she asked.

He nodded. "That's where I'm headed."

"Me too. Maybe we could walk together." She was prepared to say anything to keep this guy interested.

He exchanged amused glances with the man standing next to him and asked, "Are you spoken for yet?"

"I don't think so. How would I know for sure?"

"Have you selected any man from the gauntlet arena?"

"No." Valerie frowned. "What's that gauntlet arena thing again?" Better to get her answers from this hunk than a hostile blue alien.

He narrowed his eyes, then explained. "The gauntlet arena is a large room filled with men seeking a partner. When you enter and walk down the gauntlet aisle, the interested men will step forward and try to get your attention." He looked her up and down. "I expect you'll garner a lot of attention."

"Why?" His interested appraisal brought a grin to her lips. In her non-dream life she seldom rated a single look of interest from the men she came into contact with on a day-to-day basis. Attractive men like the man before her never saw her at all.

He smiled in return. "Well, first of all, you're a blonde. It's rare in this place, for some unexplained reason. And second of all," his eyes ran down her body with definite interest once again, "you aren't frighteningly skinny like the majority of the women here."

Valerie frowned and looked down at her crappy jogging suit. And while she'd always dreamed of being frighteningly skinny, she'd also always considered herself pleasingly plump. "Does that mean you think I'm fat?"

His eyes widened with panic. "No. Of course not. I meant absolutely no insult. It's just that the slightly curvier women are, well, more kindhearted in this place." He leaned in and whispered confidentially, "The bony, skinny ones are mean. It's not their fault. It has something to do with the alien vortex process when they're brought aboard."

Alien vortex process? Valerie drilled a look into his beautiful eyes, trying to understand. "How are the skinny chicks mean to you? What do they do?"

He shrugged. "It's their temperament, I guess. They go out of their way to aggravate all around them and especially men, but only after they've selected a group. By then it's too late. The new men here always go for the skinny, mean ones and subsequently they're stuck. Those women with a little meat on their bones are always selected first by the seasoned men here."

Valerie nodded, but didn't quite believe what he said. Her slightly hazy memory, which seemed to fade with each passing moment, recalled an incident very recently where a man she was with had suggested that she should go on a diet.

Even now the feeling of shame washed down her insides in a burning, hurtful rush. She shook her head to dissolve the remembered sting and lifted her eyes to his face. This was *her* dream, after all. She would control it and she most assuredly didn't want to think about diets.

This man's seductive gaze drilled through to her soul. His face reflected an expression suggesting that he liked what he saw in the deep, dark recesses of her mind.

"The men who have been here a while understand that principle, anyway, and I certainly do." His eyes traveled appreciatively down the rounded figure hidden by the boring jogging suit. "Yep, they're going to love you, all right."

Valerie nodded, released him and brushed her hands down her blah gray jogging shirt, which probably didn't enhance her round body in the least. "So after the interested men select me, then what?"

His gaze narrowed. "Then you select the one man you like best out of those who are interested and he takes you to meet his group."

"Oh yeah, the group. They mentioned the groups when I first got here.

How many men are in your group?"

"Five."

Valerie nodded and smiled. "I hear that's the average."

"I guess."

"Then what?"

His eyebrows lifted. "Then if all of us agree you're the one for us, we seal the deal."

Sex? Did 'seal the deal' in this dream mean sex? Of course it did. It was her dream. It could mean whatever she wanted.

Valerie studied the man before her. He had a nice face. A patient face. He was tall and his wavy strawberry-blond hair and general body build reminded her of an Iowa farm boy. He perhaps also had a touch of Irish in his blood. Sexy, as far as she was concerned.

Valerie wanted to ensure she could find this man again. "What's your name?"

"You can call me Hauser."

"I'm Valerie." She reached out and touched his shoulder. She squeezed it. The muscle in his arm was solid, not like in her usual dreams, when you reached for something that you wanted and it vaporized.

He laughed nervously. "Are you sure you're okay, Valerie?"

"So can I just pick you? And you would be one of the men I spent time with here in this place?" She glanced around the sterile hallways where they stood as if someone might witness her molesting his shoulder with prurient intent.

His eyes widened and he looked over at his friend. The other man shook his head. Hauser chuckled and said, "I believe we have to make our selections in the gauntlet arena for it to count."

"Okay. Let's go there. I'd like to choose you. Is that okay?" Valerie ran her hand from his muscled chest to his fine flat abs. He made a sound somewhere between a grunt and a surprised growl. "Will you step up at the gauntlet arena so I can choose you?"

"Yes. I believe I will."

"Excellent." Valerie sighed. She knew she'd wake up before anything 'good' happened, but planned to enjoy this dream for as long as it lasted.

Hauser's smile dissolved and his expression hardened. "You understand what the five of us in our group want, right?"

She laughed. "Yes. You all want sex. I get it."

Hauser exchanged a knowing smile with his friend, who sent his gaze to the ceiling as if in disbelief. Perhaps he was looking for a partner too. The man who accompanied Hauser was attractive in a long-haired, rebel guy sort of way, but Valerie much preferred Hauser.

The three of them strolled down the blue-lit hallway. After two or three turns that completely made her lost, she noticed they now moved towards a group of people. There were several of the painted aliens dressed just like the first alien guy, only these two had green skin and blond hair.

Approaching slowly, Valerie saw that they stood outside a set of over-tall wooden double doors. A line of girls waited for entrance, and each time the door opened to admit one, a rousing cheer went up, cut off only by the door closing.

"So let me get this straight. I wait in line while you go inside. Then when it's my turn to go inside, I walk down the gauntlet, they cheer and then you'll come and get me."

"For the most part, yes, that's right. Keep walking as far as you can, I'll be towards the end of the gauntlet row. They'll be lining the ropes on either side. Sometimes it gets a little crowded by the time you get to the end, but I'll grab your wrist when you get close enough to me. If you still want to be with my group, just touch my skin anywhere. When the crowd clears, declare that you've chosen me."

She reached out and stroked her hand down his arm. "Should I yell out your name?"

Hauser shook his head. "Probably not. We shouldn't have met ahead of time. Some of the other men might complain that I took unfair advantage." He winked.

Mesmerized by his wink, Valerie finally answered, "Oh. Okay."

They were within shouting distance of the group waiting outside the tall doors, but no one had looked up to see them approaching yet. Hauser slowed his stride. "May I ask you a question?"

"Sure."

"If I select you as the mate for my group, how often will you allow sex for each of us?"

Valerie shrugged. "I don't know. What's the average for that sort of thing?" She expected to wake up before any actual sex took place, but she played along.

"The Others think that once every other month is enough."

"The Others?"

"That's what we call the multicolored aliens here."

Nodding, she asked, "And sex every other month isn't enough?"

"I've been here for almost two months already. I'm starting to get shaky. I hear at three months I'll want to die."

Valerie sympathized. She didn't want him to suffer for a second. Glancing back at the hallway they'd just come from, she wondered if she could talk him into a quickie in some remote closet. Just looking at him made her want to climb up his body, licking all the way. Given all the rules they seemed to have, she imagined that wouldn't happen. They probably had rules against closets and any licking taking place inside them.

"Hmm. Well, how about twice a month for each guy. What's that, ten times for me each month? I could do that, easy." Besides, it was a dream. Not like she would ever get to have any real sex with this gorgeous guy anyway. She would be on the verge of ecstasy, about to experience multiple orgasmic delights, and then her alarm clock would shrilly ring before the first ripple of climax hit her unsatisfied body.

That was the way her dreams always worked, frustratingly enough.

His eyes widened. "That would be very generous of you."

Valerie shrugged. "If they all look like you, it will be my pleasure." She suspected that even if the others looked like Quasimodo, the elephant man, king of the lepers and Satan, Hauser would still be worth it all on his own. He was a walking advertisement for the kind of insatiable sex appeal she'd only dreamed about. The kind of immediate attraction she'd waited for in her awake life. Could she drag Hauser back through this fabulous dream to her awake life? Likely not.

Hauser winked at her and separated himself before anyone noticed they'd walked down the hall together. He entered a smaller door next to the double doors where all the women in line entered one at a time.

Stepping up to the last woman in the long line, Valerie studied the other females while she waited for her turn. They'd obviously changed clothes. Many were attired in fancy dresses, sported freshly coiffed hair and wore makeup. The majority of them were frighteningly skinny, as Hauser had mentioned.

Valerie looked down at her sweat outfit and suddenly felt sort of foolish. Her hair was pulled away from her face and secured with a gray scrunchy, which matched her equally boring gray cotton jogging suit.

Over her shoulder, she noticed a fresh batch of four women, also dressed up in very fancy clothing, approach to stand in line behind her. She probably should have gone with the initial group to change, but she guessed it didn't matter. Valerie had a guy lined up and Hauser hadn't cared about her clothes. Undoubtedly, sex was more important than fashion from a male perspective. Suddenly, a disturbing thought occurred to her and she hoped Hauser hadn't been teasing her. It wouldn't be the first time a man had stood her up.

The gauntlet arena door opened and another exuberant cheer sounded as the woman in line directly ahead of Valerie disappeared through the tall entryway. She took a long step forward and into the attention of the new alien guy. He glanced up and down her body a few times as if with curiosity. His gaze finally landed on her face with an expression that said although he found her attire completely inappropriate, he didn't want to argue over it or stop the speed of the line to question her.

She broke the ice by speaking before he changed his mind and expressed disapproval of her clothing. "Let me guess, your name is Aqua."

"Correct." One light-blond eyebrow on his aqua-painted face lifted. "Are you ready to make your selection in the gauntlet arena?"

Valerie answered with a hesitant, "Yes," even as unease slid through her veins. Hauser had seemed very interested. She closed her eyes and sent up a little prayer that he wasn't lying about wanting her.

"When I open the door, make your way down the roped off areas. Look for those men you find appealing. Touch the skin of the one you want with your open hand and further instructions will follow."

"Right." Valerie nodded and shrugged as though she'd done this a hundred times before.

Without a further word, Aqua opened the door and ushered her through. Valerie was unprepared for the sheer volume of men in attendance. There must have been hundreds of them and another rousing cheer went up when she crossed the threshold into the large darkened room. She took two steps inside, and the door closed solidly behind her.

Valerie brushed her hands down the sides of her clothes and took a step forward. Perhaps gray sweats were the new black. At least many of the men didn't think she looked stupid. Each man she passed had one of two distinct reactions. They either looked up and down her body and moved forward, trying to get her to come nearer. She guessed they weren't put off by her jogging suit, either. Several other men took one look at her, rolled their eyes and backed away from the roped off areas, allowing others to fill in the empty spots. Apparently, a lot of men fell into the first category of having distinct interest in her gray sweats.

Dismissing them quickly, Valerie searched the crowd for Hauser. She remembered that he'd said he'd be at the end of the row and headed quickly for what she thought was the end of this long line. Searching the hordes of men now closing in, she was panicked when she didn't see him right away. The uneasy feeling of his possible betrayal tugged at her.

The men she passed grabbed at her clothing, screaming at her to pick them. She kept her hands to her sides, but after a few steps the men were snatching at her arms, trying to entice her to touch them. She pulled her elbows in close to her torso and marched forward, looking right and left for the man she'd seen earlier. Didn't he say he would be at the end of the line of men? Where was the end of the line?

Looking down the gauntlet, she revised her opinion from hundreds of men to possibly thousands. She tried not to look into their desperate eyes, but a few launched themselves at her. The space in which she traveled narrowed and the men were able to take hold of her more easily. The hands of several unseen men reached out to caress, tap or smack her for her attention. She couldn't even see faces anymore, just hands attached to arms waving in a frenzy trying to gain her notice.

Panic engulfed her brain. Her heart pounded in her chest. She could barely move forward. Looking over her shoulder, Valerie saw that the path she'd just followed was no better. She was surrounded and she couldn't move. She crossed her arms and tucked her hands against her body, not wanting the flat of her hand to touch someone accidentally.

Male hands attached to unseen bodies were now gripping and yanking at her sweat pants as well as her sweatshirt. A bubble of fear lodged in her chest and a sob escaped her throat.

Where was Hauser?

Valerie stopped very briefly and the men closed in around her. She screamed, but they wouldn't stop. Suddenly, she was being pushed side to side by the massive bodies surrounding her. Valerie was afraid she was being smothered. She tilted her head back and screamed, "Hauser!" Her voice was lost in the din of shouts.

Valerie couldn't move forward any longer. With each and every step, she encountered a leg and no place to put her foot. She started to fall sideways and without meaning to her hand shot out to break her fall.

A firm hand snaked around her wrist the instant it left the safety of her body.

Oh God, someone had hold of her.

Chapter 2

Valerie tried to dislodge the hand that had a death grip on her wrist by shaking it off, but the man held fast. Was it Hauser? She wanted to believe that it felt like his hand, but she wasn't certain.

Afraid to look and see who held her, Valerie sank to her knees and the man with the death grip on her wrist went down too. The pressure of the bodies all around her intensified. She looked up, but the bodies were piling up over her. She tried to see the man attached to the hand and with the shifting of several bodies, she got a glimpse of Hauser's hair. He *was* the one who gripped her arm.

Thank heavens.

Valerie slid her free hand along Hauser's arm and gripped the shoulder muscle under his shirtsleeve. It felt even better to touch his firm, smooth shoulder than it did just touching him through his shirt. The moment her hand gripped his firm skin, an obnoxiously loud air horn sounded and the men around her shuffled and departed clumsily.

She held fast to Hauser's shoulder even as he released her wrist.

The air horn sounded once again with a riotous blast that she felt all the way into the depth of her chest. She clenched her hand into Hauser's shoulder more firmly, refusing to let him go. Her other hand became free and she clutched it around his waist. They kneeled on the floor of the cavernous room as the echo of one horn blast faded, only to be replaced by another.

Valerie closed her eyes as if it would help block the strident sound of the horn. After only a few seconds, she was still on her knees gripping Hauser's shoulder beneath his shirt. Her nails had pierced his skin and he grinned after they finally shoved aside the unwanted masses still vehemently trying to convince her to choose them instead of Hauser. Fat chance.

Hands in the air, as though participating in a bank robbery, he didn't seem to notice the injury she wrought on his skin. Or he didn't care.

"What are you doing?" It was a grass-green alien this time and Valerie assumed his name was Green. "Let go of him."

"No. He's the one I want." Valerie slung her free arm around Hauser's neck. His hands remained in the air and his gaze rested on the floor, but she saw his lips form a subtle smile at her passionate statement.

Green glared and put his hands on his hips. "You have to let him get up and retreat back to his place."

"No, I don't. I don't want to lose him. What if I can't find him again?"

"It's been recorded. The moment you touched his flesh with your palm he was chosen by you. Release him."

"I don't believe you. You're trying to trick me." Valerie sealed herself to Hauser and buried her head in his throat. "The second I let him go, I'll never see him again."

Mr. Green alien huffed with extreme exasperation. "You've already selected him. He must be allowed to go back and inform his group. They have to approve his choice before we can move forward."

"Why can't he just call them? I'm not letting go and you can't make me." Valerie hugged Hauser even tighter, if that was possible.

Green stiffened. "Your behavior is highly irregular, human."

"May I speak?" Hauser, his gaze fixed on the floor, hands still in the air, asked.

An orange alien approached from the sidelines of where all the rest of the noisy gauntlet arena men now fidgeted. Green huffed as if affronted by Hauser's request. "Go ahead. Speak."

"If you check my files, you'll see that I have authority to select a female without consulting my group as long as she understands our requirement to sexually service all five of us equally."

"Yes. That's right. I want to select him and his group and service them equally," Valerie parroted.

"We have been without sexual service for almost two months. It is imperative for my group to engage a female at today's gauntlet arena. The next scheduled gauntlet arena night is past our sixty day maximum sexual drought."

Green again sighed very deeply and promptly consulted with Orange in a whispered conversation she couldn't hear. Valerie frowned. She thought these aliens should be a little more understanding of the situation. Orange looked at the screen of the hand-held device he carried, pushed several buttons and spoke this time. "Very well. Both of you stand up."

Over his shoulder, Green called out, "Bring the contract seal device."

Valerie didn't release Hauser, but she did help him stand up. He kept his hands well away from her person. She guessed he wasn't allowed to touch her until the bargain had been struck.

The device was as large as two clipboards stuck together. Each side had a place to put a handprint. Hauser placed his hand on the left side. She snuck her hand out from under his shirtsleeve and flattened it on the right side of the large device. The flat gray panel warmed beneath her hand and a beep sounded after several seconds.

"All right. You are officially sealed. You may kiss now if that is your wish."

"It is." Hauser removed his hand from the clipboard and immediately clinched his arms around her in an intimate embrace. Now that they were 'sealed,' Valerie guessed he was allowed to touch her.

Hauser hugged her to his frame and whispered. "Thank you." His lips grazed her temple and the sensation of his lips touching her skin sent a zap of electric warmth straight to her clit. If he kissed her mouth she'd probably climax.

"No problem," she responded breathily, raising her face. She wanted a kiss in the worst way.

Trailing kisses down the side of her face, Hauser had her panting by the time he got anywhere near her mouth. She tilted her head back further to encourage a more intimate kiss to test her theory.

Licking her lips to moisten them in preparation, she thought she'd scream bloody murder if her alarm went off and ruined this perfect kiss dream.

Hauser's head bent close, his lips were suddenly a whisper from hers. The breath from his mouth caressed her skin sending a shard of heat to her core and then, the door to the arena banged open with force. Out of the corner of her eye, Valerie saw Blue march through the entrance . He fixed a gaze on her and shouted, "Stop! Do not kiss her!"

Hauser hesitated, his face rose slightly to see what the interruption was. He loosened his grip, but Valerie ignored the shouted warning. She wanted this kiss. She wanted it now before anyone or anything stopped it. Not to be deterred or deprived, Valerie closed the distance between them by lifting up on her tiptoes and planted her lips firmly on Hauser's mouth. He groaned and his tongue immediately shot inside the warm confines between her lips.

As their tongues curled around each other, a wave of blissful and near orgasmic power bolted down her body. She stiffened, broke the seal of their mouths and cried out as every nerve in her body sang. It wasn't an orgasm exactly, but close enough to feel amazing. She was ready for another.

Valerie's knees went weak as Hauser shuddered. He bent at the knees still clutching her hard in his arms, but stayed on his feet. She clung to him, unable to get her legs to function.

"What have you done?" Blue shouted. "I told you not to kiss her. Release her, this instant!"

"He didn't do it. She did. She kissed him," Orange said as Valerie recovered from the near blissful moment. Grateful that Hauser still held her close, she'd likely be on the floor in a satiated puddle otherwise.

Blue made a strangled noise. "She hasn't gone through orientation yet. She never officially volunteered for gauntlet duty."

Everything stopped in the room.

"What?" Green shouted. "Then how did she know about the gauntlet arena?"

Blue pressed his lips together into a flat line before saying in a low tone, "I mentioned it in the preamble before leading her group to the orientation area. We had to make some sudden changes that were not fully rehearsed."

Green seemed unconvinced. He sent Valerie a disgruntled look. "She seemed to understand the rules."

Raising his arms, Blue yelled, "She's not even supposed to be at this advanced gauntlet arena! Look at how she's dressed. Could you not tell she hadn't gone through orientation?"

"You were the one who lost her from your initial pre-orientation party. I can't be blamed for this. Besides, the only one complaining is you. They seem very happy." Orange clamped the large clipboard beneath one arm.

"Of course they do, they experienced pleasure when their mouths met, you idiot. If she hadn't kissed him, we could have reversed everything."

Orange raised his dark brows and sent her a terse look. "It's too late now. They've been sealed. She's stuck with his group for the duration of her journey. They can't return to Earth unless she cooperates."

Valerie, now partially recovered from the best kiss she'd ever experienced, was abruptly worried about why the aliens were arguing.

"Explain to me why everyone is so upset. What's the big deal?"

"The 'big deal' is that because you have circumvented our process, you must sexually service the other men in his group."

Valerie shrugged. "So?"

"So, you haven't even met them yet. You don't know what they might like and you have to service all of them."

Valerie shrugged. "I knew that already." She wasn't sure what he meant by his statement of "what they might like." She assumed they liked sex.

Blue crossed his arms. "And you have to do it for the next three years."

"What! Three years?" She turned to Hauser. "Did you know this?"

He cleared his throat and nodded. "Yes. I knew the length of service. I thought everyone did. I'm sorry you weren't informed."

The three aliens and Hauser surrounded her and they were all a lot taller than she was, making for a claustrophobic feeling.

Three years?

Edging closer to Hauser, Valerie whispered to herself, "I'm just in a very intense dream. I'll wake up in a few minutes." She mashed her eyes shut and started counting backwards from ten in a whispered chant. When she got to one, she opened her eyes. Everything was the same. With the exception that the aliens regarded her with stern expressions. Perhaps they thought she was even crazier than they had originally suspected.

Green heaved a long sigh. "Put her through orientation. She will return here and go directly to meet the others in Hauser's group. We can't deviate from our practices any further. You must remain with this man's group. Do you understand?"

Valerie nodded and glanced at Hauser. His tender smile reassured her.

Orange turned to Blue and with a stern tone said, "Take charge of her. See that she goes through orientation this time and understands her role. Then bring her back to Hauser in the lounge. He will wait for her there. And get her some other clothing. She looks too human."

Valerie frowned. Too human? What did *that* mean?

Hauser squeezed her once reassuringly before she was led away.

Three years. Five men. Sex two times a month with each of them.

Somehow this didn't seem like a dream any longer.

Deep in her soul, Valerie knew the kiss she had shared with Hauser felt too real to be a dream. She hadn't ever felt an attraction to another man like the one she experienced with Hauser. At least she didn't think so. She shook her head in frustration. The memories of her life before this place continued to fade. She would do as she was asked and play along. She didn't have much of a choice, did she?

Valerie held onto one single thought in the face of three years of sexual servitude to five men. Regardless of how Hauser or any of the others made her feel, she wanted to go back to Earth.

She would do anything to ensure her return.

Chapter 3

"These are the laws you will need to familiarize yourselves with," the monotonous tone of the tan alien intoned. "It's unfortunate that you've been brought here, but the fact is now that you are here, you must follow our rules or dire consequences for your fellow human males will result."

Valerie wanted to raise her hand and ask several questions as to what their definition of dire consequences was, but the subdued atmosphere didn't lend itself to a sharing of ideas. She'd already been labeled a troublemaker for going missing from the original group she'd come in with, not to mention somehow circumventing their eight-step process. Valerie decided silence was the better course of action in this instance.

"Rule number one states that each female volunteer will be matched up with their choice of a group of men…"

The alien's monotone voice continued as her attention drifted. She'd never been very good at sitting quietly and listening to lectures. This scenario was no different. She wanted to get back to Hauser and glanced at the door. If she'd seen any form of clock, she would have been watching it. Unease seeped into her mind. She wasn't convinced that the multicolored aliens would be true to their word. After all, they freely admitted to sucking humans up into their vortex. *Were they truly trustworthy?*

"Rule number three states that there will be no adultery allowed between mated humans…"

Rule number three? What happened to rule number two?

Valerie's fingers twitched with the desire to raise her hand and ask about rule number two, but decided against it. She made a concerted effort to focus on the alien giving the orientation. He continued on and on about rule number three and adultery. Valerie didn't remember much about her life on earth, but didn't think she was the type to be a cheater.

Given that she was about to embark on a three-year sexual odyssey involving the carnal health of a group of strange men, the concept of 'cheating' was sort of stupid anyway.

"Rule number six only applies to males of your species, however…"

Rule six? Geez, pay attention.

Although, if rule number six only concerned men, why did she have to know it? Valerie let loose a long quiet sigh and glanced around the room again. She caught the eye of another female fidgeting in her chair, who seemed even more restless than Valerie. Her dark curly hair brushed agitated shoulders until she noticed Valerie. She stopped moving and her quick grin made Valerie smile in return.

"Now that all eight rules have been explained," the tan alien said, "we have refreshments in the back of the room for you. Then you'll be taken to the staging area to receive further instructions on daily living."

Valerie wondered how she'd managed to miss the explanation of so many rules. Perhaps there was a handout she could read later. A hand in the front row went up from a female dressed in a pink fluffy robe with matching slippers and the dark tan alien narrowed his eyes. "What is it?"

"Do we get new clothes? I heard something about new clothes."

Dark Tan crossed his arms. "After refreshments and the next class, you'll be sent to wardrobe for new attire."

Another hand went up. "How many outfits do we get to pick out? And also, do we get jewelry and other accessories?"

"This is unimportant information."

Valerie thought so too and tuned out both the women and their foolish fashion questions. She was more concerned about the other four men in Hauser's group. Didn't these women understand what they had to do here?

"What if we refuse to have sex with the men we're assigned to?" Valerie's mouth had gone ahead and asked the question without her brain's permission.

The room stilled. Slowly, all eyes turned to her. The dark tan alien frowned. "That's not an option for you. Once you're sealed to a group of men, you must provide what you've agreed upon."

"Or else what? Listen, I didn't agree to be here." Valerie gestured to the room around her and arched a brow. "You're the ones that brought me to this place, against my will, I might add. Why should I cooperate?"

"Because if you don't help your group of men with their sexual needs, then none of you can go back to Earth after the allotted three years."

"Why?"

His expression darkened. "Your question is irrelevant."

"I want an answer."

"These are our rules." The original blue alien who'd been assigned to her approached Dark Tan and whispered in his ear. Together they turned and stared at her as Blue pointed and gestured.

After listening a long moment, Dark Tan smirked and said, "You are apprehensive because you already circumvented our established policy. The men you've been assigned to during this trip require you to fulfill their sexual needs so that they might function while temporarily ensconced in our world. Are you truly going to deny them a sexual outlet, thereby forcing their permanent incarceration? It's not their fault that you didn't attend orientation before *demanding* to be assigned to them."

Valerie narrowed her eyes. "And you're deliberately being obtuse. It's not my fault that I was brought aboard. Tell me why I'm even here."

Dark Tan took a half step forward as if he might forcefully stop her questions, but Blue blocked him. "That information is immaterial. It doesn't matter why. You are here now. Do you wish to release your group of men and allow them to find another female?" Blue's question was accompanied with a gleam in his shiny brown eyes.

The dark tan alien started to object, Blue held up a fist and he stopped.

"I was led to understand that it didn't matter. I'm trapped."

"If you do not wish to service the men in your existing group, then another group can be assigned. I will see to it personally. However, once you've allowed yourself to be sealed the initial time, then no other option exists. You must service *one* group while you're here. Do you wish to change groups?"

Valerie came to her senses, even though she hadn't met the majority of Hauser's group. "No. I'll keep the group I have." Given the look on Blue's face, she knew he'd choose a collection of hateful, deviant men. At least she knew Hauser.

"Carry on, then. We've wasted enough time."

She turned and headed for the table in the back of the room that displayed a bounty of food. Opting for a cup of coffee, Valerie pondered her circumstances and did her best to pretend this was all a very vivid dream.

"You already have a group of men assigned?" The voice came from behind her.

Valerie turned. The dark-haired woman she'd noticed earlier during the endless orientation sipped a cup of coffee as well. At least, Valerie hoped it was coffee.

"Yes. But I'd better warn you I'm a rebel. You may not want to be seen talking to me."

The other woman laughed. "Well, since I'm a troublemaker too, I think we'd better become best friends."

"You think so?" Valerie took a long, strengthening sip of the best coffee she'd ever tasted.

"Yes. Besides we have the same sophisticated style in clothing."

Valerie noticed that the other woman was wearing a darker shade of similar gray sweats.

"I'm Daisy, by the way."

Valerie extended fingers warm from the coffee cup and said, "Valerie."

"What is the gauntlet arena really like?" Nodding over one shoulder at the group of aliens gathered at the front of the room, Daisy added, "They make it sound very romantic."

She snorted. "You want the truth?"

"Of course. We're best friends now and the complete truth is required at all times."

Valerie liked Daisy. Checking to make sure the aliens couldn't overhear her, Valerie whispered, "It's scary. They crowd you and grab at you. But once you make your selection, they all back off."

"Are you afraid of the men you'll be with?"

"Not yet, but I've only met one so far." Valerie shrugged. "After this illuminating orientation I'll go to meet the other four."

Daisy lowered her voice. "I must be a slut, because the truth is I find the idea exciting and a little arousing."

Valerie tilted her head and smiled. Leaning in confidentially, she whispered, "I can't remember if I'm the type to kiss and tell, but the first time Hauser kissed me, I nearly climaxed."

A giggle escaped from Daisy's lips and she slapped one hand over her mouth. She spared a glance over one shoulder, but the aliens didn't look at them.

"The trick is to find a man beforehand and make a deal," Valerie said. "I don't think it's allowed, but there's a reason I'm labeled a troublemaker."

"Where did you find him?"

"I was wandering in a hallway that I wasn't supposed to be in."

Daisy sent another quick glance at the aliens before turning back to whisper, "Will you distract them so that I can escape to search for my Mr. Right?"

"Sure. After the next orientation lecture, I'll cause a scene so you can search for your own Prince Charming…if you tell me the eight rules again. I missed half of them while day-dreaming."

* * * *

Valerie trotted along the endless maze of hallways, again trying to keep up with the fast pace Blue set with his angry strides. It was quite possible that he was justifiably livid this time.

"You engineered that little stunt, didn't you?"

"I don't know what you're talking about." Valerie fought the smile trying to erupt. Daisy had slipped out of the room during the loud and distracting scene Valerie had enacted by asking all sorts of foolish questions about fashion accessories.

Ten minutes later, Daisy returned to the room in the arms of the man Hauser had been walking with when Valerie had met him. She had given Daisy a surreptitious thumbs-up regarding her choice.

"How did she know what would happen when she kissed another human male if you didn't tell her?"

Valerie shrugged. Daisy had apparently wanted an almost orgasmic experience too and had locked lips with her now-future mate, Brandon, seconds after finding him. "I told her what happened to me. How was I supposed to know she'd want to do it too?"

"Because the two of you are exactly alike: Trouble."

"Then send us back to Earth."

He increased his strides and Valerie had to run to keep up. "You know that isn't possible."

"As a matter of fact, I don't know what is or isn't possible. The reason for my presence aboard this vessel has never been fully explained to my satisfaction."

Blue stopped so suddenly, Valerie slammed into his back. Her hands shot up to deflect her body from plowing into him. His skin was cool, soft and moist to the touch. Almost as if the paint he'd been dipped in hadn't quite dried.

He whirled about and stepped out of her reach. "Hands to yourself. You may not touch me." His expression probably mirrored hers. Icky. She drew her arms back, hands level with her ears.

"It was an accident!"

"Regardless. Take care where you put your limbs in the future."

Hands still in the air, she snapped, "Whatever."

Blue continued forward down the hallway and she kept her distance so that she wouldn't accidentally touch him again.

Valerie had changed into what she considered a very sexy pink dress. She couldn't wait to see what Hauser thought of it. And truth be told, she hoped the other men she was about to meet appreciated the effort.

Daisy's opinion regarding the arousing idea of being with five different men was only an echo of Valerie's own deep desires.

Chapter 4

Valerie was brought to the advanced gauntlet arena lounge where Hauser waited. His face was pensive; she smiled in an effort to reassure him.

"Wow. You look great." He stood from his chair and reached out a hand to grab hers. "How was orientation?"

She took his hand, threading her fingers through his. Thankfully, Daisy had given her a cryptic overview of the eight rules governing this place. "Illuminating, but I don't want to talk about it. So what's next?"

"Since we bypassed the initial meeting with the entire group, we'll continue forward in the process and head for the individual meeting area. They have our palm prints, but the documentation needs to be finalized with our DNA link as well."

"I thought the palm prints sealed us."

"It sealed us from further negotiations of others," Hauser explained. "After the kiss, we were supposed to go meet the others in my group. Once they all agree you're the one, then all of us will physically sign the document to make our union binding."

"Did you call them, let them know about me?"

"I did. They're all very excited to meet you."

"Because they need sex."

Hauser sobered. "And because they want to get to know you."

Valerie took a deep breath and with it came his scent. Even though the quality of her experience felt like a dream, there were times when it seemed more vivid. Spending time in Hauser's personal space made her vividly aware she was a woman. A woman with needs. She turned and stared at his mouth, wondering if they had time for another kiss.

His eyes crinkled at the corners and he asked, "You okay?"

"Will you kiss me again?"

"Sure." Hauser pulled her to his chest, lowered his mouth and kissed her like he was making love to her lips. A climax started building in the center of her body, but the sensation was now slightly subdued, not as vibrant and urgent as before. He released her after several lip-licking moments. "Better?"

She managed a smile. "Yes. Thanks."

Hauser squeezed her once. Resting his forehead against hers, he asked, "Ready to sign some alien papers and get mated?"

"Okay. But I bet I wouldn't be as anxious to sign up for five men on Earth as I am here."

"I bet I wouldn't be as willing to share you with my friends on Earth as I am here."

"Really? Makes me wish we could meet on Earth. I bet a guy that looks like you would probably never be interested in a plus-sized girl like me back there."

"Plus-sized?" His eyes scanned her body quickly and ended focused on her face. "You don't even qualify and besides you'd lose that bet. I prefer curvy women." His wolfish grin validated his claim.

"Oh yeah? Why is that?"

"Because I hate picking bones out of my dick after I screw skinny women."

She laughed out loud and threw her arms around his waist. "I think we'll get along just fine here."

"I think so too."

They filled out the paperwork required—one document stating that she would allow each man in Hauser's group to have sex with her twice a month for a total of ten occurrences each month.

Across from the document signing room was a hallway. They entered it and along each side were several doors. Hauser led her to a door towards the end of the hall. "The others are probably waiting inside."

She paused and stared at the door, but couldn't quite take the step needed to open it.

"What's wrong?" he asked.

"I'm a little nervous. What if they don't share your interest in me? What if they prefer...a different kind of woman?"

"They won't. I was selected to find the best choice for us. And I did. You have nothing to worry about."

Hauser opened the door and ushered her across the threshold. Inside was a small living room-like space with a sofa and loveseat, but the space was empty.

"Where is everyone?"

"I guess they're down the hall. They probably didn't want to overwhelm you. I'll send them in one at a time once you're settled."

Valerie turned and flew into his arms, burying her face in his neck. Now that it was about to happen, she was horrified by this situation. If this were not a dream, as she was coming to believe, she was about to meet her entourage of lovers. Strangers she'd agreed to have sex with.

A tremor ran down her spine. These were the men she was required to satisfy for the next three years. Oh, God. Valerie held onto Hauser for dear life. He didn't speak. He simply held her and stroked her back.

Kissing her forehead tenderly, he asked, "Are you okay?"

"No. I need a minute." Valerie hated to cry. She hated that she was so inexperienced with men. At least, that was her impression from her fading memory. Even in her dreams she paled at the thought of sex with one man, let alone five.

"This is just a first meeting. A kiss is required, but no one is allowed to attack you. There are stringent rules in place to keep us in line."

"The idea that you need anything to keep you in line doesn't make me feel better."

His deep sigh didn't give her comfort. "Women are more revered here than you realize."

"But not revered enough to only share themselves with one man versus several men. And for three years. What if I decided mid-way that I can't do it?"

"You understand our predicament and you're aware of what happens when we go without." She nodded, but couldn't look him in the face. What happened to men here was cruel and unusual punishment when they went without sex. The video she'd watched during the second orientation was disturbing. A man with sunken cheeks, as if he'd been starved, was strapped by his ankles and wrists to a hospital bed. Screaming and writhing in obvious agony from lack of sex, his selfish mate had refused to relieve his sexual needs and abandoned him to a fate worst than death. A voice over on the film explained that if he were allowed to escape, the delirious man would even endure the blazing pain associated with forced sex to end his excruciating pain. At the end of the movie, the man disappeared from the screen all of a sudden. At that point the lights had snapped back on obscuring the rest of the final scene. Valerie wondered if he'd died, faded into oblivion or something much worse. She vowed not to let it happen in her household.

"While the five of us aren't exactly angels, none of us would intentionally hurt you, regardless. Okay?" He put a finger on her chin and tilted her head to stare deeply into her teary eyes. Tenderly, he brushed some residual moisture away from her cheek with his thumb.

Valerie nodded again. "Okay. Send them in. I'm as ready as I'll ever be. What are their names, by the way? I should know that at the very least."

Hauser kissed her forehead once more, and then surprised her with another gentle chaste kiss to her lips before answering, "First will be Johnny, then Frasier, then Mark and finally Dominick. I'll come back after you've met everyone." He released her, and winked before departing.

After several nerve-wrenching minutes of waiting, Johnny came into the room for his introduction. He was, in a word, gorgeous. Slightly shorter than Hauser, he had dark brown hair, hazel eyes and a big toothy grin. Scanning her from head to toes, he remarked, "You're as lovely as Hauser said you were."

"Am I?"

He nodded and approached her stealthily. "Do you like playing games?"

"Games?" Valerie shrugged. "Sure. I like games." She was worried that they'd only be interested in sex. Not other pastimes. She guessed it wasn't always all about carnal knowledge and three years was a long time. She inwardly calmed down a notch.

Johnny moved almost close enough to touch her, but at the last moment he skirted around until he stood behind her. He grabbed a lock of her hair and leaned close enough to take a long sniff. Releasing an appreciative-sounding breath that fluttered against her ear, inciting a tingle, he dropped the length of hair.

Heart now pounding in her chest, Valerie didn't move as he rested his chin on one of her shoulders. "Marvelous. And did I understand correctly that you've agreed to spend two nights a month with each of us while we're here?" His fingertips grazed her waist and she jumped at the unexpected thrill of having another man's hands on her body. She was barely used to Hauser. So far, two out of the five men in this group were sinfully sexy.

Seriously, I have to be dreaming.

Valerie pretended his casual touch wouldn't end too soon and leaned back into his chest with a murmured, "Yes."

He kissed a sensitive spot below her ear, but before she could melt further backwards, he quickly darted around to face her. Fingers gripping her shoulders lightly as he pulled her into his chest, Johnny asked seductively, "May I kiss you now, lovie? Your lips are a delectable sight for sore eyes."

Lifting her chin, she nodded and fairly quivered in suspense. He pressed his lips to hers and the rush of excitement she experienced was almost too much to bear. He traced her lips with his tongue gently and Valerie sagged in his arms as another wash of exquisite passion flowed over her sensitive skin.

"Exceptionally responsive. Very nice," Johnny whispered along her mouth and kissed her chastely once more. "I'd love to stay all night with you, lovie, but I fear the others wouldn't like it." He winked and drew away.

When she faltered, he steadied her with hands still clamped to her shoulders. She wanted to slither to the floor. Pulling herself together, Valerie placed her hands on his forearms and took a deep breath.

"Wow."

"Ah, lovie, we're going to have such fun together." He squeezed her shoulders again and released her. "See you soon."

He glided to the door and exited after one more salacious look over his shoulder. Valerie shook her head once and placed a hand over her chest trying to calm her riotous heart beat.

Johnny was hot.

The next man to enter the room, Frasier, was the tallest so far. His brown hair was highlighted in golden blond and his wide smile displayed very straight, white teeth. But it was his eyes that had her entranced. They were a vivid blue and focused directly on her. Frasier's rugged good looks made him look like an adventurer. He'd probably traveled the seven seas and explored his way across every continent on the globe.

She also wondered if he were the strong silent type when he didn't speak. After several minutes of smiling at each other, he quietly uttered a,

"Hi."

"Hi, yourself." Was he really shy? How sweet.

He cleared his throat. and sent his gaze at every other place in the room except for her. "This is sort of an embarrassing situation to be in, isn't it?"

"I guess so." Valerie got the distinct impression that he was the one who was uncomfortable. She pressed her hands together in front of her like a schoolteacher about to deliver a lecture. "So. Do you have any questions for me?"

He focused his wandering stare to her face. "I'll be straight with you, Valerie. I'm a fairly uncomplicated guy. I appreciate that you're willing to give each of us your time twice a month, but I don't want you to worry about it. Not with me."

Valerie widened her eyes. "Why would I worry about it, with any of you?"

He stuck his hands in his back pockets and approached her hesitantly. "I only mean that you shouldn't be apprehensive about spending time with me. I hate to admit this, but I'm not a very daring type. I'm fairly straight-laced and I don't want to disappoint you or make you angry."

"Telling me the truth won't ever make me angry." She smiled encouragingly. "Is there something you *do* like?"

"The truth is, I'm a numbers guy. That's my passion. I don't want you to think I'm ungrateful, but I'm fairly tame in the sack. Will that be a problem for you?"

Valerie shook her head. "I'm sure we can work something out. I don't want you to suffer. So we'll just go slow and take it one day at a time. Okay?"

"That would be great. Thanks, Valerie." He turned to leave.

"Don't you have to kiss me before you go?"

Frasier turned back. "Right. You're absolutely right." He nodded and slowly crossed the room to stand before her.

When he grabbed her face between his large hands, Valerie braced herself for a quick peck on the lips. Frasier laid a kiss on her that she was *so* not expecting. It was filled with passion and longing and lots of clever tongue movements that she could barely keep up with. Valerie leaned into him, slipping her hands around his waist to clench him closer.

He stopped kissing her abruptly and she almost cried out loud. Panting and trying to catch her breath, Valerie managed, "Wow. That was an amazing kiss for a guy who considers himself tame in bed."

A small laugh escaped. "You took me off guard. Maybe it's your scent, but you awaken something in me." His sudden frown was unexpected. "I hope I wasn't too forward."

"No." Her sigh filled the room. "It was wonderful." She put a hand to his chest, mostly to steady herself. "I think you're teasing me. Once you get me in bed, you'll rock my world, won't you?"

"I hope so. I look forward to seeing you again, Valerie." Frasier brought her hand from his chest to his lips, kissed the tips of her fingers and then promptly left the room.

Mark came into the room next. In overall looks, he reminded her slightly of Johnny, but he wasn't as forward. Nor was he as visceral as Johnny. He had the friendly, approachable aura of someone she could confide in. Until he smiled. He watched her from across the room with a wicked grin playing around his sensual mouth.

Short, dark brown hair, chocolate-brown eyes, and a body that was whipcord lean, Mark suddenly reminded her of a bad boy heartthrob from teen magazines. Girls likely chased him, so he didn't have to put forth much effort in the area of romance or sex. His expressive eyes were certainly intended to entice and seduce.

He didn't have to make a move or say anything at all. Everything he was about was stated clearly in his cocky stance. He just looked at her with those I-want-to-make-sweet-love-to-you, sensitive eyes and she was all melted honey on the inside.

Mark flicked his tongue along his lips quickly before saying, "You're beautiful. I expected you would be."

"Did you?"

He nodded. "Hauser definitely knows how to pick women. We knew he'd do a good job."

"All of you are very attractive. How did I get so lucky, I wonder?" Watching this smooth bad boy entice her from across the room without so much as a touch made Valerie wary.

She went back to her dream theory. But since it was so vivid and exceptional, maybe she was in a coma somewhere and that made this experience very intense. Each man brought to her was almost more attractive than the last. When did that ever happen, even in dreams?

Out of the four she'd met, it would not be a chore to have sex with them on a regular basis. Especially not for three years as the aliens had insisted she'd have to do.

He shrugged. "I think we're the lucky ones, honey, but I'm glad you like the scenery."

"What will you require?"

He laughed. It was a slow rumble followed by a flash of those beautiful teeth. "I'll require that you don't force me to perform in the missionary position for the next three years."

"I don't imagine I can force you to do anything."

His amusement faded. "Now there's where you're wrong, honey. All of us are trapped here. You alone hold the key to our sanity."

"What's wrong with the missionary position?"

Mark laughed again. "Well, if I had to have sex in the missionary position or no sex at all, why then I'd get on my knees, spread your legs and vigorously choose the missionary position. But I can think of so many other satisfying positions for us to explore. The thought of three years in the same exact pose is, well, excruciating."

"I won't force you to be in any position exclusively," Valerie promised. "But I don't want to take any positions off the table, so to speak. Maybe we could consider the missionary style once or twice a year for kicks."

"Sure, honey, whatever you want. I appreciate your willingness to try new things." His gaze traveled her body from head to toes and back again as if considering a plethora of exotic sexual stances.

She gave him a mock frown. "I'm not going to be dangling from a chandelier, am I?"

Mark shook his head and finally started walking towards her. "Nope. Unless you have some light-fixture fantasy. I prefer beds. More comfy and easier on the knees, regardless of the position."

"Are you going to kiss me now?"

"Yes." He slid into her personal space. "Are you ready?"

Rooted to the floor, she found she was unable to move anyway. "Not sure. I'll let you know when you're done."

His wide grin captivated her as his fingers danced along her arms, tickling a path to her shoulders and distracting her. She turned to one side to watch his hands caress her arm and he ducked in close. Kissing a sensitive place on her neck halfway between her shoulder and her ear, Valerie tingled from his kisses all the way to her soul.

He licked the spot he'd kissed and another voracious bolt of electricity went straight to her core. A moment later she was enclosed in his arms. She slipped her hands around his waist and clasped them behind his back.

One of his hands cupped the back of her head and the other wound around her in a tender embrace. His lips blazed a path from her jaw to her chin and before she could take a breath or prepare, his lips were firmly planted on hers in the most sensual kiss she'd ever participated in. Well, it was the most seductive kiss since the last man she'd met had been in the room.

Mark was aggressive. His tongue stabbed inside her mouth, dominating the space. Hips rolling against her belly with each stroke and lick, he quickly possessed her mouth, her body, her very essence and she could only cling to him until he was finished seducing her.

If he'd whispered a vague request for a practice screw, she knew she would have peeled her clothing off and denied him nothing.

After several long seconds, during which she'd begun to vibrate from shoulders to knees, he released her and separated himself from her body. She moaned and tried to reconnect.

"Sorry, honey, we'll have to wait until we're together again the next time to finish this. You still have to meet Dominick. He's probably about to burst in here and throw me out. He's the only one with the muscles to pull it off."

"Dominick?" Valerie trembled from sexual overload from the four men she'd already agreed to have sex with. At this point, she hoped five men would be enough to quench the thirst built up over the past several minutes that was testing her unsatisfied libido.

"He's the last in line for introductions." Mark backed away from her slowly, hands firmly on her shoulders to keep her upright.

Valerie swallowed hard and did her best to calm down. "Right. So, is he nice?"

Mark's eyebrows went to his hairline. "Dominick? Nice?" He tilted his head to one side as if trying to find a way to tell her bad news. "Nice is not a word I'd use to describe Dominick. He's big and quiet, but he'd never hurt you."

Valerie knew that after having four studs in a row, the fifth would have to be scary or ugly. "How do you know that?"

"Because I wouldn't, and the five of us were supposedly matched in temperament. If I wouldn't, then neither would he." His hands squeezed her once more as if in assurance.

Valerie sighed. "Forgive me if I don't jump for joy. Today is only day one and three years is a long time to endure whatever you would or wouldn't do."

"None of us are the brutal sort." A genuine smile accompanied his statement.

She nodded, but the wariness didn't leave her mind. She turned her back on the door as Mark left. Valerie didn't want to be a baby about meeting Dominick. She trusted Hauser, if no one else. If she should need to be worried about any of the five, she was certain that Hauser would have warned her up front. But he didn't.

After a few minutes, she heard the door open and close again. She felt a large presence in the room, but he didn't say anything. She gathered her meager courage and turned to face her final future mate. Dominick, who was described by Mark as being not mean, but not necessarily nice either.

Fighting to keep her eyes from slamming shut, Valerie had her face turned to the floor. She saw his booted feet initially and the bottom legs of his jeans. Her curious gaze crept up the rest of his body and by the time she'd made it to his hips she was nervous. He *was* big. Very big. And she hadn't even made it to his chest yet.

Her eyes stopped momentarily at the vivid six-pack abs evident beneath the soft shirt he wore. His shirt was the only soft thing about him, she figured. His massive, barrel-sized chest had muscles on top of muscles, which led to a surprisingly nice average-sized neck. It wasn't as thick as she would have expected, given all his other muscles.

Dominick's shaved head only added to the frightening visage he represented. He looked like a biker mercenary. God help her.

"Holy cow, you're...big." Valerie swallowed hard and stared at his warrior's face, complete with a slash of a scar on one cheek and another crescent-shaped one over his sensual lips. Brutally attractive in a scary sort of way, she wondered if he'd break her with a mere touch.

He nodded slightly at her statement. "I am."

Valerie didn't know what to say to him. The other men were so different. In her mind, he stood alone as a man who wouldn't put up with crap and who might not stop if she asked nicely.

"Do…do you have any questions for me?" Valerie stuttered her question, embarrassingly enough. To prolong the arrival of the inevitable kiss they had to share before he left to join the others, she might play twenty questions. It wasn't like she could change her mind now. She was stuck with this group of men. Four out of the five men in her group didn't scare the crap out of her. That had to be a good record for anyone.

"Will you service me?" he asked so quietly she almost missed it.

Valerie startled and focused her gaze on his face. "What? Service?"

He sighed deeply, but the expression on his face didn't change. "Will you fuck me regularly for the next three years?"

Unable to find her voice, Valerie nodded. She had to say yes anyway. "I have to."

"No. You don't."

He'd stayed on his side of the room since he'd entered. He hadn't so much as twitched a muscle to make a move on her and truthfully she was becoming intrigued by this silent giant. Her gaze slid to the scars adorning his face.

She was intrigued, wanting to know where his scars came from along with a host of other secret information. What made Dominick tick? What made him smile? What made him needful? What would make this man want her like no other?

"How did you get those scars on your face?" She blurted out her question before prudence could screen her words.

His eyes widened as if surprised and sent his eyebrows to his non-existent hairline. "I don't exactly remember." He lifted one large hand and swirled it in the air simulating a tornado. "This place doesn't allow much in the way of memory. Were I to guess, I must have been misbehaving." His sudden smile softened the harsh planes of his face.

Valerie nodded in understanding. "I feel like I've been dreaming since I got here. I'm going to wake up any minute to my alarm clock and have to face my real life. Whatever that is."

He crossed his arms again and murmured quietly, "I don't think this is a dream anymore."

"Why?"

"I've been here for almost two months and my dreams don't last that long. You?"

Valerie shrugged. "I've only been here for about a day. I guess I'll have to let you know in a couple of months."

"I'll look forward to that." Dominick watched her for a beat and then grinned. His whole face lit up and Valerie's heart almost stopped. He was, in truth, very attractive. Not in the classic sense and not at all like the others, but in his own brutal, scary way.

"So how about it? Do you think we could come to some sort of arrangement?"

"Arrangement?"

"For...servicing."

Valerie glanced down his body and then back up once more. He was so big that he'd be able to take whatever he wanted from her regardless of any arrangement. He was behaving, for now. She hoped that he would remain civil once they were alone together for their two nights a month.

Her instincts told her that he was dangerous in some way, but she couldn't tell if it were just in general or specifically targeted at her.

"Yes," she squeaked out.

If he was surprised by her affirmative answer, he didn't show it. "Good. I'll look forward to our time together." He glanced up and down her body as if taking inventory and making plans to do any number of erotic sexual acts.

"Should I be worried?"

His eyes narrowed. "Worried? I don't know what you mean."

"In the future, when we're alone together so that I can 'service' you, should I be worried about what you'll do?"

The stunned expression that slipped out before he could hide it disappeared quickly, but she'd seen it anyway. He pierced her with his stern gaze. "I won't do anything harmful."

Valerie didn't think she liked his answer one single bit. Not doing anything harmful wasn't the same thing as not hurting her. Perhaps he had dark, insatiable desires and she'd be his to do with as he wished twice a month for the next three years.

From across the room, he watched her cycle through his last words and attach meaning to them. He didn't explain further, so she focused on the good news that it was only twice a month for thirty-six months. Seventy-two times she'd have to be fearful over the next three years. God help her.

Valerie knew they'd have to kiss, but she couldn't move her legs yet. The uncomfortable silence grew too quickly between them.

"Come here." His darkly passionate voice beckoned.

It was time to go. She took a deep breath and on shaky legs, she walked towards him. Valerie couldn't believe her body cooperated.

His head tilted to one side as if in surprise as she crossed the room. He let her come all the way across until she stood an arm's-length away.

Another long space of time crowded the room. Valerie trembled as she looked into Dominick's eyes. "Kiss me."

His eyes went opaque at her simple, quiet invitation. After a few moments she added, "I want to kiss you." It might give her a hint of how he'd treat her later on.

"Do you?" A sardonic smile formed on his lips. "That's fortunate. I want to be kissed."

Valerie teetered on tiptoes, tilted her head all the way back, and watched as he leaned in to give her access to his mouth. She slid her hand around his neck and pressed her lips to his before she could change her mind. Dominick tasted like sin. His full lips parted, but did not engage. She twisted her mouth across his, preparing to take things to the French level, if he would allow it. He seemed to be letting her determine the level of heat for this kiss. At first, anyway.

Once she licked her way into his mouth, he grabbed her to his chest with a growl and dueled with her tongue in the most salacious and intriguing way. A rush of pleasure slid to her already achy core. Valerie was so turned on, she moaned with every thrust of his tongue.

Her hips took on a life of their own and pressed into his groin. She felt his hand slide down to cup her ass so he could grind into her as well. She launched from her tiptoes and surged forward so fast that she pushed him into the wall behind them. Their lips didn't break apart and the kiss ratcheted up another level to volcanic. He twisted them until her shoulder blades pressed into the wall.

Valerie wanted to have sex with this man. No problem. Right now. Please. She heard his moan and realized that one of her legs had slipped around his thigh to secure him against her body. The ridge of his cock now pressed perfectly between her thighs and rubbed deliciously against her clit. With every move he made, pleasure pounded upwards through her body. His hips rolled into hers rhythmically as a vibrant climax built in her core. She curled her hips and met each and every stroke searching for relief. They devoured each other with the carnal kiss until, without warning, Valerie broke away from him and fairly howled at the electrifying climax that bloomed from her core, saturating her in pleasure.

Trembling, she relaxed against Dominick's chest, hoping he'd continue to hold her up since her legs didn't seem to want the job any longer. He kissed a path along her jaw as she focused on breathing in and out.

"Did you just come?" he whispered. The fine hairs in her ear tickled with the breath from his seemingly awe-filled words.

Panting wildly, trying to catch her breath, Valerie nodded since she couldn't make her mouth form words just yet.

"Damn. I guess I don't have to apologize for pinning you to a wall and taking advantage." Laughter rumbled in his chest. He kissed her throat gently and repeatedly until she came back to her senses enough to answer.

"No. I don't expect you to say sorry. It was..." she paused, trying to think of a word. "It was stupendous. Unbelievable."

Dominick leaned back and stared into her eyes. "I don't think I've ever made a woman climax from just a kiss."

"If it hadn't just happened to me, I wouldn't have believed it either." The near orgasm she'd had with Hauser had been fabulous, but it paled in comparison to the one that Dominick had just rocked her soul with.

Another sardonic smile formed on his luscious lips. "Three years might go by faster than I thought."

Valerie didn't say anything. She was still vibrating from the orgasm. Dominick didn't scare her any less, but she decided her body was aroused enough that perhaps her brain could suspend her fright long enough for sex with him twice a month.

He slid his warm, wide palm from butt cheek to knee before he pulled her leg away from the back of his thigh. "I'd better get back out there before someone busts in here to see what's taking me so long." He extracted himself from her slowly.

Valerie remained against the wall and straightened her clothing. Her lips felt swollen. She wiped the back of one hand across them to remove any moisture and put her gaze on the scant space between their bodies. "What happens now?"

He cleared his throat. "The official ceremony to seal us."

Valerie glanced up in surprise. "I thought it was already done."

"There is an official ceremony where all of us link our DNA with yours. Adultery is not allowed here. Ever."

"Really? How can they prevent it?"

"It's some sort of implant they place in all of the males once they are brought aboard. If a male tries to penetrate a woman with whom he isn't sealed, my understanding is the pain will make the man want to cut his own dick off to make it stop."

Valerie raised her eyebrows in surprise. "So then I don't have to be worried about being raped by a stranger."

"No."

But the question regarding force and a man she was sealed to remained unanswered. Dominick didn't say anything further. He glanced at the door and his demeanor became that of a man who had overstayed his welcome. Pointing his thumb to the door, he followed and exited the room without saying anything else.

Valerie waited a few minutes more and Hauser came back.

Pensive expression on his face, he asked quietly, "Are you ready to go to the permanent ceremony?"

"I guess. What do we have to do again?" Her mind was all a flutter from her recent and visceral orgasm. She hoped Hauser didn't notice her still quaking legs. Already she felt like she'd cheated on him. Three years was going to be an eternity.

"We link our DNA then move on to the...consummation phase."

Valerie sucked in a deep breath. *Consummation phase? Oh God!* "Right."

"Do you know about the initial night?"

She shifted her gaze from the bland wall to Hauser's faded blue eyes. "What 'initial' night?"

He stepped close enough that his unique male scent drifted across her conscious. He didn't touch her as if sensing her reluctance to touch another man so soon after the vivid experience with Dominick, but he leaned an elbow on the wall. Hauser's quiet voice washed over her. "Where you'll be with each of us in a twenty-four-hour period?"

Valerie's eyes widened. "At the same time?" She really should have paid more attention during the orientation they'd forced her to go through.

"No. No. Each of us will get three hours with you to…um…consummate. But it's only a single time with each of us. Just so we can stop shaking from our enforced abstinence. Plus, it's sort of the alien version of a honeymoon night. They even refer to it as that. Following the honeymoon, you'll be directed to our regular living quarters after the fifth man has…finished."

Heart pounding nearly to her throat, she asked, "And who is going first?"

"Me." His quick grin relieved her anxiety a notch. "You'll consummate in the same order you met us."

Her brain sifted through the information. Hauser being her initial lover was good. The scarier proposition was that Dominick would be the final man to slake his long-awaited lust. That auspicious event would take place after she'd already had sex with four other men. She didn't mean it when she said, "Okay."

"You don't have anything to worry about."

"That's easy for you to say, you don't have to sleep with five strangers tonight."

"It's been two months since any of us had sex." The low tone of his voice caught her complete attention. "We can't come any other way. Trust me, tonight will be about immediate relief."

Valerie nodded. "I know. I'm sorry."

Hauser kissed her lightly on the mouth. "There's nothing for you to be sorry about." Without saying another word, he led her to the ceremony room to seal her with finality for three years. God help her.

Chapter 5

Valerie squeezed Hauser's hand as they entered the room where the group would finalize their sexual arrangement. The other men were already in position awaiting them.

They stood on one side of a chalkboard-sized, thick pane of glass. Hauser joined them. It looked like a prison visitation scene. Lined up like human dominoes, each of the men she was about to become intimately acquainted with had his left hand resting on a countertop behind the glass panel.

Five hand-shaped impressions were embedded in the countertop and they each had a hand resting in the indentation. On the other side was a single hand-shaped impression waiting for her to begin this unholy partnership.

Valerie put her hand down and closed her eyes for strength. Something warm emitted from beneath the space where her hand rested, and an unexpected pinprick of pain centering in her palm ended it.

Jerking her hand up, she checked to see if her skin had been broken. Her hand was clean. No wound. No blood. It wasn't even red. Hauser slid around the panel, threw an arm around her shoulder and led her from the room.

"Okay, it's just you and me for the next three hours." He squeezed her shoulder and a flutter of arousal zinged from where he touched her arm all the way to her clit.

The tingle of pleasure now causing a flood between her legs made her want to hurry to their destination. "Where are we going?"

"The honeymoon suite." Hauser led her through a maze of hallways similar to the one she'd met him in. They encountered few people along the way.

"It's pretty quiet here." Valerie glanced left and right as they marched along the corridors of the alien craft.

"This section of the alien ship houses only human admission and mating administration. Once we move to our permanent quarters, there'll be more people around." He stopped before an ordinary door with a keypad on the left side. Hauser pressed his thumb on the illuminated white pad and the door slid open.

"After you."

Valerie took a deep, silent breath and entered the room. Much like the room she'd originally met all of her men in, there was a sofa, two chairs and table in an arrangement, but beyond the entry was an open set of double glass doors leading to her perception of a fantasy bedroom.

What looked like miles of white gauzy fabric was artfully draped and swirled over a huge canopied, four-poster bed that was also covered in yards of white linen.

"Wow," she whispered. "Nice room. Like out of a fairy tale."

Hauser's hands landed on her shoulders. "Does it relax you enough for what's about to happen between us?"

Valerie turned to face a smiling Hauser as heat rose to her cheeks. "I'm not sure."

"Well, why don't we start with a kiss and see where that leads us." Hauser gently slipped his hands through her hair to cup her head. He leaned in for a kiss in the next second and the utter pleasure of his skillful tongue was enough to make her forget absolutely everything else.

He cradled her face with one hand as the other slid around her back to clench her solidly against his body.

It was no secret why they were here. Hauser hadn't had sex for a long time and she was here to relieve his discomfort. That was her job. Her primary purpose in this alternate reality.

Hauser's tongue brushed tenderly against hers and a tendril of desire unwound in her body. A moan escaped. He squeezed her tighter as more moaning ensued from her throat. Her vocal response prompted his hand to blaze a trail down her spine on a mission to massage her ass. His thickening cock pulsed between them, sending a shower of sensation and moisture between her legs.

The dress she wore was silk and she hadn't bothered to put any underwear on beneath it. Hauser broke the kiss to dip his hand beneath the hem at her knees. His light stroke skimmed up the outside of her thigh. When he discovered her lack of undergarments, he growled and thrust his hips forward.

He pulled away far enough to catch her eye and say, "My, aren't you just full of surprises."

"One or two." She pulled his head down for another sultry kiss.

His cock, huge and hard, pressed firmly into her stomach as a shudder rippled down his body. He squeezed her bare butt cheek once before sliding clever fingers between her legs. Two long fingers thrust inside her wet slit before she could protest. Not that she would have, but his intimate touch was a little shocking.

Her Swiss-cheese memory gave her little in the way of a foundation from her previous sexual experience. Given that every touch from his fingers seemed alien and overwhelming, she decided that she might be fairly inexperienced. His fingers slid in and out of her slick entrance easily and the feeling, while deliciously decadent, also felt incredibly naughty.

His thumb rubbed across her sensitive clit and she jumped backwards in surprise, breaking not only the kiss, but the intimate connection.

Panting, Hauser asked, "What's wrong?"

"I…um…nothing. I'm…just not used to…you know." She ended her stuttering sentence with a whisper.

The rate of his breathing said he was still trying to get it under control. "No. Tell me."

"I don't remember much about my life on Earth, but I get the feeling that I'm not very experienced…sexually. What you're doing to me…seems very unexpected…and naughty."

He laughed. "That's okay. I think naughty pretty much describes this whole scenario. But don't worry, I'll teach you everything you need to know."

Valerie nodded. "Okay." She took a deep breath and released it.

"God, you're sexy." He grabbed her shoulder with one hand, hugged her close and planted his lips sensually across her mouth, teasing her lips open with his tongue.

He danced her backwards slowly, through the double glass doors and into the bedroom. His tongue dipped and swirled inside her mouth, dueling with hers to a tempo only he could hear. Valerie slung her arms around his neck to hold on as they traveled. The thick ridge of his cock ground into her belly and aroused speculation regarding his size. She now knew he was huge and a ripple of arousal trickled down her body in anticipation as her core throbbed in readiness for him.

Once next to the bed, he yanked the zipper of her dress from neck to ass in one smooth, loud zip and a blast of cool air brushed her bare back. Hauser separated them enough to pull the pink dress off of her body. She was completely naked underneath.

She boldly grabbed his cock, which pulsed against her belly, and squeezed. He was indeed huge.

"Jesus, that feels incredible." Hauser gave her a salacious grin and quickly pulled his clothing off until he, too, was completely naked. He reached past her and pulled the comforter down, exposing the sheets. As he straightened, he latched his lips onto her breast, sucking one lucky nipple into the depths of his warm mouth.

Valerie slid her hands to his face to hold him in place as the most acute pleasure rode wildly inside her. He suckled and a delightful zing shot straight to her clit and a gush flooded the core of her pussy. Hauser didn't linger, but soon kissed a path from breast to mouth and drove his tongue languidly inside her mouth as he pulled her snugly against his pulsing erection. She nudged him with her hips and he clutched her even tighter.

"You feel so good, Valerie," he murmured against her cheek. "I don't think I can last too much longer."

"You don't have to. Take me to bed. I don't want you to suffer anymore."

"Trust me, I'm not suffering at all." He latched his mouth to hers.

They tumbled onto the bed, never breaking the kiss. Hauser's cock rested between her aching thighs. He shifted his hands, sending one to stroke the nipple of one breast. The other slid carefully between her legs to rub her clit. The sensations in her body accumulated quickly, and with little effort, a surprise crescendo of pleasure ripped through her, arching her spine off the bed in its intensity.

Hauser didn't wait long before thrusting his thick cock deeply inside her pulsing core. The remnants of her climax tightened and rippled around his huge shaft as he sped his thrusts.

Suspended in the moment of supreme bliss, Valerie relished the satisfied groans he made with each push forward. She kissed his jaw and buried her face against his neck. His seductive masculine scent invaded her lungs with each breath as he pumped his cock all the way inside her pussy.

With his final thrust, Hauser stiffened, whispered her name and flooded her insides with a rush of liquid heat. An unexpected climax squeezed her core and she cried out, arching against his chest. After several pulse-pounding moments, Valerie slumped back to the bed.

Hauser stilled atop her and whispered, "That was amazing. Are you okay?"

"Yes. I'm just trying to remember how to breathe." She hugged him close and kissed his cheek.

"Good. Kissing you in the arena didn't quite make me come, but it certainly took enough of the edge off so I didn't fall on you like a ravening beast the moment we stepped into this room."

"I appreciate that. Not that a ravening beast isn't just a little bit exciting, but perhaps we could save animalistic behavior for when we know each other a little better."

Resting on one elbow, Hauser fixed a soft gaze on her eyes, brushing light fingertips from her face to her collarbone as he asked quietly, "Are you going to be okay with all of us for three years?"

Valerie shrugged. "I guess I'll have to be, won't I?"

"I'll do everything I can to make our time together tolerable."

"If what you just did is your definition of tolerable, I'm dragging you back to Earth when we leave."

Hauser laughed and kissed her mouth tenderly. "After what just happened between us, I'll let you." He wrapped long arms around her, snuggled close and soon his even breathing signaled that he was likely asleep.

Valerie, sated enough to fall sleep herself after the incredible lovemaking, only managed to catnap until it was time to go. A foolish phrase bounced around in her mind: One down, four more to go.

Surprisingly, she wasn't apprehensive about what would happen next. She wondered if the aliens had somehow drugged her to be more accepting of sex with five men in a single day. Was that what the pinprick was during the ceremony? Tranquillizers for the bride?

Perhaps there would be repeated shots of a calming drug in the hand for acquiescence over the next three years. The next time she saw Blue, she'd ask him.

Like five first dates wasn't bad enough without five equally awkward moments of let's-have-sex-with-a-stranger to go with them. Although in bed, Hauser had been exactly as she expected. Sifting through the names of her new 'mated men,' in order, her only heart-pounding worry had to do with the last man on the list. Dominick had given her pleasure during a kiss but hadn't received any reciprocation. Would that make him more aggressive when she got to him?

A light bell chimed, apparently signaling that her time with Hauser had come to an end. Hauser woke, shifted to his elbows, kissed her lips and pointed to a door she hadn't noticed.

"Go through there. There'll be instructions in the room for you. I'll see you tomorrow morning at our permanent residence."

"Okay." She turned and slid naked from the bed.

"And Valerie," he called. She looked over her shoulder with raised eyebrows.

"Thank you."

She winked and exited. Three years with Hauser would not be a chore.

Inside the small adjoining room, Valerie found a clear cylindrical tube positioned vertically against one wall. She'd seen a picture of one during the orientation. She hadn't paid much attention to any instructions during orientation, let alone ones explaining the use of the showers. Hopefully there were pictographs somewhere.

What looked like a space-age clear sink and toilet was tucked in a corner across the narrow space. She availed herself of the facilities and studied the room. The instructions posted on the wall next to the see-through tube told her to disrobe completely and enter for body cleansing.

Her first alien body cleansing. Great.

Valerie stepped into the tube. She positioned her feet in the two spaces marked on the floor with pictures. At shoulder level on either side of her were hand holds that looked remarkably like toilet roll dispensers. She gripped the handles and the door shut.

Exposed as she was, it was a little disconcerting when a forceful wind rushed up and around her nude body. With her legs spread wide, she was brushed with air all over. Even between her legs pushing up inside her pussy, which was more than a little disconcerting. The air eventually turned cooler, then warmer and finally a light jasmine fragrance was introduced in a misty, scented application.

After several minutes the wind stopped and a sign lit up stating, "Cleansing process complete." Valerie guessed this was the aliens' version of a shower. She felt clean, surprisingly enough, and climbed carefully out of the cylinder. A second door lit up around the frame and in the center a display read, "Enter when prepared."

On the wall next to the welcoming door, a peach-colored robe hung. She slipped into the soft silk garment and tied the belt in a bow at her waist. Taking a deep breath, she entered the appointed door not knowing exactly what to expect next.

Johnny, dressed in a white button-up shirt and with faded blue jeans clinging to his hips, waited by the door and greeted her immediately when she entered. "Right on time, lovie."

Valerie closed the door and he moved very close. Circling behind her, Johnny pressed his front to her back, as he had in the greeting room, and whispered in her ear, "Are you hungry?"

She cleared her throat. "No. Not hungry." The utterly sexy and delectable scent of him was all around her. She closed her eyes so as to inhale and focus on him and whatever he planned to do. A prickle low in her belly tightened and her nipples pebbled and became very aware of the silk caressing them.

Johnny's arms wrapped around her from behind and she was pulled against him intimately. One hand gripped her shoulder and the other hugged her at the waist. He nibbled her earlobe and whispered, "May I touch you?"

Valerie sucked in a short breath and moaned as she released the air from her lungs. "Yes. Please."

Johnny's body remained perfectly still and pressed firmly against her, but his lips trailed light, tingling kisses from neck to shoulder. His arms slid down until both hands rested on her hips.

The silk robe shifted and fell open slightly at the neck, exposing the inner curve of her breast and the barest edge of one nipple. Valerie suspected that she had never felt as sexy as she did in this moment.

Chin resting on her shoulder, Johnny, who towered over her, tilted his head to look down her body. After an appreciative-sounding groan, he whispered, "Ah, lovie, you're exquisite."

His hands slipped to the opening of her robe and parted it to fully expose both breasts. She watched with rapt attention as his tanned fingertips stroked and kneaded the mounds of her sensitive breasts. Aggravatingly enough, he avoided stroking the peaks of her very hard nipples and, after several minutes, she moaned.

"Touch me," she whispered.

"I *am* touching you." His low, seductive rumble of laughter followed, but he stopped teasing and squeezed her distended nipples. Ripe, hot pleasure shot from the tips of her breasts, through her veins and landed in the wet space between her legs. She sucked in an audible breath and her eyes drifted shut to enjoy the sensation of being touched.

On some level, she'd worried about being 'in the mood' so soon after her experience with Hauser. However, as she'd strolled through Johnny's door, a rush of exhilaration washed through her body. Perhaps the pinprick additionally provided an aphrodisiac when needed. It was as if she'd been without sex as long as Johnny had. The anxious swell of arousal rode roughshod over her inhibitions the moment she came into contact with him.

"I'm ready. Take me to bed, Johnny."

"I don't want it to be over so quickly, lovie, and if I get into that bed with you," his arms squeezed her shoulders and held on, "I fear I won't be able to control myself. Nor will I be able to last very long."

Valerie shivered. "I'm not sure I care about that. You feel so good."

"The longer we stay vertical, the longer our fun will last." He nibbled on her earlobe and rained soft kisses along her neck as if to convince her.

She was very convinced.

"Okay."

Johnny resumed his tactile torture, making her so aroused she could smell his attentions in the form of her pungent arousal. He pulled away suddenly, spun her to face him, and kissed her hard on the lips. His passionately delivered oral copulation opened a well of emotion inside her heart that threatened to boil over. The sensation of her naked breasts pressed to his warm fully clothed body was wickedly sexy.

After a few sensual moments, he broke the kiss and fell to his knees. Parting her robe completely, he kissed a path to her belly, veered off course to kiss one hipbone and then lowed his head to lick the most imitate place between her legs.

Clit fluttering and pulsing in delight, Valerie nearly came after he stroked his clever tongue across her incredibly sensitive hot spot.

"Oh, Johnny." She plunged her fingers into his dark wavy hair, pulling him closer. His face buried between her thighs sucking tenderly on her clit, Valerie thought she might climax standing up. He slid two fingers inside her pussy and her knees buckled.

"Please, Johnny."

He stopped sucking, but his fingers remained inside her body. "You don't want me to stop, do you?" He kissed his way back up her torso until he closed his warm, wet mouth over one nipple, sucking it between his lips. Valerie trembled with the desire to climax.

"No. Not really. I just thought you'd be more anxious to have sex, since you've been without for so long."

He pulled his lips from her nipple with a pop and laughed. "Oh, we *are* having sex, lovie. This is what I call foreplay."

"Ah," Valerie said as if in sudden understanding. "Foreplay, you say? I like it."

Johnny laughed again and kissed his way back down to the pulsing nub between her legs. Fingers continuing to move in and out of her body, his tongue found her clit and after only one circle, she came.

The blissful waves of pressure centering in her core burst brilliantly and she screamed as the surprise orgasm flashed across her body. Johnny's fingers moved seductively in and out of her body and as the climax vibrated, Valerie dropped her head and watched him kiss a path to her belly.

She couldn't hold herself up any longer. Collapsing to her knees, she rested her head on Johnny's shoulder. He removed his hands from her and picked her up in his arms. Snuggled close, she sighed as he carried her to the bed and deposited her on the soft surface.

He kissed her mouth and whispered against her lips, "I can't wait to plunge my cock inside, lovie. Tell me you're eager."

"I'm desperate, Johnny." *And she was.*

"Brilliant." He stripped his clothing off quickly and climbed on the bed next to her. His cock was as huge as Hauser's. Not that she had intended to compare. Perhaps they all had similarly sized cocks and that was the true reason the aliens had placed them in the same group together instead of their comparable temperament.

Johnny kissed her and all other thoughts left her mind. He climbed on top and her knees fell apart as if by magic when his cock brushed the sensitive inside part of her thigh.

"Take me, Johnny," Valerie whispered. She angled her hips so that his cock slipped between her legs and found the entrance to her pussy. Brushing her over-sensitive clit slightly, he grabbed her hip one-handed digging his fingers into her flesh and promptly plunged his shaft deeply inside. A resonate groan of appreciation escaped his throat with each following thrust.

Valerie looped her legs around his thighs and grabbed his ass to encourage a deeper connection. He growled and pushed even harder until the telltale stiffening of his body signaled his orgasm.

The warmth of his climax shooting inside initiated an orgasm Valerie didn't expect. She bucked in surprise, arching her back as she came. Waves of pleasure rained across her nerve endings and she could hardly catch her breath. Johnny seemed to be having the same problem, but he held her close until they were both relaxed. He curled his body around hers snugly and buried his face in her neck.

Once he stopped panting enough to speak, he kissed her cheek and whispered, "When we're together again, we'll make time to play a game."

"Okay."

He yawned and his eyes slid shut, right before he mumbled, "What's your ...word...?"

Valerie shrugged at the odd question. "Word? I'm not sure what you mean."

He muttered something she didn't hear and snuggled closer.

"What kind of games do you like?" She asked, but Johnny was already fast asleep.

Valerie dozed off and dreamed of all her favorite board games from childhood. When she woke up sometime later, Johnny had migrated to the other side of the bed.

The outline of the door across the room lit up in red. Valerie sat up in bed, glanced back at a soundly sleeping Johnny and slid from the sheets without waking him.

One more trip to the bathroom area. Valerie was more comfortable with the vortex shower of wind the second time around. It freshened her again, but this time with a different fragrance. A light gardenia scent dusted her skin as she exited the tube.

Searching around for the robe, she cocked her head to one side when she noticed the clothing waiting. Not a robe this time. Instead, a modest white blouse and navy silk skirt with accompanying undergarments hung on a padded fabric hanger next to the door. Her fashion sense was not keen, but the outfit looked like something out of a mid-twentieth-century movie. Classic and expensive, but definitely from the Veronica Lake fashion era. A low stool beneath the hanger sported navy patent leather pumps and tucked inside were stockings and garter belts. Garter belts?

Frasier apparently wanted her to look like a forties movie starlet. Valerie relaxed and donned the clothing. She left the panties hanging on the hook and the thrill of going commando again lit her libido on fire. She couldn't wait to get inside and have him peel off these clothes. She'd watch for his expression when he found that she lacked undergarments.

He was across the room when she stepped inside. The room looked like it was out of a movie set. Lots of dark wood and flashes of hunter-green accents greeted her once she crossed the threshold.

Frasier was dressed in a white shirt complete with a cravat and dark riding pants with boots. He looked like a historical romance hero ready to sweep her off her feet.

Valerie was ready to be swept into the bedroom. Her pussy ached as if she hadn't had sex or relief in months. It was as if the more sex she had, the more she wanted. Strange. Dream-like. Hot.

She crossed the room with the intent to get him into bed, now. She didn't want foreplay. She wanted sex. Immediately.

"Hi, Valerie. You look great."

"Thanks. Did you pick out the clothes?"

He ducked his head once and blushed. "Are they okay?"

"They're perfect. But they don't need to stay on for very long."

Frasier's brow furrowed. "I'm sorry. What?"

Valerie slid close and tucked an arm around his waist. "I mean, don't feel like you can't rip them off whenever you'd like. I'm ready for you."

He coughed into one hand and jumped when her hand landed on his ass, squeezing one cheek. "Hold on a minute. I thought we'd have a nice dinner before…you know."

"I don't want to hold on for a minute. Let's have sex and then we can eat. You don't have to spend a lot of time on foreplay. I'm a sure thing and I really want you."

Frasier narrowed his gaze. "I believe that some things are worth waiting for." He tenderly brushed a strand of hair from her face.

"Well, I believe that some things deserve immediate attention." She grabbed his cock, which stiffened in her hand. His eyes fairly budged in surprise. He bent in half at her bold touch. "Wait, Valerie."

"I don't want to wait any longer. I need you."

"Share a meal with me first." He removed her hand from his pulsing erection, kissed her fingertips and added, "Please."

Frasier nodded at the table behind him. She glanced at the elaborate dining table filled to capacity with formal glassware, dinnerware, a large centerpiece with a riot of colorful blooms and more silverware than she'd probably know what to do with. He'd obviously gone to some trouble to arrange for this food.

Turning back, Valerie forced herself to relax. She promptly sighed, "Right. Dinner would be lovely. Thank you."

Placing an arm gently around her shoulders, Frasier led her to the dining table and promptly held out her chair. The formal atmosphere was a little difficult to adjust to given her previous liaisons. Valerie took a deep breath and allowed herself to be pampered just a little.

Once she was seated, he kissed her forehead and removed the silver cover to reveal roast beef, potatoes and carrots in an artful arrangement on her plate.

"I hope you enjoy it."

"I'm sure I will." Valerie found that she was very hungry all of a sudden. "Thank you."

"Wine?"

"Yes. Please."

Frasier lifted the wine bottle off the table and went about opening it. A calmness settled over his features as if he were finally able to operate in his element. Spontaneous sex was apparently not something he was comfortable with, but the ritual of a formal intimate dinner for two obviously fit very nicely into his purview.

She'd have to take notes. Each man would of course have

idiosyncrasies.

He popped the cork on the dark green bottle, filled both glasses with a deep red wine and finally seated himself beside her. Beneath the table, his leg brushed hers intimately and he didn't remove it. Valerie would have to pay attention to each man as an individual while she was here. Naturally, they would all have a different system of seduction.

The fresh flower arrangement on the table sent a fragrant wisp of floral scent around them. Frasier ate slowly and watched her with a smolderingly passionate gaze throughout the meal. Valerie ate little, but drank two full glasses of wine.

Once she'd pushed her food around on her plate for a long time, Frasier placed his silverware on the plate and stood.

He studied her for a few seconds, bent at the waist slightly and held out a hand. "I think we should dance."

Valerie perked up. If sexy glances were tactile, there wouldn't be a single place on her body left untouched.

"Dance?" She stood with his help and he pulled her close to his body.

"Do you like to dance?"

"Sure." Valerie didn't know whether she did or not. She couldn't remember. "I don't remember being very good at it though."

He placed a light kiss on her lips. "I'll lead, then."

The chaste kiss might as well have been a stroke across her clitoris. Valerie shuddered as if he'd fingered her intimately.

Pulling her across the room without releasing her, Frasier pushed a button on the wall and the strains of a slow jazzy instrumental filled the room.

He tightened his grip on her hand, slid his other arm around her back, pulling her close to his warm frame, and smiled as he stared deeply into her eyes, drawing her complete attention.

Valerie melted into his arms as he led her deftly around the small space. His mesmerizing gaze never left her eyes for a second and after several turns around the room, she wanted to slither to his feet and beg for sex. His seduction technique, while tamer, slower and certainly more formal, was no less effective on her heightened libido.

The music stopped and before a new song started, Frasier stopped moving and leaned in for another kiss. Soft and sweet turned wicked and wanton very quickly as his lips moved over hers in seductive pleasure. Valerie fairly burned with need. Frasier distracted her with the kiss and moved her backwards toward the bed. The scent of fresh flowers melded with the spicy fragrance of his cologne and another gush of moisture shot between her legs.

There was something to be said for anticipation. As he'd done everything else since she entered the room, Frasier undressed her slowly and reverently. His eyes darkened when he saw she wore no panties. He peeled his clothes off slowly as she watched. Once he was nude, he moved closer. His cock was magnificent. She hadn't been able to look at anything else since he'd kicked his pants aside.

"You're beautiful," he whispered. He cupped her head with one hand and kissed her lips. His fingertips slid from shoulder to breast and he kneaded her flesh with tender appreciation. Brushing the nipple with his thumb sent a pulse of desire straight to her clit. She was desperate and he'd barely touched her.

Valerie was incredibly turned on from the entire evening. Everything Frasier did to her was amplified to an unbearable need.

She slipped her hand down to caress his cock. He made an articulate noise the moment she touched his stiff flesh and groaned with need when she gripped his cock in her fist. Caressing her fingers up and down his shaft gave Valerie a feeling of power as he reacted. His hips thrust forward with every stroke of her hand until she was abruptly on her back in the center of the bed.

"Take me, Frasier. I can't wait a second longer."

"My pleasure, darling." He entered her with a slow, deep thrust. She cried out as his thick shaft filled her completely.

"You're so tight," he whispered. "God, you feel great,"

Valerie couldn't do more than make inarticulate noises of encouragement as he pumped his cock leisurely inside her pussy. Her arousal built to a hot frenzy of need. Frasier slid his hand between them, stroked her clit once and as she came, she screamed.

He buried his face against her throat, kissed her skin repeatedly and continued thrusting his cock inside her drenched pussy with reverent patience. Each powerful stroke hit her womb and sent a vibration of pleasure through every cell in her body.

Several minutes later he shuddered and groaned quietly as he unleashed a torrential flood of warmth inside her core. The rush of another orgasm blazed through her. She arched against him in surprise.

"Valerie." Her name whispered through his lips over and over until she relaxed against the bed. He followed her down still pumping his glorious thick shaft inside her body, albeit at an even slower pace. As Frasier kissed a path from her neck to her collarbone, she released a long sigh of utter contentment and kissed the top of his head.

"That was amazing, Frasier. You aren't quite as sedate in bed as you led me to believe." She laughed and ruffled his hair between her fingers.

"It's all you, darling. You bring out something powerful in me." His voice was barely a coherent whisper. Shortly thereafter, he drifted to sleep snuggled against her.

One more...and then...him.

Valerie shivered and hugged Frasier closer. She closed her eyes, drifted into a light sleep and tried not to worry about her final 'date,' Dominick.

* * * *

The light around another door came on when she opened her eyes. Frasier didn't move when she left his bed. She was getting the hang of this strangeness and that bothered her on some level, but she was tiring and didn't take time to analyze her feelings.

Another trip through the vortex shower of wind, a new fragrance and another outfit of clothing awaited her before meeting Mark. He'd left a t-shirt and jeans for her to wear.

Mark sat sprawled on the center of the sofa when she entered. A sports station displayed a football game on the flat-screen television against one wall. On his knee rested a bottle half filled with what looked like beer. His shirt was completely open and displayed his mouth-watering physique.

Studying his nicely defined chest muscles, she caught the glint of gold on one flat nipple. The visual sent a pulse of sexual longing from sensitive nipples to her now unsatisfied clit.

How could she still be horny?

"A nipple ring?"

He laughed. "Yeah. Does it turn you on?" Mark tipped the beer bottle to his lips and took a long swig.

"Yeah." She relaxed a little. "Actually, it does."

"Come on over here. Sit with me for awhile."

Valerie strolled across the room without hesitation. She fairly licked her lips in anticipation of the coming few hours.

A chill raced down her spine at the thought that after Mark, she'd have to deal with Dominick. Her unreasonable fear would have to be dealt with later. For now she lowered herself into the seat next to Mark with the wicked intent of licking his nipple ring to see his reaction.

"I won't stop you," Mark said and tilted the bottle for another long drink.

"Stop me?"

"If you want to explore." He ran a thumb distractedly over his nipple and the gold ring flat against his skin.

Valerie leaned forward and licked the tip of one flat nipple, flipping the gold circle over her tongue. He pushed out a surprised breath, put a free hand on the back of her head to hold her against his chest and her panties flooded.

"Jesus." He set his bottle down hard on the table next to the sofa where they sat.

She sucked the ring between her lips unable to stop playing with it. His hand slid from her head, down her back and cupped her ass.

"Straddle me." His panted whisper sent a zinging thrill straight to her clit. She released his nipple and scrambled to position herself astride his lap. His cock tented his jeans and Valerie reached out to grab and squeeze his thick shaft. He groaned and shut his eyes.

Mark's solid fingers went to her breasts. She'd neglected to put the bra on that he'd left for her. His realization of this fact was priceless. An inarticulate sound passed through his lips and he thumbed her nipples to hard pebbles beneath the soft material of her shirt.

"Can we have sex right here?" Valerie was so turned on she didn't think she could make it off the sofa without an orgasm.

"Whatever you want, sweetheart," he panted. Both hands snuck beneath her shirt and fastened to her bare breasts. He pulled her shirt over her head and replaced one hand with his mouth. Sucking her nipple between his lips sent a pulse of hot achy pleasure straight to her pussy.

Valerie pushed her breast into his face and he nibbled at the tip. The tug of sensation teased her arousal to a fevered pitch.

She scooted backwards off his lap and grabbed at her jeans to pull them off as quickly as possible. Mark also stood and yanked his clothing off. When they were both naked, Valerie moved forward and pressed her body to his. The hard circle of his nipple ring pushed into her flesh eliciting a fresh spasm of pleasure through her body. Valerie kissed his mouth and in return, he devoured her.

His fingertips stroked and tickled her spine as he plunged his tongue between her lips in carnal abandon. Valerie pushed him back and they tumbled to the sofa.

Her wet pussy lips grazed his cock, but it didn't penetrate.

Mark jerked beneath her. "Not that I'm complaining, but I think we're supposed to go missionary for this initial time. It can be our one time for the year—"

"I don't want to," Valerie interrupted. She lifted her hips and impaled herself on his thick shaft until he was balls deep in her pussy.

"Jesus." Mark's eyes nearly rolled back in his head as he arched forward. Valerie lifted her hips and started moving over him.

"I want to ride you."

His arms snaked around her back and clenched her torso as his mouth landed on one breast. He sucked her pebbled nipple hard into his mouth and bit the tip lightly as she moved up and down on his cock. The bite sent another pulse of hot need straight to her clit.

Suddenly his hand shot between their bodies and his thumb stroked her pulsing clit. She slammed her pussy down on his cock as an orgasm exploded within her body. His teeth on her nipple sent the electricity of release careening through her nerve endings. Valerie heard a screech of satisfaction and realized it came from her throat.

Mark shifted his hands to her hips, held her in place and thrust upwards until she thought he would split her in two with his wide cock.

"Look at me," he panted after several minutes. "Watch me come."

Valerie tilted her head to gaze into his lust-crazed eyes as he pierced her again and came. He blinked as a growl of ecstasy tore from his throat. The moment he climaxed, Valerie did too.

The rush of heightened release was almost too much to bear. As waves of pleasure rode over her, Valerie stiffened and then slumped forward. She shuddered once and collapsed against Mark's chest in satiated wonder. The glint of the nipple ring caught her attention and she ran her thumb over it then flattened her fingers over his chest and rubbed.

"You're playing with fire, sweetheart." He covered her hand with his and brought her fingers to his lips.

"What kind of fire?"

"The kind that leads to more sex."

"I'm okay with that."

He laughed. "I am too, but there are rules for the honeymoon night." He put her hand on his chest and ran a finger down her face.

"Rules? I'm not really in the mood for rules."

"This rule is what's best for you, sweetheart. Only one time for each of us on this honeymoon night."

Valerie wondered if she could talk him into more. "So if I were to entice you to fuck me again, you'd turn me down?"

"I have zero willpower, so don't tempt me." He kissed her forehead.

A tendril of dread crept down her spine at the thought of only a couple of hours separating her from Dominick. Valerie hated to be such a child about it. He wouldn't hurt her, would he?

"Can we get in bed? I haven't slept much."

"Sure." Mark stood up with her attached to him. He carried her to the bed and they snuggled beneath the covers together.

Mark fell asleep right away, but Valerie couldn't sleep at all. Her thought strayed to the inevitable. Dominick was her final lover for this evening. He hadn't climaxed when they'd met and kissed. He'd been without sex for months and he was so big. Nothing would stop him from getting what he wanted from her. Dread became her sole thought. She worked herself into a nerve-wracked ball of fear after only a few minutes.

In an act of pure defiance, and to keep her mind off her anxiety over her next liaison, she slithered over next to Mark and stroked his cock until it was stone hard as he slept. Before he woke completely, she climbed on top and rode him.

He woke seconds before his climax showered her pussy. Valerie also came, proving that something had been done to ensure she had an orgasm after each of her partners did. Perhaps it was incentive for her to make it easier with five men to satisfy.

"Jesus, sweetheart. What did you do to me?"

"I couldn't sleep. I wanted you again." The panic registering on his face confused her. "What's wrong?"

He ran a hand down his face. "I was told to only have sex with you once tonight. I'm not sure of the penalty for disobedience."

"You didn't have sex with me a second time. I had sex with you. I purposely lured you in your sleep. It was all me."

"I hope the aliens see it that way."

Valerie frowned. "I'm sorry. I just—"

"Don't be sorry. I didn't try very hard to stop you, now did I?" Mark flashed her a quick grin, slipped his arms around her and hugged her against his body.

Valerie was despondent. She'd coaxed Mark into having sex with her again to take her mind off the fear of having sex with Dominick.

Ashamed of herself for breaking the rules and possibly causing trouble for Mark, she dozed off in his arms, uneasy.

The bell woke her. She didn't know how long she'd been asleep, but Mark was gone. Alone in the bed, her fear escalated at his absence. The light around the door across the room flashed as the bell sounded over and over again, reminding her that she had one last man to service tonight.

Beyond her worry about Mark, she didn't think she wasn't ready to face her greatest fear.

Dominick.

Chapter 6

Valerie took her sweet-assed time in the changing room between Mark and Dominick's rooms. She went through the vortex wind shower twice until another light started flashing around the door she was to enter when complete.

As with Johnny, another robe hung on the wall waiting for her to slip into it and face her doom. Hand shaking, Valerie slipped the soft flannel robe on and tied the belt securely around her waist.

Taking a deep breath she entered the room where Dominick waited for her.

"You took so long I thought you'd changed your mind." Dominick's deep voice greeted her through the darkness of the room. She couldn't see him, but he sounded like he was straight ahead.

"I was a little nervous." Valerie closed the door behind her and flattened her shoulder blades against the center of it.

"Why?"

"You're big and you scare me." Holy crap. Did she say that out loud? A hand slid to cover her lips. She needed a filter on her mouth in this place. Her emotions were riddled with fear. She needed to calm herself.

"What do you think I'm going to do?" This time his phantom voice came from somewhere to her left.

Dropping her fingers from her face she said, "I don't know, but I wouldn't be able to stop you, and that scares me."

He didn't respond and the silence was unbearable. Not being able to see him moving around the room sent a fresh warning to her heart which already thumped wildly.

A dim light snapped on, finally illuminating his room. He stood by the light, next to the sofa, but it didn't reveal his expression. She only saw a sofa and chair surrounding a floor rug. The bedroom beyond was shrouded in shadows.

"Do we need a safe word?"

Valerie swallowed. "I don't know what that is."

"It's an established word used during sexual submission and domination."

Domination? Ohmigod! What was he going to do to her? The words submission and domination sent twin streaks of terror directly to her soul. A sudden emotional sob burst forth through her lips without permission and a single tear escaped over one lower eyelid streaming quickly down her face. She absolutely hated to weep, but couldn't seem to control her emotions now that she was ensconced in the dark space with Dominick.

"Are you crying?"

"No." Even if a torrential flood of tears were to suddenly gush forth from her eyes and drown the two of them, Valerie refused to admit to even the single tear coursing down her cheek. "I'm frightened. Are you satisfied?" An unexpected sniff accompanied her query lending certain disbelief to her words.

"Not yet." Through the shadows she heard him release a long sigh. "And I guess I'm not going to be."

"I don't want to be dominated."

"Fine." He didn't say anything else. She glanced at where he stood, but couldn't see his face clearly enough to determine what that single-word retort meant.

"What are you going to do to me?" She swallowed hard, hating the quiver lodged in her voice almost as much as the loathed water seeping from her eyes.

"Nothing."

Valerie straightened against the door. "I thought you needed sex."

"Oh, I do." His sardonic laugh floated across the room. "You have no idea."

She wiped the tear from her cheek and considered his answer. "Aren't you going to just take me?"

"Not against your will." His affronted tone surprised her. "I just don't 'get off' that way."

"How do you 'get off'?"

He laughed. "I don't, babe. That's the problem. I need sex like you can't imagine and while you're my singular outlet, I won't force you."

Valerie digested his words carefully. "I see."

"Do you want something to eat?"

The sudden change of topic threw her off guard and the need to weep thankfully evaporated. The unexpected scent of appetizing food wafted across the room and her stomach rumbled in hunger.

"I'll take that as a yes."

A few seconds later another light snapped on and she could see a modest table set for two between the living room and the now less shadowy bedroom.

Dominick stood between the rooms. He was a tall, imposing figure towering over the space he occupied, but apparently he wasn't going to force her to have sex.

A warm fuzzy sensation low in her belly warned her that the wicked, wild side of her libido found Dominick very attractive and eminently desirable. It was the same exact sensation as when they'd met. The memory of her climax when he'd pushed her against the wall and kissed her senseless breezed through her thoughts. It was as if his barely restrained desires pulsed through the air to tempt her with a siren song of unfound pleasures.

Valerie shook her head and tamped down her arousal.

He leaned over, pulled out a chair from the table and motioned for her to sit. Valerie walked on unsteady legs towards him. She glanced down and almost stumbled when she saw the tent of his trousers and his thick cock straining to get out. He couldn't help it, she supposed, and bucked up when her stomach growled loudly again.

Valerie seated herself, keeping her spine in the upright and locked position. Dominick leaned down and whispered, "Did one of the others mistreat you tonight?"

She twisted in her chair and her cheek brushed a stubbly part of his jaw. The scent of food wasn't the only scrumptious flavor in the air. Dominick smelled good enough to eat. She recovered from the urge to lick his chin and said, "No. Not even close." She glanced into his eyes and saw genuine worry. No one had abused her.

"It's just that if I think about what I've been doing too closely, I'll run screaming through the maze of this place and out the nearest airlock."

"I see." He sat across from her and she lifted the lid on her plate to find a sandwich cut in half. She picked it up and took a bite. Buttery, toasted, gooey grilled cheese filled her mouth and she moaned in appreciation. There was nothing like comfort food to soothe a troubled spirit. They ate in companionable silence and Valerie thought about what Dominick had said.

He wouldn't force her. She glanced across the table. He'd finished eating and sat with arms crossed, head tilted backward, staring at the ceiling. Her gaze shifted to his lap and the rampant erection still straining his pants.

The tingle of arousal saturated the space between her legs. Her skin prickled as if ants were marching up and down her limbs at the thought of all that restrained power he possessed. Was that what frightened her? The power of his brawny body. Or was it something else? Was she afraid that she'd enjoy being dominated?

Worst of all, her nipples hardened as she contemplated what Dominick would do to her in bed if she let him. *If?*

She *had* to let him, didn't she? He'd kissed her to a screaming climax the first time they'd met. Besides, she'd promised to 'service' him just like the others. The others had had their turns. It was currently his turn. She was obligated.

Valerie stood. His eyes had closed, but now popped open to watch her. Making a decision that no matter how much he frightened her, she would fulfill her promise and have sex with him, she walked two steps and straddled one of his legs.

"Before you touch me, you need to know that while I won't force you, if you get any closer, I *will* persuade you to have sex with me to the best of my ability." His growled warning was delivered in a tone lower than she'd ever heard him emit.

Valerie released a soft sigh. "Okay."

His uncertain eyes widened, as if he didn't dare hope she was serious. "Don't tease me, babe."

"I'm not teasing you. I promised to have sex with you. Thank you for dinner and for giving me a little extra time. I'm ready." A hard ache vibrated deeply in her pussy and a gush of wetness coated her lower lips in anticipation of her readiness.

She placed her hands on his muscular thighs. His dick strained and pushed the cloth across his lap. She grabbed his cock through the fabric of his slacks and stroked her fingers up his stiff erection and then back down again. When she squeezed his shaft around the base, there was only a moment's pause before he launched himself at her, wrapped her in his arms and had his mouth plastered over her lips in a brutal kiss.

The table bumped his leg when he stood, tipping over in a crash of ceramics. Seven seconds later, she was horizontal on the bed in the next room with his body crushing hers. He devoured her with his aggressive mouth until she was left limp and wanting. His cock pressed a deep valley into her lower belly and she couldn't wait until he thrust inside her pussy for the first time.

Dominick pulled himself from her, groaning as if the effort of separating was difficult. Hovering over her on his knees, he pulled the tie on her robe loose and opened the garment with a snap.

"Perfect," he whispered glancing up and down her naked body.

Valerie watched as he stripped his clothes off quickly. She couldn't keep herself from staring at his cock. It was huge, like the rest of him, and she wanted it embedded in her body.

He climbed back onto the bed slowly and kissed his way from her knees to her throat. His warm breath and firm lips lit a fiery trail along her skin. By the time his lips caressed one hip, she wanted for him to fuck her senseless. Once he'd aligned their bodies, he pressed his groin to hers rhythmically, as if in simulation of sex, and kissed her mouth aggressively.

Writhing as her pussy clenched with need, she murmured, "Just take me. I think my orgasm is built in." Valerie opened her legs and maneuvered her hips in such a way as to persuade his heavy cock to enter her body.

Even his rumble of laughter turned her on. "Patience, babe. I've been dreaming about this for a couple of months."

"I'm not sure I can wait. Besides, I want to test my orgasm theory." She slipped her arms around his neck and pulled him down for a kiss. As he consumed her mouth yet again, she lifted her hips and tried to maneuver his cock between her legs. The very tip of his shaft slid across her clit during their kiss and Valerie nearly came off the bed from the illicit sensation.

She broke the kiss and whispered, "Fuck me. Please, just do it. I don't want to wait."

Dominick stared at her without saying anything. She didn't think he was going to do anything at all, until his hips moved slightly and the first inch of his cock entered her body with warm satisfying invasion.

"I was going to eat your pussy," he said, thrusting his cock inside a little further, "but I guess that can wait until next time." He rammed his stiff shaft all the way inside her slick hot core and Valerie thought she would faint from the utterly delectable sensation of being filled to her absolute brink with his wide cock. The muscles in her thighs strained to widen and accommodate him.

Dominick gazed deeply into her eyes and watched as if to record her reaction. And then he slowly fucked her. The deep, dark part of her libido gloried in it as he thrust inside her pussy with calculated movements. The sensation of his thick penetrating cock nudged her hips into action to meet his unhurried momentum. In and out his cock moved increasing the tempo with each thrust. The friction of his careful rhythm built a yearning inside her body that she'd never felt before. The pressure of his cock driving deeply sent spasms of pleasure spiraling through her body with each push. After several minutes, Valerie was panting so hard, it was a wonder she didn't hyperventilate. It was the single most overwhelming sexual interlude thus far.

And, she admitted only to herself, she liked it best of all, too.

During the course of the vivid coupling, Dominick's hands slid to her wrists and tautly gripped her. His forearms trapped her elbows to the bed as if to hold her down while he ravished her. Powerful thighs locked her legs firmly open while he pumped his cock in and out of her pussy with forceful thrusts. Valerie trembled inside and out from his focused attention. She teetered on the edge of climax with each push against her womb.

The experience, while inherently exciting and very satisfying, was a little scary. While Dominick's gaze was still locked intently on her eyes, she registered the instant that he came. His eyelids dipped halfway as a dark, sexy growl of pleasure rolled from his throat.

Valerie's orgasm theory was proven correct the moment his warmth spilled inside her body. A rich climax rocked her with a force that took her breath away. Pinned beneath Dominick as she was, she couldn't move much, but her shoulder blades lifted from the bed an inch and a scream tore from her lips as her pussy tightened hard on his cock.

Shuddering pulses of pleasure rode across her skin from temple to toes. She sucked in a breath of air and screamed again as a second ripple of sensation danced across her body, radiating out from where their bodies met intimately.

"Fucking amazing," Dominick murmured and planted his lips on hers in a kiss that devastated her senses further. He released her wrists and rolled to his back, cradling her limp body against his until she was splayed across his chest. Still deeply connected, he kissed her thoroughly yet tenderly as he rubbed her back and neck with methodical strokes. Valerie was so satiated from the rapturous experience, she dozed off during the kiss.

An undetermined length of time later, Valerie woke. She was still on her stomach, but no longer draped across Dominick. She lifted her head and promptly yawned. Beside her, she felt Dominick shift on the bed. Turning her head, Valerie noted his hands were clasped behind his head. He watched her intently as a smirk played around his lips.

Why was he staring at her? Valerie rose to her elbows and narrowed her eyes. "What?"

He twisted towards her onto his side and propped his head on the heel of one hand. "Do you feel okay?"

She yawned again. Remaining on her stomach, she lengthened her body into a deeply satisfying stretch. "I guess so. Why?"

He reached out and stroked his hand down her back from neck to ass. "You slept quite a long time."

"How long?" She twisted to face him and his gaze fell to her exposed breasts. She yawned for a third time trying to get the cobwebs in her brain to clear.

"Nine hours."

Valerie squinted. "Really?"

He nodded. His hand rested on her hip and as she became more aware, she realized that his touch was having a profound impact. Scooting closer, she placed her hand on his chest, looked into his eyes and registered his amused smile.

"Now what happens?"

He shrugged and glanced at her hand still stroking his chest. "That depends."

Valerie ran a fingernail across one flat nipple. He didn't even flinch, but his focused gaze drilled a hole through her.

"On what?"

"Your immediate intentions."

Valerie felt his cock thicken against her leg. "Perhaps I'd like more."

"More?" Dominick leaned closer and whispered, "As in sex?" His warm breath caressed her jaw and sent a rush of heat pounding between her legs.

Valerie's cheeks heated. "Maybe."

He ran his finger tip down one side of her face and tapped her chin. "No need to be embarrassed, babe."

"But we aren't supposed to have sex more than once, are we?"

"I don't give a shit. If you want more, trust me, I'll give it to you." He laughed, and as before when they were in the initial meeting room, she thought Dominick was perhaps the most darkly beautiful man she'd ever seen.

"All you have to do is ask."

"I have to ask?" She rolled her eyes in mock offense.

His grin was contagious. "Or I could just read your mind and ravish you whenever you stare at my cock and blush."

"Kiss me."

Dominick didn't respond nor did he hesitate. He cupped her head one-handed and laid a kiss on her that warmed her all the way from her lips to her clit.

Valerie scooted against his warmth. The crisp hairs scattered across his chest tickled her breasts. She was about to voice her desire and beg for more sex when someone pounded on the door. Startled, she broke the seductive kiss and clutched the sheet to her breasts. Dominick frowned and sent a glare across the room. He rolled from the bed naked and snatched her robe from the floor. Tossing the flannel garment onto the bed he said, "Put that on."

As she struggled to cover herself and fight with the uncooperative sheet, Dominick crossed to the door where further pounding had erupted and snatched it open.

"You're late." Blue crossed the threshold and stormed into the room as Valerie tied the belt and slipped from the bed.

"I'm on my honeymoon." Dominick crossed his arms and adopted a guarded stance. Standing completely naked as he was, Valerie was embarrassed for him. He didn't seem to notice or care.

Blue frowned. "You were supposed to be at your permanent residence two hours ago." He sent surly gaze over to where Valerie hovered next to the bed. Dominick snapped his fingers, catching Blue's attention, and the alien looked away from her.

"She was tired. I let her sleep. Perhaps fucking five guys exhausted her. I'm just guessing, though. Relax. We'll be on our way in a few minutes."

Blue pursed his lips and turned the sharp look from Dominick back to Valerie. "You need to report to the High Committee chambers located on level eight with your partner Mark in an hour. I suggest you refrain from being late to *that* meeting."

"Why?" Dominick asked. Valerie guessed that having sex more than once with each man on the honeymoon was punishable by a trip to the alien version of the principal's office.

"That's between the two of them and the committee members." The blue alien turned and exited the room without another word.

Dominick slid an uneasy gaze to her. "Do you know what that's about?"

At first she shrugged, but then closed her eyes and heaved a deep sigh. Opening her eyes, she murmured, "I have a guess."

He arched an eyebrow in silent question.

"I broke a rule. And now I'm late on our first day in our permanent residence."

Dominick strolled over and took her into his arms. Squeezing her close, he said, "Don't let them push you around, babe. It isn't our fault we're here in the first place."

"I keep telling them that, but they don't seem to care," she muttered.

He kissed the top of her head and released her to get dressed.

Valerie would have asked Dominick to go with her, but didn't want him to find out about the rule she'd broken with Mark. That would have to remain a big, fat secret. Likely it wouldn't be the last one either.

Secrets. That was why it was a bad idea to share herself so many men at the same time.

Keeping secrets for three years was going to be her downfall.

Chapter 7

Valerie dressed in clothing that Dominick had picked out for her. The snug blue jeans and form-fitting pink t-shirt didn't look half bad. She said good-bye to Dominick with a kiss and was directed to her 'meeting' on level eight. He handed her a navigation device to aid her. It was the size of a cell phone and told her left, right or forward at each intersection to help her get to her destination.

In between twists and turns along her trail to level eight, Valerie considered what she would say to the members of this committee. *Kiss my ass*, came to mind first, followed quickly by, *Stop watching my private honeymoon, you perverted alien kidnappers.*

She couldn't remember the intimate details of her life before coming on board this alien ship, only that she had one and wanted to return to it.

Flashes of the past twenty-four hours of debauchery and decadent sex with five different hot, sexy men slid uncomfortably into her mind. Considering she was probably about to be chastised for daring to have sex twice with one of them after being advised against doing so only made her angry.

Being with the five of them in such a short period of time had been equal parts exciting and wicked. The vortex shower between each interlude was an experience in and of itself.

Mark was waiting for her outside the chamber doors as she rounded the corner to the last direction. His smile said he didn't care about this meeting either. He opened his arms and she stepped inside them for a hug.

"If this is what I think it is, I'll tell them it was my fault. I got greedy and wanted more."

"Is that why you were gone when I woke up?"

"I don't know." He shrugged and a half smile lifted one side of his mouth. "Maybe they were afraid that we'd go for round three. You were so sound asleep I couldn't wake you up before I was commanded out of the room."

Valerie shook her head, closed her eyes and put her hands to her face in embarrassment. If this was what she and Mark were here for, it meant they were being watched. She decided servicing five lovers was only marginally worse than having aliens watch her do it.

"It's stupid. Don't worry about it." Mark slung an arm around her shoulder and kissed her cheek.

The double doors to the committee chamber opened and Blue stepped out. His frown of disapproval at their embrace was evident. A blue finger lifted and pointed at her. "You. Come with me."

"I'm going with her," Mark said.

"No. You'll remain here to escort her to your permanent residence."

Valerie turned to Mark. "I'll be okay." His uncertain look made her sigh, but if any punishment was doled out, he didn't deserve it.

"I'll be waiting right here." He kissed her mouth before she stepped away.

Blue strode through the hall with a purposeful gait. He didn't speak, which she found agreeable.

At a large double set of doors, he slowed and twisted both knobs, pushing them inward. Without stopping, Blue breezed through the opening and stopped at another door. He turned around and motioned her forward. "They are waiting in there for you."

"Who?"

"The High Committee." An exasperated sigh punctuated his scornful expression.

Valerie pulled at the hem of her shirt to straighten imaginary wrinkles and entered through the door without sparing a single glance at the hostile blue alien.

Once inside, she was surprised to see three unfamiliar alien men seated at a modest table. As with all the other aliens in this place, they had odd skin-tone colors. The three of them had been dipped in sparkly paint the colors of gold, silver and bronze instead of shiny primary hues. They all sported shockingly white hair slicked back, puffed up like a pompadour and secured with a small ponytail in back.

Valerie remained by the door until the gold alien in the center motioned her closer. He lowered his gaze, picked up a flat device from the table in front of him and said, "My name is Golden. I've read your file, Miss Thornhill. You've been here less than seventy-two hours and you've already either bent or completely broken more than one of our rules regarding transport and management of humans."

She crossed her arms in defiance. "Maybe you should quit transporting us. Then you wouldn't have to manage us. Think of the time and effort you'll save." Her sarcasm likely wasn't appreciated or welcome.

Golden looked up sharply. "I understand your concerns, but the practice cannot be helped. Our wormhole is located near the gravitational pull of your planet and it's our only way home. Our forefathers have traveled this way for many millennia. Only recently has your planet developed enough humans to cause this phenomenon. We've done the best we can and made elaborate allowances. We will put you back within minutes of when we took you. However, while you reside aboard our ship and in order to keep stability here, our rules must be followed."

"So, what rules have I broken that were so horrible?"

"The most recent one is having carnal relations with one of your partners more than one time on your honeymoon."

"How is that any of your business? Were you watching me, you pervert?"

He frowned until the bronze alien whispered in his ear. His frown deepened. "We keep track of your DNA and when you mate with one of your partners, we record it to ensure the male's sexual health is maintained."

"Great, so every time I'm with one of the five of them, I'll know you're out there recording it. That does not make me feel any better."

"Be that as it may, we have established these rules for the good of all humans residing with us. Once you go back to Earth on your Return Day, you won't have any memory of this place."

"How does that work, anyway?"

"Didn't you pay attention at all in your orientation class?"

"Not really. I was stressing over having to have sex with five strangers. Could you explain it slowly?" Valerie forced a smile.

He inhaled deeply and exhaled. "You were brought here onto our ship by accident. Your physical body was placed in stasis as soon as you arrived so that when we put you back on Earth, you'll look exactly the same.

However, a human can't remain in our stasis compartment for three years without stimuli. Your mind needs input and exercise regularly or you'll die before we are able to put you back. The environment we have created supplies the needed stimulation that humans require.

"Additionally, human men brought here need a regular outlet for their sexual needs or they will perish before the end of four Earth months. Unfortunately, the ratio of men to women is imbalanced and men must share women, as it is done in our culture. While on our ship, we ask that you follow our rules.

"You are sealed to five men. You may only have sex with these five men and no others while you are here. Self love is not allowed and adultery among any other human you are not sealed to is forbidden.

"The human race is very complex and after centuries of study, we've learned that for our environment and rules to be successful, humans also require goals and socialization."

"Goals and socialization? What does that mean?"

"It means that your day-to-day life needs meaning. Men function best when they have an occupation to keep them busy. Women have different needs. Therefore, you will prepare the morning meal for your group of men before they go off to work each day. And you will abide by the monthly sexual schedule you've agreed to and signed."

Valerie narrowed her eyes. "I'm required to provide sex and breakfast? Is that all?"

"You will also be required to accompany your partners to a social event a few times per year. All the other humans will also attend. It is a festive event with ritual dancing and food."

"Party a few times a year. Got it. Anything else?"

"We ask that you do not play favorites with the five men you live with."

"Favorites?"

"Yes. For example, giving one of your partners more sexual attention and experiences than you gave the others on your honeymoon." Golden tilted his head to one side. "If the other men in your household found out, they might be jealous. Jealousy in any household can be very dangerous. You have three years to occupy yourself, to make your lives together work, and we prefer that it be done with consideration and cooperation. Do you understand?"

Valerie understood, but it didn't make her a robot housewife or the epitome of a team-spirit cheerleader. "I guess. We'll have to see, won't we."

"Your goal is to make it to Return Day. If you don't play nice, then none of the men in your group will make it either. You don't want them to have to stay another three years, do you?"

"I think you're asking for a lot given that you're the reason we got sucked up onto your ship in the first place." Valerie didn't remember if she was a fighter by nature in her life on Earth, but she was sure compelled not to be a doormat here.

Golden narrowed his eyes. Valerie didn't want to find out there was a punishment, so she said, "I'll take it day by day. That's all I'm promising."

The silver alien stood without warning and handed her a small sheaf of papers. "The orientation rules are written here. For your reference," he said and returned promptly to his seat.

Golden inclined his head. "You may go."

Valerie clutched the papers in both hands and exited the room without saying anything else.

Outside the committee chamber, Blue waited. He didn't speak, but led her back to Mark.

Public displays of affection were discouraged, it was the one thing she remembered from orientation, but Valerie hugged Mark as soon as she got close enough. Burying her face in the curve of his neck, she kissed the pulse at his throat and sighed.

"Are you okay?" He rubbed the spot between he shoulder blades as they embraced.

She pulled away, nodded once and together they left the frowning blue alien. "I'm fine."

Mark kissed her forehead. "What did they say?"

"They view what happened between us as favoritism. I'm to avoid it in the future." She rolled her eyes and shook her head.

"Fuck 'em. No one else would have even known about it. Don't let them boss you, honey."

Valerie grinned. "That was my assessment as well. Thanks for siding with me."

"I'll always side with you, I promise." Mark squeezed her once more and they headed away from the committee chambers.

He led her through the mazes of the administration building, across a long, rounded tunnel an into a different section of the ship. The walls were wider and taller. Plus, there was actual plant life decorating the pathways. The residence part of the ship reminded her of a biosphere. White plastic walls lit from behind towered to at least twelve feet above her head. The loamy fragrance of moist earth from the plants greeted her as they walked along. There were more people milling around, too.

They turned a corner and entered large open doorway revealing a small community of homes. Rows upon rows of cottage-style houses with tiny green yards and flowers greeted her as far as the eye could see.

They walked straight to the first brick-lined street. The white washed sign on the corner read Main Street. How quaint. Mark guided her forward and they turned at the second right onto a road called Lilac Blossom. Easy to remember, since lilacs were one of her favorite flowers. The street had ten houses on each side and Mark stopped at the third on the left. He pointed down a short brick path lined with flowers to a small house.

"This is ours. Listen, I've got to get to work. Grip the handle of the door and it opens to only our DNA. Can you find your way inside?"

Valerie nodded.

He kissed her cheek. "I'll see you tomorrow morning at breakfast."

She watched him jog back out of the area then turned to her new home. Before she got halfway down the walkway the front door opened and Dominick stepped out.

He lingered in the frame once he saw her, an unreadable expression on his face. Was he angry? Delighted? She couldn't tell.

"Are you going to give me the grand tour?"

His lips quirked. "No. I'm headed to the target range for weapons practice and then on to work."

"Where do you work?"

"I'm in security. So I need to keep up my skills."

"Are you ever going to teach me any weapons skills?" Valerie was just making conversation. She didn't actually want to shoot a gun.

"No. I don't share what I know with others."

Startled at his harsh attitude, she was compelled to ask, "Why?"

His eyes narrowed. "Too many people already know how to shoot guns. I don't need to add any more fuel to the mix. Nothing personal, babe."

"Right." Valerie nodded and skirted around his large frame to enter the house. "I'll just entertain myself alone inside."

His features softened. "I'm running late or I'd show you around. Take a look inside. It's not fancy, but it's adequate for us, I suppose."

"Okay. Have a good day."

Dominick nodded without ever really smiling and walked away. Valerie closed the door and contemplated her new existence. She was back to her dream theory, even though a part of her rational brain knew this was truly happening. This life was so strange, she couldn't let go of the possibility. Perhaps she was in a coma somewhere and until she woke, she was stranded in this fantasy world where she had to have sex with five men in a cottage on a brick-lined street in the middle of a spaceship in a wormhole on the way to oblivion for three years.

Or I'm crazy and this is my prison.

Valerie shook off her dismal reverie and perused the entryway to the little house, figuring that for the time being it was just easier to play along. She took a deep breath and scanned the small foyer.

The scent of fresh flowers hung in the air as she walked into her new home. It was more spacious than it looked from the outside. The décor seemed slightly masculine, as it was filled with lots of warm wood, dark colors and more greenery.

A large kitchen with an eat-in dining table was situated to the left and a small living room was on the right. A sliding glass door opposite the front entry led to a small patio with a grassy backyard and a small garden to one side.

Further exploration yielded the discovery of her spacious bedroom, located directly off the living room in a hallway of its own. Next to her large closet was a special door resembling the ones she'd gone through during her honeymoon to greet each partner. She opened it to find a long hallway where five separate doors existed. On the nights she spent with these men in sexual servitude, she would go to them. Whichever door was lit up would be the one she entered to 'service' one of the men in her group, according to the posted instructions on the wall in her bedroom.

Her sexual duties didn't commence until the next week, so she went back to the kitchen to familiarize herself with the 'required' breakfast duties. It resembled a standard kitchen, but what she thought was a very large microwave was labeled with the words food synthesizer. It produced various Earth dishes at the push of a button. Easy and requiring little thought. Perfect.

Quickly bored, she grabbed her sheaf of papers and went out to the patio. The walled-in space was the perfect size for private moments to read, with the exception of the low white picket fence separating the backyard of her cottage from another. If the occupants of the other house were in their backyard, it would afford no privacy at all.

Strolling over to the edge of the yard, Valerie rested her hand on the waist-high fence and peeked into the sliding glass door of the house bordering hers. She didn't see anyone at first, but then Daisy appeared and walked past the large window carrying a cup of something steaming.

Valerie smiled for the first time since waking in Dominick's arms this morning. Lifting her hand, Valerie waved and caught the other woman's eye.

Daisy, poised to take a sip of her drink, stopped, waggled her fingers and came out of the house to join her in the backyard.

"Hi, neighbor."

"Hi, Daisy. I'm surprised they put us troublemakers so close together."

"Me too. I'm sure it's an oversight, but I won't say anything if you don't."

"I won't." Valerie was overcome with emotion all of a sudden. Until she'd seen Daisy, she'd been worried about her own sanity.

Daisy leaned over the short fence and hugged her, as if sensing she needed comfort. "After the men in my household left for work this morning. I was wondering what I'd do to keep from going crazy." She glance down at the papers in Valerie's hand. "What have you got there?"

Valerie sighed and crushed the paper in her hand. "The rules. I've already gotten called to the High Committee chamber. Now I'm permanently labeled a troublemaker."

"I'm sure it's only a matter of time before I have a meet and greet with the same group." Daisy pushed a wild strand of curly dark hair behind one ear.

"So how was your honeymoon?" Valerie asked confidentially.

Daisy blushed and laughed. "Amazing, to tell you the truth. Thanks for helping me escape and for the thumbs-up on Brandon. He and his group turned out to be perfect for me."

Valerie nodded very pleased that she'd helped. "No problem. I'm grateful to find another troublemaker like me. We'll have to stick together."

"Want to go exploring tomorrow?"

"Sure. We can check out the place and maybe keep each other in line. Or not." She grinned.

They spent the afternoon chatting and made plans to meet the next day. Valerie retired to her room with the sheaf of unread rules. She fixed a light dinner and ate in her room, fearful that one of the men would come out even though they supposedly had their own studio bachelor apartments and didn't exit until the morning.

Next week the regular sexual schedule began. It was set up so that every other week thereafter, she'd spend five nights out of seven with a different man each night.

She fought the rising panic that insisted the three years was a lie and that she'd be stuck here for all eternity as the whore of five men using her for their sexual survival.

Despite the unexpected and repeated pleasure from the honeymoon with the five of them, Valerie couldn't help feeling that tonight was the first night of her three-year sentence to whoredom.

Or her permanent place in Hell.

Chapter 8

1,094 until Return Day

"Where do you want to go today?" Daisy asked Valerie the next morning after their men left for various jobs on the spacecraft.

"I don't care. Let's wander around and see where we end up."

"Okay, but I want to check out the marketplace. I need to see what sort of shopping is available."

Wandering through the shopping area, which reminded Valerie of a large, sprawling flea market only with nicer merchandise, they looked in every conceivable enclosed shop, stall and kiosk for new sights and diversions.

Stomachs rumbling, they headed for the small food court area on the far side of the market. Rounding a corner as their noses led them toward the delicious, smoky grilled scent of roasted meat, Valerie and Daisy nearly ran over Dominick on his way somewhere for what she assumed was his security job for the Others. He gave her a pointed stare at first, as if concerned over why she was out and about. He quickly shifted his gaze to Daisy and his look visibly softened. He never spoke, just gave them a single curt nod and kept moving along his original trajectory. She watched him disappear down a narrow dark hallway she never would have noticed if she hadn't been watching his butt.

Daisy whistled. "Is he one of the men in your group?"

"Yes. Why?" Valerie directed her attention away from the empty hallway to stare at her friend.

"He's huge."

Valerie nodded and shrugged, but didn't say anything. Dominick was overwhelming.

"So is he as scary as he looks?"

"I don't want to talk about it." Valerie hadn't resolved her unreasonable feelings for him yet. He hadn't done anything to earn her distrust. It was the intimidation of his size which did her in. Dominick wasn't Mr. Sunshine and Rainbows as far as his attitude, but he hadn't hurt her.

Daisy put a hand on her shoulder. "I'm sorry. Are you okay? Does he…"

"He isn't frightening in bed, if that's what you're worried about. But I'd be lying if I didn't admit that his size makes me slightly nervous."

Daisy relaxed into her chair. "Brandon is the biggest guy in my group. He's a pussycat though. If it makes you feel any better, I'd be slightly nervous about a guy that size too."

"Thanks. I'd also be lying if I didn't admit that he intrigues me as much."

Valerie and Daisy ate a leisurely lunch, chatting about anything and everything that came to mind as they speculated over the collective loss of memories from their lives on Earth and possible scenarios of what might happen when they returned. Valerie ensured she faced the hallway, which would allow her to see if Dominick returned.

He didn't.

Intrigued about where he'd gone, Valerie led Daisy in the direction of the mysterious passage as they continued their heated discussion regarding the distant social event being mandatory and why the Others would care if they were social as long as peace reigned in the households.

"I can read your mind, Valerie." Daisy stopped walking, crossed her arms and sported an amused smirk.

"I don't know what you mean."

"You led us down here to see where Dominick went."

Valerie narrowed her eyes and shrugged. "So? Exploring is exploring. What's wrong with a dual purpose?"

"I don't think we're supposed to be in this area."

"Since when do troublemakers like us care about 'supposed to'?"

Daisy shook her head. "Since the hallway we're exploring is completely unexciting. There is nothing down here except endless hallways and unless we start leaving bread crumbs, we aren't going to be able to find our way back out.

"I can find our way back."

"I don't care if we find Dominick. Besides I have a date with one of my hot men later tonight." She waggled her eyebrows. "Can't be late for that."

"Let's just turn down a couple more hallways and if we don't find anything interesting, we'll turn back. I promise."

"Fine."

Valerie led Daisy through several intersections without turning or finding anything remotely interesting. She was just about to give up when further down the hall, a shaft of green, iridescent light fell across their path, accompanied by an eerie creaking sound like the exaggerated rusty door hinges of a haunted house.

They stopped in mid-step and looked at each other. Daisy looped an arm through Valerie's and leaned close. Without speaking, they tiptoed towards the shaft of light to explore the hallway where it spilled from.

"Stop!" a familiar voice called from behind them.

Arm in arm, they turned together as Dominick approached, rapidly eating up the hallway with his long strides. "What are you doing here?"

Valerie swallowed hard and found her voice had dried up.

Daisy squeezed her arm tighter and answered, "E...exploring?"

Dominick frowned. Three more steps and he towered over the both of them.

Valerie found her voice and pointed a thumb over her shoulder. "What's down that green hallway?"

"Don't know." His brows furrowed menacingly. "Don't need to and neither do you."

"But why—"

The rest of her words were cut off. "This area is off limits. Go home. Both of you."

"Can you lead us out of here?" Daisy asked. "We're totally lost."

His deep sigh of disapproval accompanied a single nod. Without another sound he turned and lifted his arm gesturing them straight.

Valerie knew her way out, but wondered if Dominick would lead them the correct way or directly to the High Committee chamber for further discussion of her behavior.

Thankfully, he took them right to the hallway near the food court where they'd started their impromptu and very short-lived journey.

"See you later," Valerie called over her shoulder. Dominick stood like a sentry at the mouth of the 'forbidden' hallway and remained silent.

One of these days, Valerie intended to check the hallway out to find out the big secret. But she'd wait until enough time had passed so as not to be expected. She calculated that she still had well over a thousand days to explore the vessel.

She'd wait until they forgot she'd been interested in this place.

After finally reading the rules, Valerie discovered that the computer in the hallway would manage her liaisons. And each week would be a different lineup of men so as to keep things interesting. The words 'keep things interesting' was actually written in the pamphlet.

Whatever.

Valerie thought having five sexual partners was exiting enough, but routine was boring so she resisted the sincere urge to roll her eyes and went along without comment.

Each morning over the past week, she'd gotten up and made a breakfast buffet feast with everything she could think of and then she watched what each man ate. By day three she knew what was popular and what wasn't, making her morning chore easier.

They all shuffled out of their rooms quietly, ate with a minimum of discussion and departed with little fanfare each morning. Once they were all gone for the day, Valerie spent most of her first week exploring the alien-created environment with Daisy. An acceptable routine had been established with regard to her daily living.

Advertisements for a mandatory grand social event plastered the walls everywhere she traveled. All the groups of men with their single woman would attend the affair being held in one of the gauntlet halls. She and Daisy had already selected what they would wear from the available merchants at the nearby marketplace.

None of the men in her group seem anxious to attend, with the exception of Johnny. He loved entertainment. She planned to discuss it with him tonight, as he was her first liaison for her initial week of servitude.

She looked forward to seeing Johnny tonight. When he opened the door to her knock, she stared for several seconds before entering.

"Nice pirate outfit," she remarked and closed the door behind her. He sauntered into the living room of his small apartment. She remained out of his reach by the door. She was accosted by the fact that a lot of the time she still felt like she was in a dream while lingering in this alien place, and never more so than right now in Johnny's room.

He turned all of a sudden and flashed her a wicked smile. "Ahoy, my lovely. Aren't you a charming morsel for a nasty, horny pirate like me?" He threw his head back and laughed boisterously.

"Um. I don't know." She glanced around. Johnny's room looked like backstage at an impromptu theater where everything was available for any costume that could be imagined.

"Are you ready to play thirsty, sex-seeking pirate and naughty slave girl who needs to be punished?"

Her eyes cut to his and she knew she wasn't hiding her alarm. "Um, to tell the truth, I've never played that before."

"Excellent. It'll be my delight to instruct you, my lovely. First, come closer. Kneel before me, take my cock in your mouth and get us started."

Kneel before him?

Valerie glanced up at his sardonic expression and noted that one of his eyeteeth was gold. She stilled, unable to move or breathe as the gravity of the situation landed in her naïve understanding.

He wanted to play sex games?

Ohmigod. She didn't think she could do this. Her eyes watered up and a sob escaped before she could stop it.

His eyes narrowed. "What's wrong? Are you frightened?"

She nodded and widened in her eyes in unconscious panic. She was, in fact, terrified.

Johnny's grin widened and the glint off his gold tooth sparkled in his mouth. "Well, that's as it should be then, isn't it?" Johnny licked his lips. "The experience will be more rewarding if you're nervous about what I'm going to do to you, now won't it?"

"I…I…don't know."

"If I don't like the way you suck my cock, I'll certainly punish you."

"Pun…punish me? Please don't make me do this, Johnny."

"Oh, but we must, my lovely. That's the way the game is played."

Valerie's eyes widened further when he took a step closer. She backed up until she bounced off the door. Grasping behind her back for the handle made her realize that there wasn't one. She flattened against the wall next to the door, took a long step away from him and watched to see what he would do next.

"Ah, my lovely. I see you're going to make me chase you. That will be very thrilling." His maniacal laugh penetrated her and she screamed and turned to claw at the seams of the door she'd come through earlier.

He was on her a second later, pressed against her body from shoulders to knees. He nipped at her neck and Valerie slid to the floor. She couldn't stop trembling.

Johnny knelt behind her and gripped her shoulders. His rigid cock dug into her back. She started violently and whimpered.

"So sexy." He made a moaning sound as his hands slipped around to squeeze her breasts. Valerie shuddered, but it only seemed to arouse him. "Please don't. I'm afraid, Johnny."

"Excellent. Fear will make the experience richer." He bit the back of her neck with a gentle nip and she screamed. "Run to the bed or I'll smack your behind."

"I don't want to be punished."

From behind her, Johnny laughed again. "I suggest that you do what I say then."

"I want to stop."

He tilted his head to one side. "Then you know what to do. But please, lovie, don't be that way. You don't want to stop, do you?"

"What…what are you going to do to me?"

He leaned in and whispered, "I'm going to bend you over the bed, tie you down and fuck your pussy very hard…eventually."

Valerie took a deep breath. She stood up and turned in his arms. He kissed her on the mouth brutally hard. He overwhelmed her senses. The kiss distracted her because it was so very seductive and just like the one he'd given her on their honeymoon.

But it ended far too quickly. He released her so fast she stumbled back a step, but then grabbed her arm and dragged her across the room towards the bedroom. "Come here. Get on your knees before me."

Valerie's eyes widened and she trembled so hard she couldn't walk straight. Lurching behind him, she dropped to her knees before him as her heart pounded violently in her chest. What had she gotten herself into? Head bowed, Valerie let loose a loud sob and allowed the shaking she'd held back free reign. She curled to the floor and cried.

After several moments she felt a hand on her shoulder.

"Lovie, are you really frightened?" She looked up into his wide, surprised eyes and nodded.

A sniff escaped and she started crying harder. Between sobs she said, "I don't know how to play and...and...I don't want to be punished for not playing right."

His arms went around her and he kissed her forehead. "I'm sorry. Why didn't you say the safe word to end the game? I would have stopped sooner."

"What's a safe word? I've never done anything like this. I don't know the word, much less how to play." Tears streamed down her face. She felt like such a fool. She'd been thinking of Scrabble and he wanted to play sex games.

"No games? Never? Not once?"

She shook her head miserably.

"I'm so sorry. I must have dreamed that we discussed words on our honeymoon. I thought yours was 'accountant' for some reason, I must have dreamed it. Forgive me, I didn't know you were untried. When we met I mentioned games and you seemed to understand."

"I thought you meant board games."

He smiled. "Perhaps we could play naked twister. But rest easy, lovie, we don't have to do anything like this."

"I'm supposed to do whatever you say." She trembled in his arms. "I don't want to be punished. It's...it's only the first night. And I don't want to go back to the stupid alien High Committee chamber."

Johnny shook his head and grinned showing off the gold on his eyetooth. "Well then, tonight I want to play happy horny pirate and good slave girl that doesn't need to be punished. How about that?"

She shook her head miserably. "But that's not what you really want to do. I'm supposed to do what you say. Even if it's playing g...games." She stuttered and sobbed again.

Johnny murmured quiet words certainly meant to calm as he rocked her in his arms, but she wasn't at all calm.

After several moments he snapped his fingers. "I forgot. We still need a safe word."

"A safe word?" She looked up. "What kind of word is that?"

"A word that if you get so frightened you start crying before I get your clothes off, that I can stop and soothe you."

Her lip trembled. "I'm sorry."

"Nothing to be sorry for, lovie. That's how the game is played. If you ever say the word for any reason, then I stop everything. No repercussions. Okay?"

In a small voice she replied, "Okay."

"What word would you like to use?"

"How about zoo? That's where I feel like I am."

He chuckled and hugged her close. "Zoo it is. Unless you prefer the French term."

"What's the French term?" She sniffed again.

"Menagerie." He kissed her forehead.

"Menagerie," she whispered. "I like that."

Johnny held her until she stopped shivering. Rubbing his hands up and down her back with tenderness and soft caresses, Valerie slumped against him and relaxed. He leaned down to kiss her lips lightly. She trembled in delight. His lips were firm and he tasted like an exotic spicy rum cocktail.

"Let me make love to you. No games. I just need you."

"Thank you, Johnny." She looped her arms around his neck and he carried her to bed.

Shedding his clothing, he made love to her with infinite tenderness. The moment he climaxed with a low satisfied groan, she also cried out in release gripped by an orgasm she'd forgotten to expect.

Held gently in his arms afterward, she whispered, "I'm sorry about earlier. I didn't mean to be such a prude."

"No, lovie, it was my fault." He squeezed her lightly. "I should have waited to play my game later once we got to know each other better. I was showing off a little, but I didn't mean to scare you. Next time I promise not to come on so strong."

"This place is a little hard to get used to. But I hate being so naïve."

"Lovie, you aren't naïve. You're amazing and beautiful. And to prove it to you, next time you come here, we'll play Scrabble."

"Really?"

"Of course. What would you think of the naughty version where we can only spell out sexual references and four-letter words?"

She laughed. "Perfect. I can't imagine playing naughty Scrabble with anyone else." He kissed her cheek. The warmth from his lips soothed her. Before he pulled away, Valerie kissed his mouth.

Johnny was a very wonderful kisser.

She dozed off in his arms and early the next morning she traveled to her own room to dress.

Breakfast was slightly odd since they were all there and she'd spent the night with Johnny. No one said anything.

Dominick watched her very carefully. They all knew she'd been with one of them, but no one knew for sure which man.

She hoped.

Johnny winked at her before he left, but otherwise it was business as usual.

Throughout the rest of the week, Valerie spent the night with Hauser, then Mark, and then Frasier. Tonight was her final 'engagement' for the week. Dominick ended up being the last one again.

There had been no other surprises all week after the ill-fated pirate game with Johnny and even though she knew she shouldn't, she dreaded going to Dominick's room. If there was going to be another surprise sex game, somehow she expected it would come from him.

Dominick opened the door and wordlessly motioned her to enter. It was dark in his space. There was low jazzy music playing in the background. He shut the door and she jumped at the noise.

"Something wrong?"

"No."

"You seem apprehensive."

Valerie turned and tilted her head back. "You're still really big."

He crossed his arms and leaned his butt against the door he'd just closed. "Did you expect that I would get smaller as time goes by?" He didn't smile, and she wasn't sure if he was making a joke. One eyebrow lifted. "I promise you, nothing on my body has shrunk."

She glanced down. She couldn't help it. His cock was already fully erect. Lifting from the paneled door, he dropped his arms and walked forward.

Before he made it completely within arm's-length, she blurted out,

"Shall we get right to it then?" She sighed internally, realizing that she sounded like a prostitute doing a brisk business where time was a factor in her profits. It was the unreasonable fear she had of him. It wasn't fair to be afraid of Dominick, since he hadn't done anything to warrant her unease. He was just so big. So powerful. So overwhelming to all of her riotous senses.

He stopped in mid-stride and frowned. "Is that how you've operated all week with the others? Slam, bam, thank you—"

She broke in before he finished. "You aren't allowed to ask me that."

His shoulders lifted once. "I can ask. You don't have to respond."

Valerie mashed her lips together and crossed her arms. "Well, I decline to answer. What I did with the others is none of your business." Each night with all of the others had been very nice, but she knew she wasn't supposed to discuss her partners with each other. The rules the aliens had provided stated that discussion of sexual practices between groups of men invariably led to dissension.

Daisy told her there was a rumor that a large percentage of the other women in the community treated their mates very poorly. They pitted them against each other and verbally compared them for sport. Valerie refused to participate in this practice and not just because the aliens forbade it.

"Fine. We'll 'get right to it' then. Take your clothes off and get in my bed. I'll be there in a little while."

Valerie deflated a little. She did an about-face, stalking away from his harsh regard, undressed quickly and slid beneath the silky soft sheets of his large bed. Resting on her back, she purposely kept her gaze on the ceiling and waited for him to join her.

Eventually, she dozed off, still worried about what he would to do to her once he finally retired and joined her under the covers.

When she woke later with a start, the room was completely dark save for a few shafts of ambient light from what she surmised was the door to his bathroom. Dominick was snuggled up against her, his breath brushing across her cheek. One of his arms curled across her breasts and his thigh was slung over her hips possessively.

Had he fucked her while she slept? She took inventory of her body. It didn't feel like he'd invaded her. She would have woken, right?

He stirred and lifted his head. The dim light only afforded her the barest outline of his head and one shoulder. She couldn't see his face clearly.

"Did we, uh, do anything?" She left the question open.

He cleared his throat. "No. I prefer participation."

Valerie reached out a hand and stroked his whiskery cheek. "I'm sorry. I didn't mean to imply—"

"Don't." He cut her off. "I'm the one who's sorry. It was inappropriate of me to ask about the others. It won't happen again."

"Thank you." Valerie turned towards him, aimed for where she thought his mouth was, but kissed his jaw. Dominick, although big and scary, was a very attractive man. And never more so than when he was resting naked against her in a warm bed in the middle of the night.

Cocooned with Dominick like this made him seem less frightening for some foolish reason. Probably because she couldn't see how tall he was. Plus, he'd apologized. How many men ever did that? If she'd ever known the answer to that nebulous question from her past on earth, she'd forgotten it.

Valerie tried to kiss his mouth, but he pushed her to the bed and moved on top of her. His fingers laced between hers. He planted his mouth on hers and kissed her lips once before he pulled back, as if to gauge her expression. In case it was too dark for him to see, she pushed her hips against his groin to convey her interest. He tightened his grip on her hands and slid their entwined fingers upward until they rested above her head. His huge cock nestled between her legs, sending spiraling signals of arousal directly to her clit as he pinned her with his large body.

He didn't speak, but fastened his mouth on one breast. The suction he exerted sent an electric pulse of sensation to her pussy, which responded with a gush of wetness readying to be filled.

She arched off the bed and spread her legs wide to allow his cock to penetrate her. He trailed his lips along a path to her mouth and distracted her with a luscious mind-blowing kiss. With a relentless obsession for immediate sex, she wiggled her hips, negotiating her wet slit into position until the tip of his cock slipped inside her pussy an inch. The glorious feel of him caused a spasm. She squeezed her internal muscles as if she could suck his shaft deeper inside.

Dominick growled as if surprised to find his cock inside her already . He promptly thrust forward a few inches before he stilled the exquisite movement. Valerie moaned in delight and squeezed again. The breath from his exhale tickled her collarbone. Valerie pushed her hips forward and he responded with a slow thrust until he was buried deeply. He pulled out and plunged to the hilt again, slowly, as a satisfied groan erupted from his lips. He grasped her hands and thrust inside her again even slower than the last time. Meticulously and agonizingly measured, he overwhelmed her senses with his careful penetration.

Valerie relaxed slightly. He didn't use force. He was tender, but she felt cocooned by him as he held her arms above her head. He dominated her in a way that made her glad to share his body even if it was a little scary. His weight pressed her into the bed as his fingers gripped hers very tightly. He lowered his mouth to hers for a devastatingly wicked kiss. His tongue thrust inside her mouth to the same unhurried rhythm that his cock pushed inside her body.

A tingle low in her belly signaled an orgasm ready to rush across her sensitized skin. Dominick's pace picked up and she met his powerful thrusts, adding to the utter pleasure of the experience.

The moment he briefly stiffened, the warmth of his release showered inside her pussy and sent her over the edge of thrumming gratification. She groaned and bucked beneath him in delight as he continued thrusting his cock into the clenching walls of her satisfied body.

Dominick slumped against her. He kissed her face and whispered, "That was unbelievable. Very erotic for some reason."

"Maybe because it's the middle of the night. It seems slightly decadent to wake up and then have sex." She whispered the final two words. While she couldn't see him very well, his face was pressed into her shoulder. The rumble of his laughter caught her off guard. She suspected that he was amused by either her whisper or her conjecture.

"Maybe so. This is the second time you've thwarted me, babe. Next time I'm doing what I want."

"I don't understand."

"Next week, I'm going to bury my face between your thighs and make you scream in climax once before you trick my cock into your pussy."

"Oh." Her quiet, mousy response apparently amused him even more.

He chuckled and kissed her throat. "You came when I did, right?" His fingertips trailed along her skin from hip to nipple. "I'd be happy to remedy that if I've left you unsatisfied or simply wanting more."

Valerie felt the heat rush to her cheeks even in the inky darkness of the room. "I came when you did. I guess it's the alien version of motivation so I'll perform."

His fingers gently caressed tingling circles around her breast. The peak hardened beneath his expert touch. Each time his fingers touched her nipples a current of pleasure zipped its way to her clit.

"Let me make you come." His whispered suggestion aroused her to a level where she didn't think she could say no. Even if she was only supposed to come once. Was that even a rule? She'd have to check her pamphlet later.

Guilt made her pause and then she sighed, "I probably shouldn't."

"Not a good enough reason, babe." His hand dipped between the folds of her pussy and the second he brushed her clit, Valerie knew she wouldn't be able to stop him.

"Damn, that feels great." Her whispered expletive spurred his next actions.

Dominick's mouth suddenly covered the peak of one breast and the tip of his tongue circled her nipple. The sensation combined with his fingers dancing across her clit was unbelievably erotic. She couldn't see him clearly in the shadows and the fantasy of his sensual attention in the dark was more heightened.

Although, if she could see him better, she probably wouldn't be able to keep her eyes open. His mouth trailed to her other breast. Once his lips clamped onto her other nipple, a furious spike of pleasure riddled her senses.

Valerie climbed to another seductive peak as Dominick plied her with his mouth and fingers. His lips trailed from breast to mouth and soon devoured hers in a carnal kiss.

The sudden invasion of his fingers sliding inside her pussy caused a low moan to erupt from her throat. In and out, he penetrated her slick passage with practiced moves. A single stroke across her clit, with his fingers buried deeply inside, made her come.

Moaning and writhing as the sweet curl of climax swept from her throbbing clit to the crown of her head, Valerie arched and pushed her breasts against the warm skin of Dominick's chest.

Valerie came down off the orgasmic high and snuggled closer. She was tired. No, she was contentedly weary. A purring sound emitted from her throat as she wrapped her arms around him.

Dominick broke the delectable kiss, slid his arms around to hold her and whispered, "You make the sexiest sounds when you come, babe."

"You're amazing," she whispered, barely still awake. "I'm just so sleepy." It was her last conscious thought. If he responded, she didn't hear it. She dropped into a contented slumber and dreamed of making love with Dominick all night long. When she woke, Valerie was all alone in his huge bed.

A note propped on the extra pillow said, 'Had to go to work early. Didn't want to disturb your sound sleep. Hope the contented look on your face was because of the second time.' The letter D ended the note.

Valerie sighed and stretched her muscles. The second orgasm had been phenomenal. Quite frankly, the first had been awe-inspiring. Dominick's approach to sex was overwhelming.

She'd be lying if she said she still wasn't a little frightened by his intensity, but what a ride. Dominick had a way of overpowering her body and soul when they were together.

He was fast becoming a man who occupied her daily thoughts more than she would expect given her initial fear of him.

Dominick was a puzzle. Valerie sensed that he hid something when they were in bed together. Something she couldn't quite put her finger on, but she'd definitely keep her eyes open. Perhaps that unknown factor fed her fear. It didn't stop her from thinking about him during idle time or active time, either.

Valerie returned to her room with only Dominick on her mind. Glancing at her calendar, she noted the date of the big social party, which was marked in red.

The mandatory social event scheduled in six months would put Valerie with all five of her group of men in the gauntlet hall for a dance. She rolled her eyes at the idiocy of the forced event. The Others had a ridiculous sense of what social events happened on Earth.

Valerie did look forward to dancing with Dominick. Perhaps sliding close might yield hidden information about him.

Chapter 9

913 until Return Day

Valerie entered the gauntlet hall with a sense of trepidation. Having five men tower over her all along the hallways to attend this social event was a cause of both relief and anxiety. The last time she'd been in here a huge throng of men had been grabbing at her.

Six months had passed with relative speed and Valerie didn't begrudge her sexual servitude as much any more. And yet, after half a year she couldn't help the heart-pounding first few minutes as she entered Dominick's room twice a month.

The gauntlet hall was decorated in an earth-tone frenzy of autumn colors. Perhaps the Others thought they missed the fall holidays on Earth.

Twinkling lights danced inside wall sconces set around the room, showering the large space in more light than she would have expected from mere candles. Perhaps it was alien magic light.

Instead of a horde of men seeking partners, the grand hall had what looked a little like gazebo shaped structures with tables centered inside and enough seating for eight people. The huts for lack of a better word were erected and lined up in a loose oval shape around the rectangular perimeter. In each corner of the large room, either a bar or a food buffet awaited the attendees.

Each of the booths was also decorated with colorful strings of lights and faced the center of the room, which showcased a large dance floor. Several couples danced together, undulating to the overloud, upbeat tune from an unseen music source pumping out of hidden speakers.

"Valerie," a familiar voice called over the din. Daisy waved from a booth in the center of the right-hand side. Valerie immediately changed course to head in her direction.

Hauser dropped his arm around her shoulders and walked alongside her, as if he needed to protect her. The other four men in her gorgeous entourage drifted to the booth they'd been assigned a few places down from where Daisy waved.

"I can find my way to the booth," Valerie said, lifting eyes to Hauser's salt-water blue gaze. She wanted to chat with Daisy alone, girl to girl.

"I have no doubt, but I don't trust any of the other men here beyond the ones we entered this room with, so your choice is either me hovering over you, or Dominick."

"You," Valerie said far too quickly to hide her unfounded apprehension. Hauser's eyes widened. She flashed a quick grin to dissipate any questions. A few charged moments later, he smiled politely and nodded. Tightening his grip around her shoulders, he scanned the immediate area, ostensibly for threats.

"Glad you finally made it," Daisy called over the clamor of chattering voices and music filling the room.

Valerie rolled her eyes. "I'm just fashionably late."

The room was full of activity and a crush of people. The lights were low, adding a certain intimacy to the room even with what had to be a thousand people in attendance.

"Did a buzzer go off telling you to get your ass to the party?"

Valerie pursed her lips. "No," she said evasively.

"Then what?"

Sighing loudly, Valerie crossed her arms and muttered, "The emergency red light around every door in our house went off and blinked in rapid-fire flashes. It was very annoying. I'm sure an offensive sound would have followed if we hadn't exited."

"Why don't you like parties?"

She shrugged. "I don't understand the point of them."

Daisy shook her head as if Valerie was daft. "To dance and drink and have fun."

Valerie's annoying lack of concrete memories from her life on Earth didn't specify details of why parties made her edgy, but she knew on some primal level that she hated them. She didn't consider herself a particularly nimble dancer and a feeling of panic engulfed her at the thought of so many people watching her flail around in a public forum.

Drinks arrived via a cart propelled by unseen means and dispensed beverages to everyone in the booth. Valerie took a sip of her cranberry juice and vodka cocktail, calming herself by mulling over the number nine hundred and thirteen, which repeated over and over in her head.

The name of the ship which had sucked them up and now forced her to attend this stupid party was *Chippen* and given that the multicolored male population wielded muscles any bodybuilder would be jealous of, she and Daisy had nicknamed the ship *Chippendales Pleasure Cruise.*

Nine hundred and thirteen was the number of days that were left here on the Chippendales Pleasure Cruise. To keep her sanity, she mentally chanted the day's number when she was uncomfortable. *Like right now.*

"I can read your mind, you know." Daisy winked at her, sucked down a double shot of straight tequila, bit into a salted lime slice and promptly whooped in delight.

"No you can't. You're just overconfident." Eyeing the empty shot glass, Valerie added with a friendly smile, "Or already drunk."

Daisy snapped her fingers indicating she wanted seconds and asked, "So tell me, what's the number bouncing around in your head?"

Valerie's mouth fell open and Daisy laughed as another drink was placed in front of her.

"Nine hundred and thirteen."

"Good. That's plenty of time to do lots of wicked things with the men in my life." She glanced at Brandon, turned back to Valerie with a hearty laugh and motioned her to drink up.

"Let's go dance," Daisy yelled the moment she'd downed her second drink and smacked the shot glass on the table. She grabbed Brandon's shirt by the sleeve as she exited her booth, already rocking and dancing to the beat of the new song playing.

Hauser and Brandon exchanged looks of amused annoyance at first, but soon got into the spirit of the event. Valerie downed the remainder of her drink in one swallow for courage and allowed Daisy's exuberant attitude to envelope her unease. The four of them migrated to the center of the dance floor and gyrated against each other to the beat of the music pounding a rhythm through her chest. No one seemed to be paying attention to her, so Valerie allowed her nervousness to ratchet down a notch and focused on Hauser.

Out of nowhere, a thin woman with a tousled cap of silvery blond hair bumped hard into Valerie and sent her stumbling toward Daisy and Brandon locked together in a dirty dancing move. Hauser grabbed for her and missed as Valerie fell against Daisy's mate Brandon on her way to the floor. Luckily, Brandon caught her beneath the arms and kept her on her feet, but not before she saw the predatory gleam of jealousy in Hauser's eyes.

The look was as frightening as one of Dominick's thunderous expressions, but Hauser shook it off quickly, retrieved her from Brandon's grasp and hugged her to his frame. Valerie hadn't realized the extent of his possessive nature. The fast music ended all of a sudden and several jazzy notes of a melodic song started playing in its place. The mood around them changed from frenzied to serene in a matter of seconds. The couples on the large dance floor clutched their partners close for a slow dance.

"Hi, Hauser," the blonde who'd knocked her into Brandon said with salacious grin. She moved in close enough that Valerie was assaulted by her strong perfume before she was an arm's-length away. Given the smug expression on the blonde's face, Valerie suspected she'd crashed into her on purpose. A rapacious gleam of jealousy streaked down her spine in response.

Daisy had warned her about the rumors surrounding these 'mandatory social events' and the women with ulterior motives who often used any excuse to get close to and shamelessly flirt with forbidden men they weren't attached to. Men couldn't rape other women they weren't mated with, or have sex with them. However, just about any other sexual touching or kissing could be accomplished if the man could be persuaded.

"So have you missed me?" The blonde reached out and ran her forefinger down Hauser's arm from shoulder to elbow. Valerie resisted the urge to break the offending finger off at the second knuckle and hand it to her for the personal space violation audacity.

"No."

Her attention quickly turned to Valerie, "I'm Gina, by the way." She extended her hand, pressing Valerie's obligation to take it. Her fingers drifted forward, but Hauser threaded his fingers through Valerie's and pulled her fingers back before they touched Gina's.

Gina sent a scandalous gaze Hauser's way. "Are you sorry you failed to secure me for your group?"

"No. You shouldn't be here, Gina. Go spend time with your own partners."

"That's just it, I don't want to. Once upon a time I wanted you, Hauser. I want to know why I got blackballed from your group."

A sudden chill washed down Valerie's body. *The blonde had gotten blackballed from 'her' group of men?*

Valerie shifted her focus from the self-satisfied mug of the blonde to Hauser's face, now wreathed in apology. She felt heat rise in her cheeks and hoped the darkness of the room covered her reaction.

Hauser's gaze hardened and he sent a chill glance to Gina. "You know why. You're just being a bitch."

"I was only joking back then. I would have fucked the big monster in your group. At least enough to keep him from dying."

Turning her attention to Valerie, Gina winked and asked, "So does Dominick's cock split you in half when he fucks you?" She glanced down at Valerie's generous hips and smirked. "Or are you also big enough on the inside handle his atrocious girth."

Daisy saved her from responding. She and Brandon purposely danced past and knocked Gina out of the way before Valerie could slap that superior look off her face. "Leave my friend alone or you can deal with me," Daisy said.

Gina sneered, but kept her insufficient distance. Pinning a gaze on Valerie, she said tauntingly, "You should enjoy Hauser's mouth as often as you can. He's got the best lips here. It still makes me wet just remembering his tongue swirling around in my mouth." She clucked her tongue, leered at Hauser and licked her lips.

Valerie turned to Hauser. "You kissed her?" She didn't mean to sound so shocked or pathetically hurt by the unexpected knowledge.

Daisy passed between them, pushing Gina further away and whispered, "Don't give her a reason to gloat. Brush it off and dance, Valerie."

Hauser took her in his arms and spun her away from the volatile, upsetting situation. Valerie reeled from the repeated mental picture of Hauser kissing the other woman, his tongue swirling around in her mouth, making the silvery blonde super model-sized woman wet with desire. She shook her head to dissolve the vision.

"I wasn't your first. How foolish of me to think that I was. Of course I wasn't." Valerie whispered more to herself than to Hauser.

"I met her at our first gauntlet arena," he said. "She selected me."

She pinned him with a glare. "You don't have to explain."

"Obviously, I do."

Valerie barely registered his face in her view. Her perverse imagination shot vivid pictures of Gina with Johnny, Frasier, and Mark into her brain like repeated flashes from a lightning storm and a well of tortured despair rose in her throat. The punch to her stomach when she visualized Dominick in bed with Gina made her stop dancing. Her legs went weak.

"I need to sit down."

Hauser slid an arm around her shoulders for support and led her toward the booth where the others in her party waited.

"I'm sorry, Valerie." His utterly tormented tone conveyed his regret.

She stopped at the edge of the dance floor. "Did everyone in the group kiss her?"

"No. Only me. Because I was the scout." Hauser sighed deeply and added, "She chose me and I kissed her, but when I took her to meet the others she took one look at Dominick and refused to have anything to do with him."

"So she was blackballed."

Nodding, he continued, "Mark thought she was a bitch, Johnny said she'd suck the creative life out of us within a month. So before she met the others in private we collectively declined to pursue her as a mate."

"How many others were between Gina and me?"

"None. I was careful thereafter. We only got two free selections before someone was assigned. That's why I made the deal with you in the hall."

"Why her?" But Valerie knew why. Gina was beautiful, blond and most of all very skinny, which generated a load of insecurities in Valerie's brain regarding her body.

"She was the first blonde I saw." Hauser shrugged. "She was very persuasive that she wanted to help me with my needs until she met the group. We'd all maintained a one-for-all-and-all-for-one mentality regarding our stay here. She laughingly refused Dominick as a monster freak of nature, so we blackballed her. She obviously didn't measure up."

"So I was the second blonde you saw?"

"No. You were the first curvy one and besides, we met before the gauntlet arena. I had a chance to talk to you. I liked you. Still do." Hauser gently ran his hand down her spine and slipped it around her waist.

Valerie nodded without smiling and walked the rest of the short distance to their booth.

"Do you forgive me?" he called.

She turned and pegged him with an indifferent stare. "There's nothing to forgive. You met her first. You never lied to me. Other women never came up in any conversation. I was simply taken off guard. Especially her parting remark about your kisses."

"I only care about what my kisses do to *you*." His eyebrows rose in question.

"They do the same thing." Valerie paused. "They make me wet."

"Good to know."

From inside their booth, Dominick stood when he saw them approach and drifted onto the dance floor. "What's up?"

"Gina introduced herself and made Valerie mad." Hauser strolled into the booth and plopped down in a seat.

Dominick tipped her chin up with a finger. "She's not worth your anger. Dance with me. I'll make you forget she was ever in the room."

"I don't care about her. Not really." Valerie was ashamed to admit that what Gina had said was her initial fear regarding Dominick. His size was intimidating. After spending the past several months with him, she knew he was not monstrous by any definition. Valerie spent a lot of time thinking about Dominick, even when she shouldn't have been.

"I'm fine. We don't have to dance."

"Dance with me anyway." He gave her a bone-melting half smile and pulled her into his arms. Once secured against his warm frame, a flash of memory from the last time they were in bed together singed her mind. Dominick exuded a powerful aura and it was difficult for Valerie not to get swept up in it.

"Why?"

"I'd like to have you slither across my body to the beat of sultry music. Come on. Indulge me."

"All right. Fine. Let's dance."

Valerie followed him to the dance floor amidst the crowd of couples swaying to the thrumming beat of a slow, seductive song. He slid his hand to her ass and pulled her against his groin, separating her legs with one rock hard thigh. Her insides clenched with arousal at the sudden tactile sensation of being so close and intimate in front of other people.

As he grasped her fingers and spun them around the dance floor, she remembered that Dominick's name was listed as her first contact for next week's schedule. By midnight a week from right now, she'd likely be in his bed sucked up this close, only they'd be horizontal instead of vertical and they'd be naked. Perhaps this was the beginning of a lengthy act of foreplay.

Valerie slid around the dance floor in the arms of a man strong enough to break her in half, but with the apparent restraint to hold any hostility in check.

After six months, she'd mostly dismissed her unreasonable apprehension of going to Dominick's room. Ever tolerant of her inexplicable and unwarranted fears, Dominick never initiated anything sexual toward her until she made the first move.

Gina, with her silvery blond hair and skinny body, waltzed past with a smirk on her face and eyed Dominick with distaste. Valerie stiffened in his arms and stuttered in her next dance step.

"Relax," he leaned in and whispered. Dominick planted a kiss on her neck that sizzled straight to her soul. Her focus shifted from the couples around them to his lips blazing a path along her jaw. Seconds later, he riveted his mouth to her lips and kissed her with driven passion, enough to make her forget where she was.

"Can't wait until I see you again, babe," he murmured against her hair after breaking the sultry kiss. Their bodies were pressed tightly together from shoulders to knees. Valerie was surprised when a tingle of anticipation curled to life low in her belly. She was additionally ashamed to admit that she'd thought of him while with each of the other men in her group over the past couple of months.

A forbidden concept she wouldn't even share with Daisy.

"Can't wait to see you, too," she admitted in a breathy whisper and tightened her grip around his waist.

His rumble of laughter caught her off guard. "I find that hard to believe." He ran his hand from the middle of her back to cup her head, threading his fingers in the locks of her hair. It came across as a very possessive gesture and a secret thrill ran down her spine at his forcefulness.

Tilting her head back, she gazed deeply into his eyes. "I promise you, I look forward to our next night together."

Dominick licked his lips in a wolf-like gesture and returned the stare. The world fell away and Valerie was assaulted with image after image of remembered times with this man. Dominick filled her waking thoughts as none of the others did. Dancing so close to him was overwhelming to her already overloaded senses. He intrigued her and her body responded to him in ways she couldn't control.

Pressed so close and sliding up and down and across his torso, her nipples poked into his chest and stoked her arousal. The action had a profound impact on her libido, which purred for more.

"Hold me tighter," he murmured in her ear. The flat of one large hand slid down a fraction to cup one cheek, pulling her tighter against his groin. He squeezed his fingers lightly and his large palm sizzled her butt in a most delicious way.

"If I get any closer, I'll be inside of you."

The rumble of his laughter sent a friction of electric sensation down her spine. "My favorite place."

"Are people watching us slither over each other?"

"Yes. Every man in this room is jealous."

Valerie snorted. "No, they aren't."

His laughter caressed her. Hugging her close, he put his lips to her ear and whispered, "Oh, yes they are. Each of the men watch us on the dance floor, molded seductively to one another, and speculate if we'll be horizontal sans clothing later on. I suspect a few of the women do, too."

Valerie laughed. "So is this something that 'gets you off'?"

"Not yet. Not tonight. Next time I see you, though, I'll think back to this moment and 'get off' on the memory." He paused, gave her an odd look and added, "You should do the same thing for Hauser."

Startled at having Dominick mention one of the other men, she asked, "Do what for Hauser?"

He cleared his throat as if what he had to say was uncomfortable for him to say. "You should come out here and slither around on the dance floor with Hauser. Then every person here will wonder which of us will have you tonight. The speculation will give them something else to gossip about and rob Gina of her perpetual sneer."

Her eyebrows went to her hairline. "And you're okay with me slithering all over Hauser?"

He shrugged. "I'll be the next one in line for private, naked slithering purposes. No one else needs to know. But mostly, I want Gina to writhe in curious agony for ever distressing you."

"What makes you think she cares about seeing us together? She called you monstrous."

"After we turned her down, she tracked me to my security job and secretly begged for another chance. Apparently, her selections at the following gauntlet arenas weren't as appealing. She promised me extra sexual time if I swayed the group to choose her at the next gauntlet arena. I told her to fuck off." He sneered as if in perverse memory. "She called me a name then, too."

Valerie nodded. "Okay. Slink me back to Hauser and we'll put on a show for Gina. I'd hate for her to think she'd caused any rift in our household."

Dominick glanced over at their booth and apparently signaled Hauser to come and join them. Valerie didn't see what Dominick did, but within seconds Hauser was positioned behind her. After a few beats to the music with both of them sandwiching her, Dominick released her to Hauser's care with a wink.

After a slow turn around the dance floor, where she and Hauser practically had mock sex while swaying to the seductive beat of the sultry music, they managed to stray well into Gina's visibly perturbed view. Valerie caught her eye and sent a satisfied gleam in her direction. Once she knew she had an audience, she kissed Hauser like they were about to drop to the floor and go at it to the beat of the music while the others watched.

She thought they'd proved a point, but soon Johnny tapped Hauser's shoulder and she danced around the perimeter once with him, too. Mark cut in on Johnny and shortly thereafter, Frasier also intruded for a spin. He pulled her very close and swept her into an overtly erotic dance. Even more erotic than what happened between them when they were alone.

Dominick returned after a long while to whisk her through several more dirty dancing steps as they writhed around the dance floor yet again for their finale. After so much tactile stimulation on the dance floor, Valerie was ready to head home and jump Dominick's bones.

"Okay, enough. I think Gina gets the point. She just left the dance floor to screech at one of her poor unfortunate mates."

Dominick's laugh was rich and deep. "I don't really care about her. I just like having your body sliding all over mine." He pressed her lips to hers and licked his way inside her mouth. She didn't resist.

He pulled back and stared deeply into her eyes. She returned the gaze, thinking about how attached she'd become. Dominick fascinated her on a level the others didn't touch.

Valerie didn't know how long they looked longingly at each other, but when the lights came up signaling the party was almost over, she found she was disappointed they didn't have more time together in this seductive venue. Perhaps she'd initiate a sensuously slithering dance the next time she went to his room.

Dominick pulled away from her as if with great reluctance. Valerie felt the loss of his warmth as if he'd been cut from her. He kissed the fingers of one hand with aching tenderness before returning her to the booth.

Acutely aware that a remarkable event had transpired between them on the dance floor as the sultry music powered their intimate movements, Valerie had an epiphany. There was something elemental about Dominick that captivated her. The basic need he drove in her, which had once been a frightening chore, was now an anticipated luxury.

She was falling for him. Hard.

"Would you like to get a drink?"

Valerie nodded, although she wasn't thirsty, and opted for a drink of punch followed by a trip back to the booth to rest, although sleep was not the primary thought in her head. Her eyes strayed to Dominick while he spoke to one of Daisy's mates.

He was beautiful. Darkly perfect and she wanted to learn more about his tastes. The dancing tonight had been a huge surprise. Dominick would certainly remain fully entrenched in her thoughts going forward.

Once they'd stayed the minimum time decreed by the Others for optimal regeneration of spirit, the six of them headed home. She blew a kiss to Daisy, who was plastered against Brandon and dancing to a beat only she could hear.

Hauser and the others led the way as she and Dominick trailed behind them. With his spicy scent wafting around her and the memory of their slithering dances, she wished it weren't still seven days until her next sexual encounter.

Dominick now held a newly discovered fascination for her libido and she already contemplated how to explore this newfound treasure.

Valerie also wondered how she'd be able to wait until next week to show Dominick her eager new attitude.

Chapter 10

Hand poised to knock on Dominick's door, Valerie wondered if he would allow her to have what she craved. Would he even let her inside his room? It had been only two days since the dance and Dominick hadn't been far out of her thoughts for much of the past forty-eight hours. The truth was, she hadn't thought of anyone else. The recurring memory of the way he'd held her as they'd danced had sizzled a path to her core and boosted her nerve.

After two days of longing, Valerie had slipped into bed tonight each night knowing that sleep wouldn't come easily. Pondering her options, she made a sudden command decision. She slipped out of bed, pulled her nightgown off and bunched it in a corner. Changing into the sheerest robe in her closet, she left her room and headed down the hallway to Dominick's door.

Valerie closed her eyes and tapped on his door three times. She counted to five with no response. Maybe he was gone. But she knew it wasn't true. All men were confined to quarters this late at night unless they had to work and Valerie knew he didn't. Maybe he was asleep.

She stepped back to retreat just as the door opened. Her eyes traveled upwards as his large muscular frame filled the doorway, a questioning expression on his handsome features. Shirtless, Dominick was so overwhelmingly gorgeous and big, she couldn't speak for a moment.

"What's wrong, babe?" An appreciative gaze strayed down her barely clad body, only further making it difficult to think clearly.

Valerie couldn't find her voice and just stared at his bare chest for a few minutes, trying to remember how to breathe. She shifted her gaze to his questioning eyes.

His brows soon came together in concern. "Are you okay?"

"I'm fine." She nodded as if to convince herself and added, "Nothing's wrong."

He glanced down either side of the hallway and then found her gaze. "It's not my night," he whispered.

Nodding again she whispered back, "I know. It's actually my night."

Crossing his arms and leaning one beefy shoulder against the door frame, his features softened. "Can I help you with something?" he asked slowly, as if the answer would get him into trouble. Valerie wondered the same thing.

Garnering some courage, she placed her hand on the center of his warm, smooth chest and answered, "Yes. There is something urgent that I need help with."

His eyes slid to where her hand rested. Clearing his throat, he asked, "What can I do for you?"

Valerie sent her gaze to his and watched his reaction to her confession. "I don't want to sleep alone."

His eyes widened, but he remained silent, as if digesting the words on how her sleeping patterns impacted him.

"You want to sleep with me?" His lids narrowed. He glanced down each side of the hallway quickly before resting his amused and inquisitive gaze back on her. "Why?"

Heat flashed in her cheeks before she could reign it in. "I…I'm lonely," she managed to stutter.

Valerie was puzzled as to why he wasn't more excited about the idea, until a horrifying prospect occurred. Perhaps he was content with the current twice a month arrangement.

She removed her hand from his chest. "Perhaps you aren't interested. If you don't want me here, I understand and I promise I won't ever bother you again…"

Valerie slid a foot backwards and slammed her eyes shut in embarrassment.

Before she could take another step, Dominick grabbed her and pressed her body to his granite-firm chest so fast she almost shrieked in surprise. His strong hands slid behind her back to secure her close. The whisper of material between them in the form of her sheer robe enhanced their contact rather than subduing it. Her face pressed against the spot on his chest where the steady beat of his heart sped up with the pressure of his hug. "I always want you, babe." He squeezed her even tighter. "Always."

Valerie released a breath she hadn't realized she held and asked, "May I please come in?"

"Sure."

Peeling herself away from his perfect body, she watched his ass as he turned and led the way inside. He ushered her to the small living room and watched her carefully, but didn't touch her.

"Do you want something to drink?"

Valerie shook her head. She wanted sex. A throbbing between her legs had started pounding as soon as she crossed the threshold into his space. She was so turned on by her own audacity she could hardly get air into her lungs. Having her face buried in his chest put his scent all over her and it was playing havoc with her limited control.

Searching the room for an ice breaker, she noticed the video screen in sleep mode. "Did I interrupt anything? I don't even know how you spend your spare time here."

He shrugged. "I read sometimes. I watch video movies occasionally. Nothing too exciting. So, are you ready to tell me why you're really here?"

Valerie felt heat creep up her face. She wanted sex and didn't know how to ask for it.

Probably best just to blurt it out. "I'm tired of spending half of my time alone every month. I have five regular sexual partners, but I'm…lonely."

"So you want to spend your extra private time here, with me?" He didn't make a move towards her. On any other night when she had showed up in the past month or so, he would have found a way to have kissed her by now. Plus, she'd have something in her hand to drink and she'd be ready to peel her clothing off with the merest look he gave her.

Tonight, she could hardly get breath into her lungs. She swallowed hard and found her gaze lingering on his brawny, perfect chest. She was so used to him making the first move on the nights she came for his turn that she was paralyzed by indecision as to how to get things going.

Perhaps this was a bad idea. "You don't have to do this if you don't want to."

A seductive smile stole over his lips. "Oh, I want to." He took a step closer. "Is there anything special you'd like me to do or are you just here to sleep?"

Valerie trembled as the assault of various things she'd been contemplating all vied for attention in her brain. Like some porn video on fast forward, she couldn't single out a solitary thing. She just saw flashes of various body parts and naked flesh scanning before her eyes.

"I want to have sex with you. I'm not sure how to initiate it. Or if I should at all."

He leaned his hip against the edge of the sofa back. "Did you ask the others for extra time?"

"No!" The exclamation came out before she meant to express it, but her answer seemed to make him very happy. "I only asked you."

"Tell me, if I had turned you down, who would have been next on your list?"

"No one. I don't have a list." This *was* a bad idea. "I should go." She turned to leave, but Dominick moved with the stealth and speed of a wild animal securing its prey.

Wrapping his arms around her and pressing his glorious body to hers from behind, she almost came as the warmth from his strong body rushed to overwhelm her senses.

"I don't want you to go, babe. I'm just trying to comprehend your actions. I want to understand so there is no misinterpretation. You want to spend extra time with me, but not the others. Is that right?"

Valerie swallowed a sob. "You must think I'm a horrible person. It's not right. I know that it isn't right to feel his way. I just can't help it." Unable to hold her volatile emotions, she broke and started crying. Tears ran unheeded down one cheek and splashed on his arm.

"I don't think you're horrible. I just can't believe you chose me. How long have you felt this way?"

"Since before the dance. I can't stop thinking about you." Her knees buckled and he lifted her into his arms. She buried her face in his neck and murmured, "When I'm not with you, I'm thinking about you. It's worse on the weeks that I'm alone. After dancing with you two days ago, I haven't thought of anything else each waking moment. I just couldn't stomach spending another night by myself."

Dominick leaned down and kissed her trembling mouth softly. "I'm glad. I think about you quite a bit, too. The truth is, I've don't remember ever having such intense feelings for a woman. For future reference, you can stay here any time you want, even if it's just to sleep." He clenched her tighter. "I won't ever let you regret coming to me tonight."

"Thank you."

He kissed her again with a firm press of his lips implying serious carnal intent. His kisses always made her a little woozy, as if she were intoxicated. Picking her up, he carried her to his bedroom and placed her on her feet next to his bed.

"Tell me, what can I do to make you happy?"

"Kiss me like that again a few more times and then take me to bed. I'm really here more for the sex and not so much for the sleep."

His eyes narrowed into a smoky, sexy stare that drilled into her soul before he whispered, "My pleasure."

Another part of the thrill for Valerie was the prurient idea that the Others were recording this auspicious event. If they called her into their chamber to complain, she had a speech all prepared regarding how she should be able to spend her private time in any way she wanted as long as no one got hurt.

Dominick slid his hands slowly along the contours of her body, trapping the sheer robe against her sensitive skin. Reverently, he slipped his fingers beneath the collar and pulled the fabric apart, slowly revealing her nudity. He pushed her hips against the mattress edge with a gentle nudge from his hands and kissed her bare skin from collarbone to bellybutton. Her fingertips traced his smooth skin over the visible muscles of his shoulders. He soon knelt before her and kissed a path further down until he buried his face between her legs.

One lick across her clit and her body arched forward as if pulled by an invisible string. Legs trembling, Valerie broke the delectable sensation to sit on the bed's soft edge.

"My legs won't hold me up when you do that."

His warm laughter filled the room. "Okay. Scoot back and I'll get up there to have my wicked oral way with you."

Once settled, she rested on her elbows to watch what he'd do next. Kneeling between her thighs, he laughed and pulled her legs apart, giving himself better access to where she really wanted his attention directed. She felt his breath first. Just a wisp of air against her sensitive nub, and she sighed in anticipation.

Dominick traced her lower lips with the tip of his tongue. Again she arched off the bed when he circled her clit as his fingers separated her. Valerie slumped against the sheets as his clever tongue suddenly invaded her pussy with a deep thrust.

"You're so good," she murmured.

His only response was a grateful sounding moan, as if he devoured a mouth-watering meal he'd waited an eternity to eat. With his tongue now focused firmly on her clit, she was fast moving up to a pinnacle of what felt like forbidden pleasure.

That she wasn't truly supposed to be here with Dominick and his seductive mouth somehow made the experience more titillating.

The moment he slid his cock inside her body, the Others would know. Valerie hoped they didn't burst through the door to stop the completion.

Dominick slid two fingers inside her body, wrapped his lips around her clit and sucked repeatedly until she came so hard her toes actually curled. Her thighs trapped his head in place until the last convulsion of orgasm ceased and she became boneless in the aftermath.

From between her legs he said, "Have I ever mentioned how sexy you are when you climax?"

Valerie laughed. "I believe you've mentioned it."

He crawled next to her on the bed. Her body, still limp and sated, didn't move when he began stroking her from neck to thigh.

"You are beautiful."

"I'm glad you think so."

He pressed a kiss to one shoulder and trailed his lips to a particularly sensitive place behind one ear. His hand stroked from thigh to belly then cupped one breast, kneading it gently. Thumb circling her nipple, Dominick whispered, "Now what, babe?"

"I believe you already know exactly what do to."

"Tell me. I don't want to presume."

On fire after what he'd already done and longing for him to simply mount her and thrust furiously until he came, Valerie reached down and grabbed his cock in one hand. "I'd like this hot, hard cock inserted between my legs and thrust inside my pussy repeatedly."

"I love it when you talk dirty, babe."

"Oh yeah?" She laughed, feeling just a little bit naughty when she whispered, "Fuck me, then. I'm ready for your huge shaft to pleasure me."

Dominick nipped her earlobe, eliciting a shiver of desire that raced through her nerve endings before he shifted his body to cover her. She spread her legs as wide as possible beneath him. His heavy cock dropped neatly between her thighs, his tip grazing her clit once deliciously before settling against the wetness covering the opening of her slit.

Overwhelming her senses as he always did with his massive body, Dominick then circled her wrists with his large fingers and secured them above her head. She had little ability for movement beneath his thickly muscled arms and a second later he thrust his cock deeply.

A groan escaped her lips when he pulled out slowly and pushed inside a second time. He kissed her hard on the mouth, delving his tongue between her lips. She tasted the tangy musk of her own orgasmic juices coating his mouth as the tempo of his thrusting cock sped up.

Her hips bucked upward, aiming for a deeper connection, but his powerful thighs pressed her immobile against the bed. Dominick seemed to enjoy the power of holding her completely still as he drove his hard strokes deep into her body.

Every nerve ending inside readied to sing in glorious climax once he came. Valerie hadn't ever felt so protected as she did in Dominick's arms, or in his bed, or about to climax from the sheer friction of his powerful thrusts. His tongue matched the exact rhythm of his cock, and the second he came, a burst of furious sensation enveloped her body, starting with her pulsing clit and radiating warmth outward to each limb.

Dominick groaned and slowed his pace. He kissed a path to her ear and whispered, "You're, without a doubt, the best I've ever had."

Valerie sighed deeply in contentment, unable to speak and return the compliment. As she came back to the reality of her impetuous actions, she found she couldn't reciprocate anyway for another reason. The other men in her life were equally fabulous and she wasn't even supposed to be here with Dominick right now. It would be worse to confess to him that he was indeed the best she'd ever had, too.

So she kissed his cheek hoping to convey her silent appreciation and glanced at his door, hoping the Sex Police weren't about to rouse them for crimes against the rules and blatant disregard of previously written down regulations. The night had been too perfect to contemplate it being be the last one. Valerie already planned to be in this exact place doing the exact same thing for the rest of her week off.

Bravado spilled over with her exuberant mood from repeated orgasms tonight. Any repercussions wouldn't dissuade her from seeing Dominick again. And again.

The three member panel holding court in the High Committee chamber could blow it out their collective asses.

Chapter 11

881 until Return Day

Following Blue to the eighth floor of the administration building, Valerie knew she was in trouble. Again. She even knew the topic of discussion for today's chastisement. Extra time with Dominick.

It had been a little over a month since she'd decided her spare time was better spent in Dominick's company. Each day thereafter, she'd expected to be called in for punishment, but each day nothing happened.

She should have known they'd wait until she was lulled into a false sense of security. When Blue showed up at her door with a snotty attitude, Valerie was genuinely puzzled by what he was doing there.

"Your presence is required at the High Committee chamber. And by the way, you're in serious trouble."

"Now what?"

His bushy eyebrows went up. "You've been playing favorites."

Valerie could tell from Blue's silent tight-lipped expression on their fast-paced journey to the High Committee's chamber that she wasn't going to like what they had to say once she entered. Valerie had a big surprise for Goldie and the High Committee jerk offs. She wasn't sorry for what she'd done and she didn't plan to stop.

Blue ushered her through the chambers and before anyone else could say anything, Valerie announced, "If you think hauling me here every other month makes a difference, you're wrong. I couldn't give a shit less what you think about how I'm conducting myself here. And before you announce any ultimatums, I suggest you reconsider. I'm not likely to be swayed to change my ways by any threats from you." She crossed her arms in defiance and stared. Goldie's ivory eyebrows lifted, while Silver and Bronze's mouths fell open.

Recovering his brief, almost non-existent composure gaffe, Goldie frowned and said, "Your impertinent attitude, while amusing, will not serve you well today. You've broken a serious rule and it is obvious by your admission that you did so intentionally and repeatedly. There will be repercussions for your actions."

"I don't care. In my mind, what I do on my own time is none of your business." Valerie had a moment of panic, wondering what the consequences might be regarding her infatuation with Dominick. But it didn't last long.

Angry that they watched her private life in the first place, and furious over feeling guilty when they practically forced her to have sex with five men anyway, and that only after bringing her onto this spacecraft against her will in the second place, was bad enough. She didn't think she should have to explain her actions regarding her feelings about one of her men.

"If your other men are suffering, it *is* our business."

"But they aren't, and you know it. You literally watch every fucking service I perform."

Goldie rolled his eyes and sat back in his tall-backed chair. "We don't see the specific acts. We just keep track of your whereabouts. And we of course register the month-to-month health of the men you sexually service. We've registered a larger than normal number of sexual releases for one of the men in your household."

"Of course," she murmured under her breath before adding loudly, "So what if one of them is getting more?"

Goldie huffed and leaned forward, fixing his eyes on a blue sheet of paper on the desk before him. "The first question we must ask is whether or not this man is pressuring you for more." Goldie's expression shifted from the desk to her face and displayed his doubt that she wasn't fully complicit in the extra sex rule violation.

Valerie remembered Dominick's puzzled expression when she had showed up the first night. It never occurred to her that any of them would try to get more than what she willingly offered. "No. He would never pressure me. I sought out Dominick last month and for each of the extra nights we shared in the past month on my own time. He never came to me. Not once."

"Oh? So you led him astray over and over again. That is not a surprise, but he didn't stop you either, did he? Therefore, you are both culpable.

However, you are more so because you started it."

"Yes, I did. It was fabulous and I plan to keep doing it, too."

Bronze and Silver's mouths dropped open again. Goldie, meanwhile, mashed his lips into a thin, disapproving line. Clenching his fingers together before him, Goldie's mouth relaxed after a few seconds.

Pinning her with an inquisitive gaze, he asked quietly, "May I ask why?"

Valerie paused. She'd been about to blast him with attitude. She took a deep breath and with it came the sterile smell of the room, including a faint disinfectant scent.

"Why I continually break your rules or why I slept with Dominick during my own time?"

Goldie looked at the ceiling and shook his head before dropping his gaze to her again. "Why Dominick? My understanding was that he was the one you were most apprehensive about during your initial meeting with this group."

Valerie shrugged then narrowed her eyes. "How did you know I was nervous about Dominick?"

"We monitored your general health and vital statistics during the initial meetings when you were in the company of your potential mates before the final deal was struck. Dominick has made your heart race and your vitals spike from the very beginning." Goldie picked up a metal clipboard and scanned it. "At least until recently."

Valerie closed her eyes. She knew what had changed and when. After dancing with Dominick at the social event, Valerie hadn't been able to get him out of her mind for the immediate two days following. After having nary a single dream while aboard this alien craft, Valerie had basically day dreamed about Dominick the night after they returned from the dance. Placing herself in several very sexy scenarios, Dominick was her last waking thought before drifting off to sleep. At breakfast the next morning, the unique scent of him drove her nearly mad. Until the next night when she'd gone to his room and done something about it.

In the last month, they'd spent every night of her free time together. She refused to divulge to even Dominick that she was falling in love with him. No one needed to know.

Valerie also didn't want to confess to the assembled panel that she favored him. "What difference does it make?"

"A great deal if you plan to eliminate your other mates as sexual partners."

Valerie took an involuntary step forward. "I'd never do that. Never! Just because I prefer spending my excess time with Dominick doesn't mean I'll allow the others to suffer."

"It has happened before. I believe you saw the video during orientation." He paused and gave her a look of distaste before adding, "You did see that part of the orientation, didn't you?"

Valerie nodded and closed her eyes. She remembered the abandoned men vividly from orientation. Heart-wrenching and tortured to the point of death, those men were treated abysmally by their female mate. It was the reason why Valerie would never do that to any of her mates. She did love each of them in their own special ways.

"Well, it won't happen in my household."

"We'll see about that, won't we." Goldie straightened up in his chair. "Your flagrant abuse of our rules doesn't assure us you won't break the most important one of all."

Valerie crossed her arms and prepared to defend herself. "This is different. I think most of your rules are stupid, but I would never hurt any of my mates."

Goldie tilted his head to the side and shrugged lightly. "We'll keep a special eye on your household to ensure you are abiding by the agreement of sex twice a month for all of your other men."

"Big deal. Go ahead. I'm already on your watch list."

Goldie stood and his menacing expression gave Valerie pause.

"Is that all?" Valerie studied the floor between her feet and the desk, feeling a little deflated, and wished to be anywhere else.

"No. There is one final item that we need to discuss."

Valerie suspected that no "discussion" was about to be forthcoming, just another ultimatum or her punishment for crimes already committed.

"What else?" Valerie heaved a deep sigh of resignation.

"Do not under any circumstances tell any of your other mates what you're doing with Dominick."

Valerie hadn't planned to tell them, but she wanted to know why Goldie didn't want her to. "Another new rule? Okay, I'll bite. Why not tell them?"

"If they find out, invariably they will want to know why you didn't choose them for extra sex time. It could cause irreparable damage to the fragile peace in your household. Five men sharing one woman is a difficult enough conflict without adding favoritism."

"It's not exactly favoritism."

"Yes, it is. Otherwise you'd add an equal time to the monthly schedule for each of your mates. Which is why we waited so long before bringing you here. Initially, we gave you the benefit of the doubt."

Valerie sent her gaze to the floor again. She'd obviously disappointed the committee with her choice of a singular mate for the extra sex she craved from Dominick.

"I can't help the way I feel about him."

"Regardless, you may be jeopardizing your Return Day by disclosing this information to the other men."

She inhaled and digested the information. "I don't think the others would care."

"I'm warning you, Valerie." The grave tone of his voice and the fact that he had used her first name made Valerie look directly into his angry gaze. "Do not tell the other men in your household how you spend your free time."

"All right, fine. I won't tell any of the others." Valerie ignored the tug of conscience at keeping this secret from the other men, but tucked it away. She'd show these colorful perverts that she wouldn't allow discord in her household. None of her men would ever suffer, she'd have Dominick whenever she wanted and she'd take special care to keep their relationship private.

When she got back to her house, Daisy stopped by within minutes of her arrival holding two cups of tea and a sympathetic expression.

"I saw you leave with Blue this morning. What did you do this time?"

Valerie sighed. "Does it matter?"

"Not really. I just came to commiserate." Handing her the extra a cup of tea, Daisy seated herself on the sofa and asked, "Want to talk?"

"Yes," she murmured. Valerie would love to blurt out all the secrets she harbored regarding her fascination with Dominick, but because of all the fresh threats from Goldie hanging over her head, she changed her mind and her response. "No." She shook her head and added morosely, "I don't know." Valerie lowered herself slowly into the overstuffed chair next to the sofa and tucked her feet underneath her.

Daisy's nervous laugh rippled the air. "Sounds serious."

Confessing her secret was on the tip of her tongue, but Valerie chickened out and decided to keep her own counsel. She loved Daisy like a sister, but feared sharing this particular information. It was a rule everyone understood. No favorites among the men in your household.

Valerie stuffed the desire to share deep down inside where it couldn't escape, took a sip of tea and forced a laugh. "It's nothing. I just wasn't in the mood for a lecture on my continually disappointing conduct this morning."

"I got a wrist slap for decadent public displays of affection with Brandon the day after last month's social event dance."

Valerie lifted her cup in salute. "I got that lecture times five for showing off in front of Gina at the same dance." She almost added a clue about that night being a turning point in her feelings for Dominick. Valerie would have to bury her feelings much deeper to keep from blurting them out at every available opportunity. It could only cause an irreversible faux pas.

Daisy got a funny look in her eyes. It was the same one that precipitated her reading Valerie's mind. Admittedly, only her friend had this skill.

Piercing her with a serious gaze, Daisy said in a low tone, "Of all the men in your house, do you have one that is—"

The front door popped open all of a sudden and Frasier strolled across the threshold whistling a tune. Her gaze went to the wall clock, noting he was home hours early for the first time ever.

"Frasier. What are you doing home?" Valerie stood, slopping hot tea on her hand. Daisy had gone pale the moment he came through the door.

"Got off for good behavior." He grinned. "Sorry to interrupt you, darling. Don't let me keep you ladies from your conversation." Resuming his cheerful whistle, he turned and headed to his room.

Valerie watched until he disappeared. "That's so strange. He never comes home early. None of them do. Ever."

Daisy, still harboring a wide-eyed gaze, scrambled to her feet and mumbled, "I need to get going."

Valerie lifted the teacup, slopping more hot liquid on her hand. "Wait. This is yours."

"Keep it. I'll get it later." Daisy practically ran out the back sliding glass door.

Valerie was left alone with tea still dripping off one hand, a guilty conscience over having nearly been caught conversing about a forbidden subject, and sincere curiosity over what Daisy had been about to ask her. Suspecting she knew exactly the topic of the question, Valerie knew they'd never again pick up the thread of that particular inflammatory piece of discussion.

The illicit thoughts regarding favoritism were better left unspoken.

Chapter 12

328 until Return Day

After spending the past several days in luxurious sexual abandon with Dominick, tonight followed by the next three nights would be spent servicing her other mates.

Valerie's sexual servitude had become somewhat of an unwelcome chore shoved into the middle of her extended life with Dominick. While she adored all of the men in her household, Dominick had held particular fascination for her this past year. He grabbed the bulk of her attention.

Last night had been Dominick's 'official' night for sex with her, but mostly it marked the final night they were together before she had to administer her promised and now somewhat awkward responsibility. The night before her four-day break to spend 'time' with the others was always slightly stilted.

Guilt had tugged at her conscious the past couple of months as she tried not to begrudge her other mates the time spent away from the man she'd fallen in love with. Plus, she endeavored not to think of him while in the company of the others.

Although, trying to keep such a powerful vision of perfection out of her thoughts was fairly useless in practical application, as Dominick slid into her mind easily and often. The nagging worry of their hopeless permanent future had no place in the bedroom with any of the other four. If only it were that easy to keep her mind focused where it should be.

Valerie cleared her head of everything else and knocked on Frasier's door with a vow to keep her mind on only him until the next morning. She planned to seduce Frasier as soon as possible when she walked through the door. His usual manner of sedate evenings needed a wake-up call. She'd decided that it was time to shake things up a bit.

"Hello, darling," he remarked as she strolled over the threshold.

Across the room, Valerie saw an elaborate dinner had been set up on his dining table. The door closed behind her with a snap, startling her. She turned and noticed that Frasier seemed unusually bright-eyed, for lack of a better word. His gaze swept down her body and back to her face. His leering smile should have been a forewarning.

"Let's go to bed," she said, as she'd planned earlier in her quest for the different.

"Right now?" His surprise was expected. Frasier was obviously uncomfortable with changing the format of their regularly scheduled dates even though it was slightly over two years later. Frasier thrived on routine. They always had dinner first. They always danced afterward. They always went to bed last and had a very wonderful, sedate time together under the sheets.

"Yes." As part of her 'shake things up' evening, she wore only a silk robe. Valerie turned away and slid the light garment off her shoulders. She usually wore her most conservative clothing when she was with Frasier. The robe had been selected to further entice him to change things tonight.

"Did I do something wrong?"

She whirled at the apologetic tone of his voice. Her breasts, exposed to the sudden chill in the air, pebbled. *Why was she so cold?*

"No. Of course not. I just thought you might like to change our regular routine a bit." Her eyes couldn't meet his. The truth was, she wanted to hurry and have sex with him before her mind strayed to someone else.

"Why do I get the feeling that you want to hurry and get this over with, darling?"

She shrugged. "I don't know what you're talking about. Don't you want me?"

Standing nude before him, Valerie reached her hands up and stroked her breasts and nipples. Out of the corner of her eye, she saw that he watched her stroke and pinch herself. The fly of his trousers tented in reaction to her bold actions. That was new. She'd never seen Frasier with an erection until they got to bed.

"I do want you." His hands went to the fly of his trousers. Shockingly, he unfastened and unzipped his pants. He freed his cock and stroked his stiffening member one-handed. The very breath in her lungs stilled in astonishment. She'd expected to have to convince him to participate in her 'shake things up' evening. The prurient vision of Frasier with cock in hand, pumping his erection to full girth, was slightly unsettling. Perhaps it was a bad idea to shake things up.

"I didn't expect you to acquiesce so quickly. If you don't want to do this, we don't have to."

Frasier drilled her with a fierce stare. "Don't be silly, darling. That's what you're here for, after all." *Pump. Pump. Pump.* His cock seemed bigger than she remembered.

Something was wrong.

Even to shake things up a bit, Valerie would never be this forward with Frasier. Her initial plan had been to entice him through dinner with the fact that she wore nothing under her robe, not fling it off in the first second and flaunt her taut nipples. They never started with such aggressive foreplay and Valerie hadn't intended to go so far so fast.

On any other night with Frasier, once they did make it to bed, he practically had the lights off when they got down to the business of having sex.

"I think you're trying to change the subject." Frasier didn't seem to mind watching her play with her body. Something was *really* wrong, but she couldn't make herself stop. She pinched and rubbed her nipples until they stood at attention. The tingle of arousal spun down to her clit as she stroked her own flesh.

Feeling suddenly far removed from the action happening in Frasier's room, Valerie heard herself say, "No. This *is* the subject. I came here to fuck you. Isn't that what you want? I know you need sex. Here I am, ready to give it to you."

She never swore in front of Frasier. What was going on here?

Tilting his head to one side, a never-before-seen leering gleam came into his narrowed, distrustful eyes. "Are you ready to give it to *me*, darling, or once I stick my cock inside your pussy, will you be thinking of him?"

"Him?" She stopped touching her breasts and dropped her hands to her sides. Frasier absolutely never, ever said the word pussy.

She had to be dreaming. But she never had dreams. Not here.

Wake up. Wake up!

Frasier crossed the room, stiff cock bobbing as if leading the way, to where she stood rooted to the floor still naked with her nipples protruding. She couldn't move. She couldn't stop him or the dream. Frasier put his hands on her shoulders and squeezed too hard. "Him. The one you always think about when you're with me."

Alarm washed down her still frozen body. "I don't think about anyone else when I'm with you."

"Liar." Frasier's fingers squeezed harder until his carefully trimmed nails pierced her flesh.

This wasn't like him. Always the epitome of gentle, he treated Valerie like she was spun glass any time he was in her presence.

"You're hurting me." Valerie tried to pull away, but in what she sincerely hoped was a nightmare, Frasier held her fast to his body.

His fingers dug into her skin cruelly as he leaned in and whispered, "Am I? Good, I'll hurt you worse before I'm through." Twisting around to stand behind her, Frasier maintained his vise-like grip on her shoulders and pressed his chest into her shoulder blades. His fully erect cock pressed into one butt cheek uncomfortably. Now that she couldn't see his face, a wide swath of fear rushed down her body.

Frasier bit into her earlobe painfully and murmured, "Let's try something new, darling. How about I fuck you up the ass until you stop thinking about him? Would that work?"

"No!"

Please be a nightmare. Please be a nightmare.

Valerie closed her eyes and thought about how to get away. Nightmare Frasier was angry and forcibly physical and not the calm, rational gentleman she'd come to know and adore. He was a quiet lover, not experimental. He barely did oral sex and only on rare occasions when she asked for it. She'd only been on top twice in all this time with him and even then only because she'd insisted. He was most comfortable in the missionary position. She suspected he didn't even know what anal sex was let alone want to do it.

Valerie's rational mind tried to cope with the realization that logic wasn't going to work here in this ethereal nightmare world.

Wake up. Please, wake up!

Suddenly, there was a pounding knock at his door and Frasier screamed, "Come in, boys, I've got her pinned and ready to be punished."

The lights went out, drowning her in pitch black and Valerie let loose a scream from the depths of her soul.

Frasier, still hugged up close behind her, laughed maniacally. He removed one hand from her shoulder and brushed her butt several times as if priming her to be fucked. A sudden shaft of light came from an opened door a short distance away. The silhouette of another familiar figure emerged into the framed light. It looked like Dominick, although she couldn't distinguish his face in the darkness. He stood as if with arms crossed and watched her struggle with Frasier.

In the next moment and with a blur of movement, Valerie was immobilized further, held aloft by several arms she couldn't see. Someone was behind her. Frasier whispered in her ear, "Get ready. Get set. Go!"

A burning sensation centering between her ass cheeks prompted her to release another scream from the depths of her frightened core. Mouth wide, Valerie screamed in terror at the violation, until Johnny, holding his swollen dick, crossed her view. "Suck me. Suck me hard, bitch or I'll punish you." She tried to turn to the side, but he moved with her and shoved his cock brutally into her mouth. He didn't stop pushing until it rested at the back of her throat and she gagged.

Another dick from someone she couldn't even see penetrated and filled her pussy. She heard loud sweaty grunting all around her. She was in a sea of sweating, unidentified bodies that sounded like the men in her life, only they were raping her. She couldn't move. She couldn't breathe. She couldn't defend herself.

Please wake up. Please. I'm so sorry.

Valerie woke with a start and flung herself forward into a sitting position from her pillow. The memory of her nightmare dissolved slowly as she gasped for breath and fought panic. Fresh tears streamed down her cheeks. She wiped them away with shaking fingers. It had seemed so real.

She *had* been having a nightmare, right? *It was over now, right?*

Beside her, she saw Frasier's tousled hair as he stirred against his pillow, and Valerie slid away from him to the edge of her side of the bed as the viciousness of the dream permeated her once again.

Was she really awake?

Pushing up on his elbows, Frasier turned a sleepy-faced frown her way and mumbled, "What's wrong, darling?"

Valerie trembled uncontrollably. The nightmare had seemed very real and she wasn't convinced she wasn't still ensconced in it.

"Are you mad at me?" she whispered. Her frightened and trembling tone was telling.

"What?"

"Do you hate me for...?" She'd been about to confess her love for Dominick and admit that she'd been spending every moment with him. Damn, she hadn't even told Dominick she loved him. But she did. Valerie clammed up and scooted further away from Frasier. One cheek of her butt hung off the edge of the bed. She'd be on the floor if she moved any further away.

Frasier narrowed his eyes and shook his head. "Darling, I don't hate you for any reason." He twisted his body beneath the sheets until he sat up. Resting a shoulder against the headboard, he rubbed his face vigorously, crossed his arms like he did when he wanted to solve a problem and asked, "Now, what's this all about?"

Valerie opted not to explain her feelings for Dominick, although if she could, she'd run and beat his door down until he held her in his arms and convinced her everything would be okay.

Instead, she cleared her throat and whispered, "I had a bad dream."

Nodding, Frasier asked, "What was it about?"

She absolutely did not want to tell him about this awful nightmare. "I don't remember," she lied. "Just that I was scared."

Frasier smiled a friendly smile and opened his arms, as if silently inviting her to hug him with a promise of soothing her fears. His expression was sweet and caring, but the memory of his personality change from the dream flooded her brain. She flinched away from his reach, lost her balance and flipped off his bed, landing on her ass against the hardwood floor. She sprang to her feet and used the wall to help hold her up. It was time to go.

Valerie couldn't look at Frasier before she rushed out of his room, even as he called out in alarm. She bolted out of his room and ran down the long hallway to her bedroom. She closed the door, checked the lock and went straight to the bathroom. Glancing at her wall clock along the way, she realized she'd only been asleep for three hours before the nightmare had woken her.

The air shower wasn't as comforting as what a real hot water shower would have been, but it was better than nothing. She went through four cycles and then curled in a ball on the floor and cried off and on until morning, unable to close her eyes to rest or even think about sleep. After five hours of staring at the wall in deep contemplation of her previous evening in between bouts of sobbing over her fear of the horrible dream, the lights in the bathroom flashed.

Breakfast time.

She had to leave the bathroom soon or an annoying buzzer would sound throughout the house. The bathroom sink had a small reserve of drinking water that she splashed on her face for courage.

Unsure of how she would face her mates as anxiety pelted her nerves, she took several deep breaths and focused on just getting through the morning meal. She looked in the mirror and grimaced. Even makeup wouldn't cure her puffy red eyes.

For as much as she longed to see Dominick to secure the comfort she needed, she didn't want to explain why she looked like crap. Once in the kitchen, for better or worse, Dominick had already left for work early. He'd left a note on the table so she wouldn't worry.

A bad dream easily explained her puffy eyes to the others. Frasier hung around longer than usual and tried to catch her eye all through breakfast, but she refused to engage in private conversation, even the non-verbal kind. When Frasier acted like he would stay to ask about the night before, Valerie pointedly requested that Mark remain behind so she could speak to him privately.

Mark was her date for tonight, but more than anything, she didn't want to take a chance that Frasier would be able to coax the truth out of her. His wounded expression as he left hurt her heart worse than memories of the dream.

"So what happened to you last night?" was Mark's first question.

She cleared her throat. "I had a terrible dream."

"Must have been a monstrous bad one to make you so..." He paused and glanced nervously at her eyes once more. "Upset."

"It was." She looked away. She didn't want to explain the dream to Mark either.

"What did you want to talk to me about?" he asked politely.

Valerie was at a loss for words. She just hadn't wanted to talk to Frasier. "Nothing. It's not important. I'll see you tonight." Valerie forced a smile and while Mark narrowed his lids momentarily in suspicion, he didn't press her.

Of the five, Mark was probably the most intuitive of her moods and feelings, second only to Johnny. But Mark was more like her best friend. He understood her without the need for words. He exited their home without another word and earned her eternal gratitude for knowing when to back away slowly and not press for details she wasn't ready to reveal.

Left alone, Valerie hid in her room staying well away from the living room and the sliding glass doors. She didn't want to take a chance on seeing Daisy. They didn't have any plans today, but Valerie knew that Daisy had some sort of sixth sense where she was concerned. If Daisy were to see her moping around, she'd be over with hot tea and a list of questions before Valerie could say, "I don't want to talk about it."

Curled beneath her covers, she contemplated the idea of asking Goldie and the crew if nightmares were a sign of something dire, but figured they'd blame her or her extra time with Dominick. Either that or they'd invent some other rule she'd broken. Her punishment would be worse nightmares to teach her a lesson about following the rules, so she stuffed the guilt down and reevaluated her extra time spent with Dominick and whether it should continue.

Tonight she was with Mark, tomorrow was Johnny and then the next night was Hauser. Perhaps the nightmare would fade. Then again, perhaps if she cut back on her extra time with Dominick and spent some time alone, she could gain some perspective.

There were no easy answers. Return Day had never seemed so far away as it did at this moment. What a difference a day made. This time yesterday, she'd been so full of optimism.

One thing she decided for certain was having Dominick gone before coming out looking like crap this morning was definitely a good thing.

Unlike Mark, he likely wouldn't have departed without a carefully outlined explanation.

Chapter 13

255 until Return Day

The 'fucking' nightmare, as Valerie referred to it, continued sporadically over the next three months. It was always the same. The dialogue, the setting, the participants, the panic, the darkness, the shaft of hopeful light dashed when one silhouetted figure watched, arms crossed in anger. The pain of the humiliation of being violated by men she knew in her heart would never harm a follicle on her head endured.

Every single fucking time.

After the first incidence, Valerie had convinced herself it would never come again, until a few days later she'd woken to see Hauser's stricken face. She'd backed away from him in horror, mumbled that it was a bad dream and raced to her room to shower and cry. Spending the day after curled in the fetal position hiding under her covers didn't help much in the long run.

Knowing it was only a bad dream didn't help at all. Not even when she came to recognize the scenario. A knock on a door. Frasier answered. And then the 'fucking' nightmare ensued. She woke, ran from whatever mate she happened to be sleeping with as her heart pounded wildly in her chest and allowed the fear to promptly cripple her for the entire day afterwards.

Valerie never knew when the nightmare was about to pop up. Sometimes days would go by with nothing. Sometimes she'd have the bad dream four days in a row.

She couldn't stop it, she couldn't prepare for it and she couldn't make herself tell any of the men in her household what the dream was about or why it was happening. The pattern was consistent. She never dreamed when she was alone. She'd never had the nightmare and run from Dominick. And she didn't want to. They all tried to discuss it, but she refused. Fearing she'd accidentally say the wrong thing and end up confessing, Valerie remained stubbornly silent. She convinced herself that revealing the horrible dream would only worsen the stability of their household and the precarious relationships therein.

Breakfast had become a chore that all of them wanted to get through as soon as possible. Valerie put the food out, silently nursed a cup of coffee while they ate and refused to look at anyone. Lately, Dominick missed all of the morning breakfasts, anyway. She was glad because she didn't know what she would do if he demanded she confess. She likely couldn't keep secrets from him. So she avoided being alone with him.

Valerie hated how the recurrent nightmare impacted her extra private time with Dominick. Unable to control or understand the pervasive nightmare, she crawled inside herself in retreat. Most days she tried to sleep during the day so she could stay awake at night to fulfill her obligations.

The precious time with Dominick went back to just twice a month, like the others.

He never asked why. Not even on the subsequent nights they were together for his turn. That he never questioned why they weren't together on her free days anymore bothered her very deeply. More than Valerie was willing to admit out loud. On the other hand, she was grateful not to have to explain why things were so tense and screwed up in her mind.

She suspected saying the words to the dream aloud would end any possible harmony and patently refused to discuss the problem with anyone. Not even with Daisy.

Valerie half expected Goldie and the gang to call her in and at least ask why she was back to the regularly scheduled sexual rotation, but they didn't interfere. They had probably cheered and done a high five, happy dance in the high committee chamber when she went back to the authorized routine. More likely, they didn't care.

Even with her self-imposed time diet from Dominick, he was the only one always on her mind. She missed him desperately, but decided that the time away was the best plan for her sanity.

One other aspect of the 'fucking' nightmare, which Valerie tried not to over analyze, had to do with the fact that it hadn't occurred on any night when she'd slept with Dominick. Part of the reason for her retreat away from him was to keep her demons at bay.

Each of the others had watched her flee in terror, but not once had

Valerie experienced the nightmare in Dominick's room. Deep down she worried that if she ever had the nightmare and slipped out of his bed, he'd never allow her to escape. He'd hold her down until she'd spilled her guts. Upon further consideration of that scenario, a worse fear came to light. What if he didn't stop her? What if he didn't care about her as much as she did about him?

She couldn't decide which was worse, so she kept her distance on her own time and prayed she'd never have to find out which scenario would play out. There was less than a year left. She'd endure until it was time to go.

Valerie knocked on Dominick's door at the end of day two-hundred and fifty-five with anticipation coloring her attitude. Due to the way the schedule had worked out, she hadn't been to his room for over two and a half weeks.

After a lengthy wait, she was about to knock again when the door snapped open. Dominick ushered her inside, but kept well away from her.

"I thought we'd start with dinner," he said and pointed to the dining room table filled with food. Outwardly, he looked as dark and deliciously sexy as he always had, but several minutes of no further conversation or looks in her direction signaled his reserved attitude. He'd likely been this way the last time, but she hadn't noticed.

"Is something wrong?" she asked.

A mirthless smile surfaced. "I could ask you the same thing. You've been distant lately."

Valerie rocked back. She was an idiot. She was the one who'd stopped coming to see him in her free time. The rules probably stated somewhere that he couldn't even ask her why. She'd half expected him to demand she explain on one of the nights they were together, but in the past few months he hadn't crossed the line.

Truthfully, she'd been so preoccupied with keeping her nightmare a secret from him, she hadn't thought about why he didn't ask. She'd just been grateful not to have to answer.

Cooling herself down a little, Valerie said, "I'm fine. I've been looking forward to seeing you. The truth is, I've missed you."

"Have you?" The disdain in his tone conveyed his feelings perfectly. They stared at each other for several seconds until she looked away first. He exhaled a long, deep breath, but remained silent. He obviously didn't believe she ached for him. Although, why would he?

Valerie realized what a bitch she'd been. She'd called the shots in this forbidden relationship. That he didn't opt to serve his heart on a platter for her amusement shouldn't elevate her ire. But it did. She wanted him to have missed her, too. She wanted him to love her the way she loved him. She wanted things to be the way they used to be before the 'fucking' nightmare ruined what little happiness she'd found aboard this spacecraft.

The fear of stirring the wicked beast of her confession to the surface kept her silent. She never wanted to explain the dream. Not to anyone. Especially not to Dominick.

Before she weakened her resolve to keep that element a secret, she changed the direction of her thoughts and asked the politely inane question, "What's for dinner?"

"What does it matter?" he muttered. Turning his back, he crossed the room to the food-laden table and dropped into his chair. He picked up a platter of meat and forked some onto his plate.

Valerie's mouth fell open in shock.

Staring at his food as if it were the most fascinating thing in the room, he said, "You should eat if you're going to. It's getting cold."

Do or die, the confession she'd held inside for so long bubbled to the surface so fast her tongue itched. "I'm so sorry, Dominick."

He looked up as if surprised she'd spoken at all. "Sorry? For what? Abandoning me?" He stood. The chair scraped the floor in a loud angry movement and he approached with a dangerous expression. Valerie didn't move. "Or are you sorry for making me fall in love with you and then dismissing me without a single word?"

"You're in love with me?" she whispered.

Closing the meager distance between them swiftly, he towered over her. "They told me, you know."

Oh no. The nightmare. He knew.

Stunned, Valerie put her hands to her face and lowered her gaze. "How did *they* know?"

"How do they know anything? They just do. My only regret is that I wish you'd had the balls to tell me yourself." He stalked back to the table and scraped the chair back into place without sitting. "It would have saved me the humiliation of demanding the truth from Golden and the boys."

Valerie followed him to the table slowly, trying to keep track of the conversation. She wasn't sure they were having the same one. "What *truth* did they tell you?"

"They told me you have a favorite mate and that you're in love with him." Dominick looked away to say the last words. "They explained to me that you spent all that extra time with me to try and forget him. I can only assume that you threw caution to the wind and confessed your love to the other man you hold dear. And that's why you've been gone from me the past few months."

"They told you—"

He interrupted her. "They warned me not to ask you about it, but I find at this moment that I'm willing to face their wrath if you'll explain why you spent all of your off days biding your time with me if you only intended to break my heart and pursue one of the others."

"When did you ask them?"

"The morning after the first night that you didn't show up like I expected."

She stroked her palm down one arm from shoulder to elbow. "You went to the High Committee chamber and asked about me?"

"Not exactly." He looked away and sighed. "You aren't the only one that gets called to task for rule violations, you know."

Turning back, he grabbed her gently by the shoulders and whispered, "Why didn't you just tell me?"

"There was nothing like that to tell. Besides, they lied to you."

"Did they? Why didn't you come back?"

Valerie swallowed hard. "Listen to me carefully. I spent all that time away from you because of a completely different reason. One I don't care to explain. I spent all those extra days with you because *you* are my favorite. It has been agony to be separated from you."

His expression softened. "I wish I could believe that."

"What would it take? What do I have to do?"

"Tell me you love me. And promise to spend all your extra time here, like before."

Valerie should have jumped for joy. Now she knew his true feelings. He loved her. But the stubborn insistence of keeping the nightmare a secret intruded.

"I love you. But I won't abandon the others and you can't tell them that I favor you."

"I don't expect you to abandon anyone. I won't tell anyone anything, but if I'm really your favorite, then I want you to spend your time off here." He gathered her in his arms and kissed her hard. A sob rose in her throat as the memories of the dream haunted the forefront of her mind.

Dominick carried her to bed and made tender love to her, whispering repeatedly how much he'd missed her. He told her over and over how much he didn't want to live without her.

Secure in his arms for the first time in ages, Valerie accidentally dozed off next to Dominick. The nightmare came with a vengeance. She woke trapped underneath his beefy arm and fought like a wounded wild animal to free herself. As she'd feared, he declined to let her escape and run to her room like she always did with the others.

She screamed. She cried. He pinned her more firmly to the bed and demanded to know what she was upset about. She tried to buck his body off of hers to no avail. Once the initial terror of the dream had faded and Valerie's marginal sensibilities became clear again, she opened her eyes.

"Release me!"

"Not on your life. What the fuck is wrong?"

"I had a bad dream."

He snorted. "Bad dream? I'll say. You put scratch marks on me." Catching her eye he added, "And not the good kind."

"There's a good kind?"

Dominick's eyes softened, but he didn't remark or explain the 'good' kind of scratches. "This is why you've been a zombie at breakfast?"

"How would you know? You never attend breakfast any more."

"Hauser came to me because he was worried about you. And I stopped attending the morning meal for a completely different reason. One I decline to explain."

"I hate it when you use my own words against me."

A smile shaped his luscious mouth. "Well, I hate to see you look like a zombie, babe." He leaned closer for a kiss. Softly he pressed his mouth to hers, teasing her lips with the tip of his tongue until she kissed back.

Dominick pulled his lips away. "I know you'll likely tell me to go to hell, but what is the nightmare that has you so destroyed?"

She shook her head and closed her eyes. "I don't want to tell you."

He released a deep sigh. "You can't keep this bottled up."

Valerie's eyes popped open. "Oh, yes, I can."

"And how is that working out for you?"

Valerie inhaled and exhaled. Her lips trembled and an unwanted sob escaped. "It's bad. Really bad. I don't want anyone to know. I don't even want to say the words out loud."

"Talk to me, babe. I swear I won't tell anyone."

His anguished tone and her desire to unload the guilt associated with the nightmare conspired to force a confession. Snuffling a little, she looked away from his piercing gaze and whispered the dream from the knock on the door until the end when they left her crumpled on the dark, dirty floor, laughing as they parted, calling her nasty names.

His lips caressed her temple in a tender kiss. "I'm sorry." He released her arms and rolled to his back as if to give her the option of escape. For the first time since the nightmare had started torturing her sleep, she didn't want to get away.

"I know they'd never do this to me." Valerie sat up. "Which makes it worse."

Dominick cleared his throat. "Maybe now that you've confided in someone, you won't dream it anymore."

"I wish that were true."

"It's sounds like you have a load of guilt over something."

"What guilt?"

"I don't know. Guilt over being with more than one man. Guilt over wanting to spend more time with me than the others. It could be lots of things. Why don't you tell them—"

"I'm never telling them about this!" Valerie twisted and grabbed his shoulders. "And you can't tell them either. Swear to me! Swear that you'll keep quiet."

Dominick took both of her hands in his. "I swear they won't hear it from me. But they should hear it from you."

"No."

"You can't go on like this. Tell them you have a favorite and move on."

"I can't. I've been ordered not to by Goldie and the gang. I'm not in the mood to go back there. I don't want to undermine the harmony we've managed to accumulate so close to Return Day. Besides, it won't work."

"I disagree. If you tell them, the nightmare will likely stop."

Valerie threw the covers back and slipped out of their bed. "No. You're wrong. If I tell them the truth, it will cause a worse rift than already exists now and then I'll feel guilty night and day."

"You're the one who's wrong, Valerie. The only rift has been caused by you walking around like a zombie because you can't sleep."

She hated when he called her by her name instead of the endearment she'd become accustomed to. "Listen to me. You'd better not tell them. Don't even mention it."

Tossing the covers back to exit his side of the bed, Dominick snarled, "I'm not the one having screaming nightmares every night. And besides, they know your feelings anyway. We can all read you like a fucking book."

Her fingers flew to her face and a sudden sob of angry despair escaped. The gut-wrenching fear of guilt overwhelmed her. She didn't want anyone to know. "It's not fair. It's not fair to make me tell them that I like you best. It's just not fair." She sat down on the end of the bed.

He looked skyward momentarily and then zeroed his penetrating gaze right on her. "This isn't about fairness, babe, it's about your health. You think they don't see it? You think they aren't brutalized by the fact that you're dreaming recurrently about something they can't help you with or change? Do us all a favor and confess or I worry if you'll even make it to Return Day. And if you don't make it, then neither do we."

She popped up from the end of the bed because he came too close to her. She didn't want to be trapped with the vestiges of the nightmare so fresh in her mind. "What if they hate me? What if I tell them and they all hate me?"

"They won't." He grabbed her shoulders and squeezed. "Besides, what if you have a nervous breakdown tomorrow and we all go crazy in three months from lack of sex?"

She wrenched herself from his grasp, breaking their connection. "So it's all my fault."

Dominick shot his hands to his face and dragged them down. "That is not what I meant and you know it. God, Valerie, do you *hear* yourself? You have two choices. You either tell them what is really going on or live with it in silence. And I have to tell you that I don't think the silent gig is working for you." His anger brought her attention forward.

"I'm just so sorry to threaten your only piece of ass."

"You know better. Don't force me to turn you over my knee."

Valerie sucked in a deep breath and backed away.

* * * *

Valerie's bright round eyes filled with utter terror. She withdrew from him in fear for the first time since Dominick had known her.

What is wrong with me?

He should never have raised his voice. He was more afraid than at any other time since he'd been trapped here. This place was an endurance test at best and for a man who was always in control, Dominick found he had none.

Valerie was losing it. She was his mate in every sense of the word and he didn't know how to help her if she wouldn't help herself.

Taking a deep breath to aid in calming his raw emotions, he said quietly, "I'm sorry, babe. I'm just seriously worried about you." He walked to her slowly and took her gently into his arms.

She stared at him for a long moment, then nodded and hugged his waist, resting her head against his shoulder. "If you were one of the others, and I told you I favored, say, Hauser, would you be mad?"

Yes. Damn it! Her question was difficult to answer out loud. He wasn't able to tell her what she wanted to hear, but he couldn't lie to her either.

Dominick took a deep breath for strength. "Keep in mind that I'm not them. And, yeah, I'd be furious."

She tensed up in his arms and tried to break away, but he held her fast and talked faster. "But then again, like I said, I'm not them. The feelings I have for you are alien to me." He pulled back until he caught her eye. "Isn't that funny? I made a pun." A smile curved her lips and she relaxed in his arms.

"The honest truth is that I love you, babe. I love you deep down where it hurts me to think of you with others. Ever. It's all I can do to keep my temper in check day to day. Breakfast is difficult for me with everyone there, so I generally avoid it.

"From the first time with you, I've nursed a hole in my soul on the days when you aren't with me. Eight days a month I mourn you. Do the others feel this way? I can't imagine they could possibly feel the way I do. But I can't bear seeing you with dark circles every day. And all five of us are worried."

"I'll live. The alternative is worse. Plus, I've been ordered by the High Committee not to admit it."

"The only others you need to worry about are the ones in our household. They deserve the truth. It's your unnecessary guilt eating at you. Perhaps you need to reveal it to resolve this problem." She tensed in his arms again but he held on. "But if you don't want to, then in the meantime, why don't I teach you some hand-to-hand combat techniques."

Valerie's eyes rounded again. "Hand-to-hand combat techniques? Why? They aren't really going to attack me. I know it's only a dream."

He shrugged. "I'll show you how to fight back during the day and then if anyone tries to do anything you don't want, especially in your dreams, then pow!, you can punch them right in the kisser. I can teach you how to fight so the knowledge will be there with you in your dreams."

The relief in her eyes was palpable. "You'd do that for me?"

"Babe, there isn't anything I wouldn't do for you." *That was the truth.*

"I thought you said you'd never teach what you knew to anyone."

Dominick trailed a finger from her forehead to her chin and cupped her face in one hand. "First, you're not just anyone, and second, now maybe you understand how worried I am about you that I would break my cardinal rule to help you out in this way."

Valerie nodded. "Okay, teach me to fight back."

Chapter 14

219 until Return Day

Learning hand-to-hand combat techniques didn't help. And it wasn't because she was a poor student either. Valerie learned to block punches, anticipate what a combatant would do next during a fight and retaliate in kind. She spent weeks with Dominick in the gym practicing self-defense moves until she could practically do them in her sleep. Which was the point. But it didn't work. She was never able to implement the moves in her nightmares.

The 'fucking nightmare' continued with a vengeance, as if she'd done nothing. The mornings around the breakfast table were silent and morose. It had an impact on every part of their daily life. The worst part of the continued nightmare scenario was that the sex with each and every one of them became something to get through and not enjoy. She could feel their reluctance in the way they held her at night. She could see the pain in their eyes each morning after she screamed the night away, sometimes waking more than once if she didn't flee to her room.

However, through it all, the night before was never discussed. She never even identified who she'd slept with, but they all knew. Whichever man had the most pitiful look on his face had been the one dealing with her screaming nightmares.

* * * *

The next time they were together, Dominick offered Valerie the handle of a pistol. "This is a Glock Seventeen nine-millimeter automatic. Let's try marksmanship and weapons training."

He might as well have offered her a writhing snake baring its fangs ready to strike. She turned up her nose. "I've never fired a weapon in my life that I remember anyway. I've never needed to. To tell you the truth, I don't think I want to."

Dominick sighed, walked closer until he could whisper in her ear and said, "Take this gun or schedule a morning conference for the breakfast table and explain to the others what the problem is and why you aren't sleeping—"

"Fine. Give me the damn thing." Valerie cut him off and grabbed the handle of the gun with two fingers. She held it up like a week-old diaper and wrinkled her nose. "What do I have to do?"

He showed her how to load the gun and made her memorize lots of safety tips first before allowing her to shoot it. After deciding she understood the seriousness of shooting a gun, he took her to the firing range in the depths of the ship. A place she'd never been to before if her wide-eyed perusal was any indication.

Dominick stood behind her, his torso pressed to her back, and guided her arms into the proper position to hold the pistol. Valerie was flattened against the stand on their range lane trying to sight up the target silhouette and hit center mass. Her elbows rested on the coarse fake grass cover to keep her from skidding around. It left grass-like impressions on her elbows and smelled like gym socks.

"Hold it with both hands. One to support and one to aim. Don't jerk the trigger, squeeze it nice and easy. The hardest part is learning not to anticipate the recoil. It'll throw your aim off."

"There's something else throwing off my aim." A sweet laugh escaped her lips.

Her laugh surprised him and squeezed his heart at the same time. "What's that?"

She shifted her hips back and forth swishing her butt against his already enflamed crotch. "Your cock is digging me in the ass."

Dominick pressed his hips forward grinding his rampant erection harder into her soft flesh and whispered in her ear, "Deal with it. Watching you fire a gun makes my dick get hard."

"Everything makes your dick get hard." She giggled and his heart melted as he realized it had been too long since he'd heard her laughter.

"I can't argue with that." His rumble of laughter in return made another smile register on her sweet lips.

"What would happen if you pulled my pants down and then took me from behind against this stand, while I aimed?"

His cock throbbed against her back as if in silent answer that it was ready to go. "Goldie and the gang wouldn't let us practice at this firing range anymore. Plus, your target silhouette would look like shit."

"Pity," she lamented. "I hate it when my target silhouette looks like shit." His cock pulsed against her once more.

Dominick lowered his head and grazed her shoulder with his chin. Planting a kiss on her neck beneath her ear was as close to sex as he was going to get for now. It was all he cold do not to comply with her request and go for it here at the target range.

"What if when we get back home we pretend we're here."

* * * *

Dominick's body stiffened and he pulled away from her. "No," he grunted in anger. The draft between them was palpable. She felt the loss of his separation like she'd lost the back half of her body. He turned away and started collecting their things.

"What's wrong?"

"It's not my night, Valerie. "

Damn it, she'd forgotten.

"Now I have to picture you playing this little game with someone else." He shoved gun accessories forcefully into the bag he carried.

Valerie put a hand on his shoulder to soothe his anger. "I would never play our games with someone else."

"But I'd never know anyway, right?" His gaze pierced her miserable soul. "It's not like I even want to know the intimate details of your time with each of the others, but I still picture it. I can tell by the way you act each morning which of them you've been with."

She pursed her lips together until they hurt. "You can't either!"

"Last night you were with Hauser. The night before was Johnny. Tell me I'm wrong."

She stared at him unblinking and now unwilling to answer because he was right and she didn't want him to gloat.

"And let me take a wild stab that tonight will be Frasier."

Her mouth opened and then closed. "Do you want me to stop sleeping with them? Is that what you want?"

"No. I want you to tell them that you prefer me. I want them to know that when you're in bed with them that you really wish it was me fucking you."

"That's not fair. How can you ask me to do that? You know what my nightmare is like."

"That's how it is, Valerie. Deal with it."

"I hate it when you use my name like I'm an errant child in trouble. My middle name is Jean. Want to throw that in for an extra twist?"

"Yeah." He laughed mirthlessly. "I do, Valerie Jean."

"Fine. I'll go to bed with Frasier tonight and think of you like I always do and in the morning I'll confess my transgressions to the assembled group of lovers I currently service."

He stopped loading things in the bag and straightened. "Don't tease me. It's not nice."

"Since when do you ever care about nice." Valerie turned her back on him, rested her arms on the stand, lifted the gun and took aim at the target.

"Oh, I care."

She fired three rounds into the silhouette. Her back was stiff and her shots were off her mark slightly, albeit tightly grouped. From behind her, Dominick murmured, "Relax. Don't fire the gun when you're angry."

"Why? Because my practice silhouette will look like shit?"

"No. Because I don't want you to miss and hit me in your zeal to destroy the target."

"Very funny."

* * * *

Frasier knew something was up the second Valerie arrived in his room. She could see it in his eyes and feel it in the way he spoke even though he treated her with kid gloves as usual. His analytical mind was obviously hard pressed to deal with emotion in its rawest form. Tomorrow morning she'd tell all, but tonight was about routine.

They had dinner. They had sex. They went to sleep and the nightmare began once again. For the first time ever, Valerie felt distanced from the dream, like she watched it instead of participating. It wasn't any less horrific, but as it progressed she thought she might be able to change it for once.

She closed her eyes and thought about her defensive training.

Dominick told her to focus on the muscles of her arms and legs. He'd taught her to twist and fight. Ignoring the pain and humiliation of the nightmare, Valerie took a deep breath, focused her attention on her arm and leg muscles and wrenched herself out of the sordid abuse. It stopped immediately.

Valerie was suddenly free and in the next moment she landed hard on her ass next to Frasier's bed in a flurry of bed sheets with her nightgown twisted around her thighs.

"Darling? Are you hurt?" Frasier's sleepy voice drifted from the bed. His head appeared over her now vacant side of the bed. He was sleep rumpled and sexy, rubbing his eyes.

The vision of the recent dream slid in to haunt her. Valerie jumped up from the oak floor, flattened herself against the bedroom wall and screamed. "Stay away from me." Her sphincter contracted as if to protect itself from violation. Frasier's puzzled expression calmed her.

His eyes focused on her face and a concerned look replaced the sleepy one. "Did you have another bad dream?"

As the vestiges of the nightmare fell away, she noticed his guarded, hurt expression and nodded. Valerie felt very foolish all of a sudden. It was unconscionable to believe that Frasier would ever hurt her. Looking at his disheveled, concerned face she knew he'd never harm her in any way. He'd never try to do anything by force.

Valerie nodded. "Yes. It was a bad dream."

After over two years together, he still practically asked permission to have sex each and every time as it was. He most assuredly had never tried to penetrate her anally. He probably wouldn't do it even if she asked him to. Probably not even if she begged. As her rational wits seeped back inside her brain, Valerie realized the truth. Dominick was right. She was going to have to tell them.

Damn fucking nightmare.

She couldn't go on like this, it wouldn't wait until morning at the breakfast table. The High Committee would have her head, but she couldn't take it any longer. Perhaps it was better to tell them individually even though she'd have to repeat this distasteful news three more times.

"You've been having bad dreams for far too long, darling. Please tell me, is there anything I can do?" Frasier propped his head on one hand and watched her carefully. It was the first time in a long time that she hadn't simply bolted out of his room in terror. His expression was that of a man with a problem to solve. Frasier liked solving problems, but Valerie hoped he wouldn't be hurt by the confession she was about to make.

Taking a deep breath she said, "I have something to tell you. You won't like it, but I need to confess or I'll have a nervous breakdown from lack of sleep."

"No, you don't, darling. You never need to explain anything. Not to me."

Valerie released a deep breath she hadn't realized she'd held. "I do. Please listen to me, Frasier. I care for you very much. Of the five men in my life, you are my sensible, responsible partner. I depend on you being solid."

His faint smile belied what he said. "You mean the boring one."

"No. I don't mean the boring one." She crossed the space from the wall to the edge of the bed and sat down, albeit out of his reach. "The truth is, I love all of you. Each of you is different and I adore each and every one of those differences."

Frasier leaned back against the headboard and crossed his arms. He looked like a district attorney about to give a summation to a jury. "But something is wrong."

"Yes. The problem is that…" She paused to inhale. "Of the five of you, I have a favorite." She mashed her eyes shut, fearful of his anger and hurt. He remained silent. She peeked through an eyelid.

His eyebrows wrinkled and an amused smile slid over his mouth. "I know that, darling. I've known for a long time."

Valerie opened her eyes in surprise. "What? How do you know? I never allowed myself to express it outwardly when any of you were around."

His boyish grin reassured her. She couldn't wait to hear what he had to say.

"Darling, I suffer from no illusions about what is going on in this odd place. We are, all of us, prisoners of a race of people who have parked us into a situation that is uncomfortable at best. I'm grateful to you. In my eyes, you've selflessly saved my life. I don't care that I'm not your favorite. I don't care if you have a favorite. And besides, I believe I know who your favorite is." His eyebrows went up tauntingly.

Valerie rocked back. "So you aren't upset that I have a favorite? Not even a little?"

"Not even a little." He uncrossed his arms. "It's Hauser, isn't it?"

It was her turn to be surprised. "Why do you think it's Hauser?"

"He's the first one you met. It's understandable that you would have a stronger attachment to him. He's the one we sent out to find us the perfect mate in this insane world. And he did. I don't begrudge him. Honestly, Valerie, is this what has truly had you so upset?"

She nodded. "I think it's what was making me have bad dreams."

"I hate that more than anything. You have given of yourself to us more than is even required. You are not mean or spiteful and truthfully, for one of us to qualify as a favorite in a bad way, the rest of would have had to suffer and we haven't. You didn't stop spending nights with the rest of us to explore a relationship with Hauser."

Valerie didn't confirm or deny that her favorite was Hauser. "Do you think the others would be upset if I confessed this information?"

Frasier considered her question a few moments before answering, "I'm not sure what Dominick would say, because I don't know him as well, but the others probably wouldn't even raise an eyebrow."

Valerie pegged him with a grateful look and slid under the covers next to him. His pajamas were soft and warm. She slid on top of him and kissed his mouth. "Thank you so much for understanding."

He patted her gently on the back. His discomfort with physical gestures was endearing. "Go to sleep, darling. You need more than an hour at a time."

She kissed him again. "I love you Frasier. I truly do."

"I know." He kissed her forehead and moved her off his body. He turned her away and snuggled up behind her to cuddle as he always did after sex. Valerie would have had wild, wicked sex with him in that moment, but he seemed content just to hold her gently.

That was Frasier.

They'd made love earlier and while Frasier had done what he normally did, she'd spent their time together trying not to think of Dominick and the game they'd played earlier at the target range. And she'd failed. He'd been on her mind during the act. She just couldn't help it.

In this moment, with Frasier snuggled up behind her not at all upset that she'd admitted to having a favorite, for the first time she didn't feel guilty about her wayward thoughts of Dominick.

She slept the rest of the night all the way through without dreaming. The next morning was the best she'd felt in weeks. Her lack of nightmares had a profound impact on her physically and at breakfast the next morning everyone noticed. Including Dominick, who put in a rare appearance. He was the only one not happy about it. She didn't get a chance to explain her new plan to tell each of them individually, and decided it wasn't important.

She vowed to disclose her secret to them all, but one at a time. She hoped Dominick was right about these confessions.

* * * *

The next night, after a particularly satisfying evening with Mark, the first in months, she confessed to having a favorite mate and the nightmares it caused.

"Thank God above. I thought one of the others was mistreating you or something and I didn't know which one them I'd have to kill."

"You aren't angry?"

He grabbed her face and planted a kiss on her mouth. "No. Of course not. I care for you, honey. I need you desperately in this world. But the truth is, I'm not used to having only one woman in my bed for so long."

Her mouth fell open. "So you're bored with me?"

The horrified look started his sputtering and explaining. "No. It's not like that at all. It's just that..." He paused as if to find the correct words to keep her from being pissed off. They all hated it when she was pissed off. Every man in this strange world stepped on eggshells to avoid allowing his woman to get angry.

"If we were anywhere else, I would have spent at best a year or two with you and then moved on. That's just how I am, sweetheart. I can't help it. I like women. I like variety. Please don't be mad."

She blinked repeatedly and wondered why she'd been so sure the others would have such a problem with her deep dark secret. So far, no one had cared that she secretly pined for another.

Valerie pondered this phenomenon silently until Mark said, "I'm screwed, aren't I. Now that I've confessed, you're going to make me beg?"

"No." She slung her arms around his neck and kissed him. "Honestly, I'm so glad, Mark. I know it must be hard for you having the same old me every time."

His whole body relaxed. "Not at all, my beautiful princess. You've spoiled me in our times together. You've never turned me down once and you've never expected me to do the missionary position except once a year. And it's not like I can take what you won't give."

"What do you mean?"

"Force isn't allowed. It's built into us from the beginning. We all have implants, honey." He tapped the side of his head with a finger. "All you have to say is no and launch is a no go."

"I didn't know that. How did I not know that all this time?"

"Don't know, princess, maybe you slept through that part of orientation." Mark tilted his head to one side. "I only resented it because it was an unneeded implant for me. I've never forced a woman in my life." He ducked his head slyly. "Never needed to."

Valerie hugged his neck again and kissed his cheek. "I believe it."

"Now let me take you to my bed before you realize what I've confessed and I suffer the consequences of you banning me."

"I'd never ban you. I like talking to you. You're my best buddy."

"Best buddies with benefits?"

Valerie laughed relishing the feeling of happiness she'd missed. "Exactly."

* * * *

Valerie's litany all day had been, "Two down, two to go."

Johnny was her date mate for tonight. He never failed to come up with artistic ways for them to spend their time together. After their first night, he'd never played any pirate sexual games ever again, but still he was what she would term very creative. Full of life. Never a dull moment. She would hate to stifle his imagination by telling him that he wasn't her favorite mate.

She should have known he would read her mind before she was two minutes in the door.

"Something's up, lovie." He gave her a narrow-eyed appraisal from head to toes and then pegged her with the most serious gaze she'd ever seen him deliver.

She glanced at him with alarm. "What do you mean?"

"Each night this week you've been with one of the others and for the first time in months you aren't a walking zombie upon your arrival here."

"So?"

"So whatever was killing you one day at a time isn't taking its toll any longer. Or I'm the problem and you're about to tell me the bad news. It's not hard to figure out."

"There isn't a problem with you. I just need to tell you something. I think my bad dreams have been because of guilt."

"Guilt about what, lovie?" The concern in his eyes was palpable.

She swallowed hard and focused her gaze on the wall. "The thing is, I have a favorite among the five of you." She glanced back to assess his reaction. "I didn't mean to, it just happened and I needed to tell you about it."

He frowned. The horrified look he exhibited startled her. "Oh, God, it's not me, is it?"

"Um. No."

He heaved a great sigh of relief. "Thank heavens."

"Really? You aren't mad at me?"

"Mad?" He crossed the room with his signature saunter and took her into his arms. "I'd never be mad at you. I adore you. But you and I are so very different. You're always so serious. I've worried about your creative light."

Valerie huffed. "I was so sure you would be angry if I confessed. I agonized over the hint of anyone finding out."

Johnny kissed the frown from her brow and murmured, "What's between us is very unique, lovie, and I'm more grateful than I can tell you for all the fun we've had, but the truth is that if we didn't have to make this work, it probably wouldn't, now would it?"

"Perhaps not." Her head tilted coyly. "I'm so glad you understand."

"If it's not me..." Johnny trailed off and promptly smirked. He looked up at the ceiling as if to figure out a complex problem. "Then I would guess that either Hauser or Frasier has captured your heart."

Valerie sighed deeply and rested her head on his shoulder. "Why them?"

"Hauser because he met you first, wooed you and brought you to us. Remind me to thank him again." Johnny kissed her forehead. "Frasier because you both have a completely serious and logical mindset. So, did I guess right?"

She shook her head. "It doesn't matter. I'm just so glad that you aren't upset with me."

"Never, lovie. You should know that about me. I'm way too fun-loving for jealousy. My only concern is that whichever of the five of us it is, I hope he feels the same way about you."

"He says he does." Valerie exhaled a deep breath of relief.

"Then he does. None of us would ever lie to you. I'm so happy for you. And grateful."

"Grateful?"

"I didn't want to have to get physical with one of the others for hurting you." He shrugged. "I'm also not comfortable in the role of vengeful man."

"It won't change things between us, will it?"

"Of course not, lovie." He hugged her. "I think your newfound inspiration will take the burden off of your soul. The nightmares needed to stop." He kissed her cheek.

"Thanks for understanding, Johnny."

"Of course. Now, not to be pushy, but how would you feel about letting me eat dinner off of your body tonight. I've prepared some wonderful items for this endeavor. We can even take turns. You like chocolate-covered donuts, right?"

She laughed. Johnny was always very creative in his quest for sex. "Sounds very inventive. I can't wait."

"Thank you, lovie." He kissed her lips lightly. "You're always such a good sport."

* * * *

Hauser was the last and the most worrisome, now that she'd spoken to the others. Everyone else thought he was her favorite. Did he believe the same erroneous information and think he was the one she favored above all the others? She hoped not. After having the notion eat at her all day long, she approached his room that night with a wary heart.

Ten minutes into the room, she sensed that Hauser understood the problem she'd been suffering from and the solution she'd discovered. The others might not talk about uncomfortable things or what went on in their beds when she shared it, but they would certainly ease his mind over the anguish she'd endured for the past several months. Valerie loathed the need to tell him that he was not the man she craved with every fiber of her being.

Chapter 15

214 until Return Day

Valerie found it excruciating to watch Hauser's expression. He led the topics of discussion all throughout dinner. She didn't converse much because of her worry over what she had to tell him.

"Take me to bed, Hauser," she whispered after picking over her food for far too long.

"What's wrong?"

"Nothing. I'm not hungry."

His eyebrows rose with skepticism. "All week you've been getting better. Tonight, you seem worse, if that's even possible."

"Worse?"

He sighed deeply. "Something has been troubling you for months, Valerie. I'm not an idiot. Just tell me."

"I'm afraid to tell you."

That got his attention. He half stood up from the table. "You're afraid? Of me?"

"No. I'm afraid of telling you something that I know you won't like."

"But you told all the others?" He slumped back into his chair, but his expression was already of the miserable variety.

She nodded and a tear escaped down one cheek. "I'm not ready to tell you. I'm not sure what you'll say." Valerie wiped the moisture from her face quickly, stood up and came around the table. He scooted back and she straddled his lap. Taking his face between her hands she kissed him gently and cursed herself when a sob released from her throat.

"Tell me. I need to know. I can't touch you until I do."

"The problem is that once I tell you I'm afraid *you* won't want to touch me anymore."

He slipped his arms around her waist and hugged. "There isn't anything you could tell me that would keep me from wanting to touch you." His relaxed expression prompted her to confess.

"As you are well aware by now, I've been having nightmares. And I'm pretty sure that I've figured out why."

"Good. What caused them?"

"I have a favorite." As soon as the word came out she closed her eyes, unwilling to see what she assumed would be pain or anger on his features. Taking a deep breath, Valerie opened her eyes slowly and gazed into his confused ones.

"A favorite?" He smiled in a winsome way as if trying to figure things out. "Like a favorite mate?"

She sighed. "Yes."

His brows furrowed. "Why?"

"Why do I have a favorite? I don't know." She shifted uncomfortably on his lap and tried to stand up, but he stilled her by clamping his arms around her body.

"No. Why was it so hard to tell me?"

"Because everyone else thinks it's you."

"Me? Why me?" His panicked expression gave her hope for the first time all evening.

"I don't want you to be mad either way."

He unwound his arms from her slowly. "Valerie," he whispered. A hand came up and wiped down his face.

"Take me to bed, Hauser."

"Valerie." He repeated her name in another whisper and stood up, allowing her to slide to the floor away from him. "We need to resolve this first."

"Why? Bed first. Resolution later."

"Valerie."

"You can keep saying my name, but it won't change anything."

He closed his eyes and took a deep breath. Valerie watched him closely.

A long sigh escaped his lips. "I love you, Valerie. I have from the first moment I laid eyes on you."

"Oh!" Valerie's eyes welled up with tears. She threw her arms around him so he wouldn't see the look of anguish she must have on her face. This was bad. He *did* think he was the one. How could she tell him he wasn't?

Hauser hugged her and let out a long sigh. "Let me finish, Valerie. The thing is, I have particular tastes. And while I think you are perfect, physically you aren't quite the type of woman I typically prefer." His fingers traced the length of her spine slowly as if counting the discs along the journey.

She pulled away, studied his tormented face and tilted her head with the sudden realization that she was mistaken about his initial discomfort. "You aren't my favorite, Hauser."

His whole body slumped. "Thank God."

"When we met I got the impression that you thought I was to your tastes."

Taking her chin in his fingers. "And you are. Still want to go to bed now?"

"No. I want to know how I'm not to your tastes."

He frowned. "What difference does it make?"

"None, I guess. I just want to know."

Hauser rolled his eyes and looked at the ceiling a moment before piercing her with a serious look. "I hope I don't end up regretting this."

"You won't. I'm just curious."

"Fine. The truth is, I like women with more meat on them. When we met you were a little skinny for my tastes, but…"

"But I've lost some weight since I've been here."

"And I've mourned each pound, but as skinny as you are now, I still think you're perfect. I wouldn't change anything and I'd still select you from the gauntlet arena if I were given the option today."

"Do you know who my favorite is?"

His eyes narrowed as if considering his response before a grin lit his face. "Now that I think about it for a second, I'd say Dominick, right?"

"How did you know?"

"It's more in the way he looks at you than the other way around, but I remember a particular dance long ago at the first social event. You two moved like a single person and not two. Was that when you knew?"

She nodded. "Took me a while to act on it. I didn't want anyone else to suspect or be upset about it."

"You two are perfect for each other. I'm glad."

"Why glad?"

"Because you've never changed anything with regard to the rest of us. After you discovered your preference, you didn't suddenly put the rest of us on minimum rations. And I'm sure Dominick would not have argued the point if you'd wanted to do that. It's understandable. You shouldn't feel guilty, but it's your personality." He shrugged. "It's what makes you the kind of person you are. We're lucky that you took a chance on me and refused to accept any other back on day one. You could have."

"Good thing I hadn't gone through orientation, otherwise I wouldn't even have been allowed at that particular gauntlet arena gathering."

"Fate smiled on us." Hauser slid his hands to her face and pressed his mouth tenderly across her lips until she grabbed him close.

"Are you finally taking me to bed?" she murmured with an amused tone.

"If you'll let me."

"I'd never stop you. Nothing will change, I promise."

"Good." He pulled away to stare deeply into her eyes. "I do love you, Valerie. I've never once regretted that I chose you for our group. Not once."

"Thank you." Valerie was feeling very odd. She thought she'd feel different once everyone knew. She was her own worst enemy as far as her morals and idiot ethics were concerned. In a bold moment designed more for her own lack of audacious behavior than any other reason, she cupped his groin and gripped his cock, squeezing until she got his reaction.

It was lightning fast.

Eyes widening as pupils went black, Valerie knew she had his attention.

"What are you doing?" His whisper sent a spike of desire down her body. Hauser was usually a take-charge guy. He always made the first move. Although each time she squeezed his cock, it pulsed in her hand.

"I thought you'd enjoy a little power transfer for once." She kissed his chin and slid to her knees. "How do you feel about oral stimulation?" Without waiting for his answer, she unbuckled his belt, unbuttoned his pants and had the zipper down before he responded.

"It's not allowed here, but I love it." His strangled reply made her smile.

"Well, just don't come in my mouth." Valerie reached beneath his shorts and sucked his cock between her lips.

"Jesus." His reverent whisper gave her the courage to continue. His hand stroked the top of her head lightly, but he didn't try to stop her.

Oral sex to completion wasn't allowed for men because of the stupid rule governing sperm waste, but it was quite an attention-getter for foreplay. Valerie couldn't resist the shock tactic and as such, she'd planned ahead. Underneath her skirt she wore nothing. Perhaps she'd manage another surprise for Hauser before the night was over.

"Valerie. I can't... You've got to…" Hauser's impassioned words trailed off and he jerked once. Valerie figured he'd hit his oral sensation limit. If orgasm were imminent, he'd feel sharp pain not pleasure. She stopped sucking and pulled her mouth from his granite erection.

"Walk backwards two steps, Hauser," she commanded. He shuffled back and landed on his butt in the center of the sofa. The half-lidded expression of pure lust on his face as he looked up made her efforts worth the embarrassment.

His cock, thickly erect, thrust upwards through his clothing. Valerie stepped between his legs. Grasping the bottom front of her skirt she lifted it to reveal her propitious lack of under things. Hauser made a noise like a groan of appreciation. His eyes slid shut and his cock pulsed once.

Valerie straddled him and pressed her wet and heated pussy over the tip of his engorged dick. His eyes opened again slowly.

"Damn, Valerie. What's gotten into you tonight?"

She laughed and impaled him deeply into her body. "I don't know what you mean, Hauser. Your cock's the only thing *into* me tonight."

He groaned again. His hips thrust up at the same time that she pushed down and seconds later he was fully embedded inside her wet, slick pussy. Her vaginal walls clenched his cock once in gratitude of the fabulous feeling as soon as his tip brushed her womb.

Valerie slipped her arms around his shoulders as he buried his face into her throat to nibble. The seductive rhythm of their hips commenced as she realized what being naughty and sneaky did for her own sexual experience. She was getting hot.

Hauser trailed his nibbling mouth along her collarbone, stopping only long enough to rip her shirt open. Buttons flew across the cushions of the sofa as he scraped his teeth across the nipple of her breast over the lace of her bra.

Need engulfed her as she ripped the rest of her shirt off and pulled the bra over her head with it. Hauser's hot, wet mouth closed over the tip of her breast and she almost came as the pull of suction from his mouth registered in her pulsing core.

She slammed her hips down for a deeper connection and he sunk his teeth gently into her ultra sensitive, very wet nipple.

Valerie screamed. She couldn't articulate any words as she climaxed, which was probably good. Mindless as she was in the throes of orgasm, she would still hate to scream the wrong name.

Ripples of pleasure sped across her body and her mind went to a place she wished it wouldn't go. While she loved each of her mates independently and each gave her tremendous satisfaction when they were together, Dominick was the man she always wished she were with during and immediately after she climaxed. His name was the one she screamed in her mind each time.

Hauser thrust his hips upward, pushing his cock inside her deeply twice more and grunting his release before he whispered her name repeatedly, hugging her close. Valerie leaned forward and kissed the side of his face. *I love you, Hauser*, she said in the privacy of her own mind. A part of her loved each of the men in this crazy world.

With a deep, satisfied-sounding exhale, he leaned back against the sofa, his cock still lodged deeply and rubbed circles on her back as she slumped down and dozed against his chest.

Later she woke as Hauser shifted to lift her up. She wrapped her legs around his waist and he carried her to bed.

Valerie slept without dreams or nightmares marring her rest. Early the next morning, she kissed Hauser on the temple without waking him. She slipped out of his bed and headed to her room to change and shower so she could get breakfast started early. Then she could sit with her coffee and contemplate her future without nightmares.

* * * *

Dominick was awake and already waited for her at the table. He didn't look at her when he asked, "Did you sleep well?"

She walked past and retrieved the coffee makings from the cupboard before answering in a very quiet, "Yes."

"Do they all know?"

"Yes." She gave the second affirmative a little louder.

"Anyone have a problem with the information?"

"No. They seemed to already know without me saying anything. You didn't say anything, did you?"

"Of course not. I swore to you I wouldn't. Did you dream?"

Valerie pushed the buttons on the machine to start breakfast and twirled around, slipping her arms around his shoulders to hug him from behind. She kissed his neck below his ear where she knew he was sensitive. His only reaction was a tightening of his fists resting on the table. "No. I didn't have the dream. I haven't had it for several days." She moved her mouth and nibbled his earlobe. "You were right. Confession is good for the soul."

He jerked his head to the side and out of her reach so that she didn't nip him again. "My goal wasn't to be right. I simply wanted you to stop having nightmares."

"And I have." She kissed the side of his face. "I love you, Dominick."

"Do you?" His rumbled response sounded more amused than anything.

Valerie moved where he could see and grinned. "Yes. Want me to prove it?" He grunted once until her hand landed on his thigh and promptly inched its way up, quickly sliding to his crotch.

"What are you doing?" He didn't move, but she could tell his entire body had tensed.

"Proving that I love you." She caressed his thickening cock and leaned closer to kiss his mouth. She brushed the corner of his luscious lips before he pushed back in his chair and grabbed her hand away from his crotch.

"Jesus, Valerie." He stood up and gestured with his hands towards the sleeping rooms. No one else had emerged yet.

Valerie grabbed his shirt lapels. "It's early. Relax. It's just you and me."

She put her hand back on his now fully erect cock and squeezed. "Or we could go to my room."

His body stopped moving. "That's never allowed."

Valerie laughed with delight. "Like 'that' has ever stopped me from doing prohibited things. You of all people should know how I operate by now."

An inarticulate noise escaped his lips as he hugged her close. Pushing and half carrying her to her private bedroom, he secured the door behind him and rested his butt against it.

Valerie slipped her robe off, exposing her nude body, and curled her fingers motioning him to join her.

Lifting away from the door, he approached slowly. "It is forbidden for me to be in here," he whispered, glancing around before he followed her to the bed, fell on her, trapping her against the sheets, and shoved his hands between her legs.

"Forbidden sex has got to be the best sex, don't you think?"

His rumble of laughter warmed her from the inside out. "Undoubtedly."

"Want to go for broke and tie me up before you ravish me?" Valerie wasn't certain where that idea had come from, but the very thought aroused her to a new pinnacle.

The feral look of utter desire Dominick shot her almost brought an immediate climax thrumming through her body. His surprised expression said, "Hell, yes! Where's the rope?" However, the words that came out of his mouth were, "No. Why would I want you bound?"

Before she could respond or argue, he kissed her mouth hard. His hand cupped one breast, his thumb slid over the tip roughly and his cock rubbed against her clit with enough pressure to make her groan. Given that the first time they'd met he'd made her climax without removing any clothes, Valerie had no doubt that with her naked, he'd be able to do it this time with simply a look.

"Can we try something?" she asked.

"What?"

"Remember when we were at the firing range?"

His entire body stilled against hers. "Yes."

Valerie lifted her head to gauge his expression. "I wondered if we could try this with you behind me."

He nodded and pressed his face to her chest. "Are you sure that's what you want to do?"

"I haven't thought of anything else since that day. But only with you in mind."

Dominick lifted off and rose to his knees. "Turn over."

Grinning, Valerie rolled to her stomach as he straddled his legs over her hips. His large hands brushed down her back slipped beneath her body and carefully raised her butt to meet the ridge of his cock. She reached to grasp the bar of her headboard, thrusting her ass against his prominent erection.

"I think it's time you got undressed."

"I'll just loosen my fly. In case I need to make a quick getaway from the forbidden zone." She glanced over one shoulder to watch. He unfastened his pants and released his impressive erection into view. The tip of his thick cock grazed one butt cheek and her pussy tightened and gushed. She was ready.

"Ohmigod, Dominick, just take me."

Before she finished saying those few words, he'd pierced her to the hilt. His wide shaft was snugly ensconced as deep as possible. His fingertips tickled her outer thighs then he gripped her tightly, leveraging his cock out and in again with powerful thrusts.

Valerie cried out in near climax when he reached beneath with one hand and pinched a nipple between forefinger and thumb. She dropped her head and watched him.

"If we were at the firing range," he said between lusty strokes, "your target silhouette would look like total shit."

A low-toned laugh escaped her throat, "Trust me, I wouldn't care."

Dominick growled. "Jesus, you're so tight."

Valerie couldn't speak anymore or respond as he continued thrusting inside her body. The very nature of being in her bed with Dominick doing something they weren't supposed to be doing sent a current of arousal pulsing through her. His steady strokes increased in speed and ferocity until she had to brace herself or go flying head first into the wall behind her headboard. This was the single hottest interlude she'd ever been a part of since this arrangement had started.

A wave of pleasure washed along her spine in pre-climax just before an orgasm of epic proportion rippled along the same swell of glorious, arousing sensation, starting at her throbbing clit and radiating outward to all her limbs in trembling bliss.

Valerie screamed so loud when she came, she wondered if Earth had picked up the sound waves on radar. Dominick grabbed her ass with both hands, squeezed her hips and pulled her hard against his groin one last time. With a satisfied groan, he thrust inside deeply, releasing a hot stream against her womb before her voice died down or her reciprocal orgasm finished pulsing.

He draped his torso over her sweat-slicked spine and he kissed her shoulder tenderly. His cock was still impaled all the way inside her body and her internal muscles clamped down repeatedly as if hating for the interlude to be over already.

When she could finally speak through her panting, she murmured, "Forbidden sex is the best."

The breath from his amused laugher rumbled across her shoulder blade. "Yes, it is."

Chapter 16

Valerie and Dominick recovered quickly and exited her room before any alarms went off or any of the other men emerged from their rooms.

"I'd better go. They'll take one look at your face or mine and know exactly what just happened."

"They won't care."

He shrugged with a smile. "Still. No need to rub it in. See you tonight."

Valerie threw her arms around his neck and kissed him hard on the mouth. "Can't wait."

Patting her butt, he soon released her with a wink before exiting.

She made breakfast for the others and for the first time in months, the mood during their morning meal was light and cheery.

Daisy arrived moments after all of her men had left. "You look great."

"Thanks. I resolved an issue and things are looking up."

"Want to go shopping?"

"Of course. Let's go soon." Valerie expected she'd be called to task for luring Dominick to her room. She might as well not wait around the house for a summons. They could track her down later on, if they even bothered.

Blue found them enjoying lunch hours later. His sour expression didn't bode well. "You've been summoned," he announced with his sternest expression to date. "Come with me."

"Right now?" Valerie, in truth, wanted to go to have a heart-to-heart chat with Goldie and the gang. They'd lied to Dominick and she took issue with their underhanded interference.

"Yes. Right now. Let's go."

Daisy stood and inserted herself between Valerie and Blue before they could leave. "Why don't you call one of her mates to go with her?"

Blue shook his head. "Not this time."

Valerie winked at Daisy to reassure her. Usually, she went to see Goldie and the gang all on her lonesome for the various verbal accusations, but secretly wished that either Mark or Hauser were accompanying her this time. Dominick's face flashed in her mind, but she didn't want him near the committee if they planned to punish him in any way for his participation this morning.

In very short order, Valerie found herself back in the High Committee Chamber standing before the hostile-faced trio of Golden, Silver and Bronze.

"Well, I see you've been very busy disregarding our rules, Valerie. It's a wonder you bother with any of them."

Valerie, emboldened by the knowledge Dominick had shared, said, "Well, considering your theories and practices are completely erroneous when applied to me, it's a wonder I'm not simply dead."

Golden frowned. "What do you mean?"

"You forbade me to tell the men in my household that I had a favorite among them," she accused.

He opened his mouth as if to chastise her again until she held her hand up and silenced his words with a curse. "Damn you. I suffered for months and you couldn't be bothered to check on me, could you?"

"You performed your duties as expected. There was no reason—"

"I had vicious nightmares and couldn't sleep until I confessed to them all."

"You told them!" Golden stood.

"Yes. And they were fine with the information. They approved, even. So perhaps you shouldn't treat me like all the other rule-following sheep aboard this vessel. I'm different."

Pursing his lips, Golden glanced down at the desk between them. "You had relations with Dominick in your private quarters this morning."

Valerie rolled her eyes at the word he used for sex. 'Relations' was not the right word to describe the amazing forbidden sex they'd shared this morning in her room.

"So? No one else knew."

"This time. What about when they catch Dominick sneaking out of your room?"

"They still won't care. I've promised them that I'll continue with the regular schedule for everyone. However, the rest of my time aboard this ship will be spent with Dominick. And you better leave him alone about it. I told him he was my favorite. And that I love him."

"You told him." Golden glared, but apparently couldn't find anything else to say. He seated himself again.

"Yes. I told him and guess what? He loves me, too."

"This is highly unusual." Silver and Bronze each took turns whispering in his ear.

"Get over it. I'm not abandoning him."

The three of them exchanged resigned glances. "As long as harmony remains in your household, we'll over look the additional time you spend with Dominick. However, keep him out of your private quarters from now on."

"Fine."

Golden sighed and shook his head gently. "You're dismissed."

"Wait. I have a favor to ask."

"A favor?" Again Silver and Bronze took turns whispering into Golden's ear.

"Yes. I want to know what I need to do to remember Dominick once I get back to Earth on Return Day."

All three of their mouths fell open. Golden recovered first and said, "Impossible."

"Why?"

Silver and Bronze resumed whispering furiously on either side of Golden until he waved them off with a curt nod and they resumed their stiff-backed stances.

Surprisingly, Golden's features softened. "Your mind would be ill-prepared to handle this unusual situation. If you have any residual memories, they'll seem like a fading dream in your subconscious."

"Then tell me, how can Dominick and I be together?" Valerie's heart hurt at the thought of losing him.

"That is not our responsibility."

"Does that mean you can't do it or you won't."

"Arranging for you to 'hook up' once the both of you return is not an element taken into consideration during the elaborate complicated return process."

Valerie huffed. "Why can't you make an exception? You sucked us up here and I find the man of my dreams, but I'm not allowed to pursue him?"

Golden rolled his shoulders back and tilted his head slowly from side to side, as if considering her query. "No. Unfortunately not. We must not change events on Earth. It could cause a paradox. If you meet him on Earth you won't remember your time spent here. That falls under the heading of fate."

She started to voice a sincere plea to implore them to change their minds, but Golden held up a hand. "Enjoy your time together here. We won't interfere as long as you maintain the schedule for your other men, but there is nothing to be done once you leave."

Valerie exhaled. She did an about-face before she said anything she might come to regret and stomped out of the High Committee chambers.

She marched out the doors and straight into Dominick, bouncing off his muscular chest. He locked his arms around her in an intimate embrace.

His velvety chocolate gaze penetrated to her soul and he asked, "What did they want?"

A smile crept over her mouth. "How did you know I was here?"

"Daisy found me and told me." He squeezed her once.

Blue gave them a disgruntled look, turned away and disappeared down a nearby hall.

"Were you called here because of this morning?" He glanced at Blue's retreating back and added, "In your room?"

Valerie nodded. "I told them to get used to us spending all of our extra time together. They told me not to allow you in my private quarters any more. I don't know what the big deal is. Plus, I asked if they would help us find each other once we return to Earth. They won't."

Dominick nodded as a sharp breath escaped his lips. "Did they give you the paradox story crap?"

She hugged him tighter. "How did you know?"

"Because I asked the same thing."

"For the first time since my arrival in those awful gray sweats, I almost want to stay. I don't want to lose you."

Again his deep brown eyes bored a hole through to her soul. He leaned closer and whispered, "Maybe we'll find each other without their help."

"Even if we do, we won't remember our time here."

"Doesn't matter." He shrugged. "I just want to spend my life with you.

And in the meantime, we'll store up some quality time together before we go. Perhaps we'll remember each other in our dreams."

Valerie buried her face against the curve of his neck, inhaled his spicy, unique scent and murmured, "Okay."

"I've got to get back to work. See you tonight." He squeezed her once before releasing her with a kiss on the corner of her mouth.

Valerie grabbed his face and deepened the kiss, tangling her tongue with his. He broke away with a regretful-sounding sigh.

He led her back to the lunch place and Daisy.

Starting tonight, Valerie planned to ramp up the experience here and investigate her untested wicked side.

* * * *

Valerie entered Dominick's room with a plan to explore her darker erotic fantasy alter ego. Before he closed the door, she asked, politely, "So, what shall we do tonight?"

He secured the door and lifted her into his arms. Swinging her around in a circle, he kissed her temple. "Whatever you want."

Dominick deposited her on her feet as his gaze slid to her face.

"Okay, then, I want you to tie me up."

"What?" His shocked expression turned her on for some reason.

"I think you hold back when we're together."

"What are you talking about?" He shook his head a little too fast. "I love when we're together."

She released him, backed up and crossed her arms before he could grab her and kiss her senseless. He moved forward until his chest rested against her arms and put his hands on her shoulders.

Before he could seduce her with his lips again she said quickly, "I believe there are things you want to do, like tying me up, but you're afraid to ask."

A slight tremor ran down his body. If she hadn't been touching him she might not have felt it.

"I don't have to tie you up."

"Bullshit. I appreciate the position you're in, but I want to offer you something different. Something special."

He exhaled deeply and narrowed his focus. "And you think I want to tie you up?"

"Yes. And perhaps other things. Don't be afraid to ask."

"So why do you want something different all of a sudden?"

Valerie loved him. She only wanted to be with him for the rest of her life. What they had right now might be all they'd ever have and she wanted to experiment. "I want you to be satisfied. I don't want you to have to settle."

A harsh laugh escape his lips. "Trust me, what we do together isn't even close to settling—"

She cut him off. "I don't believe you." Then she softened her tone. "Please. I want to make you happy, not force you to endure the minimum to suffice. Tell me what you like."

A gleam came into his eye. "Tell me why."

"I don't understand."

"Why, all of a sudden, do you insist on going down a new mystery path with me right now?"

She shrugged slowly. "I don't know what you mean."

"Sure you do. What are you really asking? And why now?"

In a torturously saddened, guilt-filled voice she said, "Because we may not have much time left together." She dropped her head, embarrassed to have feelings for him that she couldn't seem to control. "The high committee won't even make an effort to ensure we'll be together on Earth. Now is the only guaranteed time for us to be together. It's also the only instance for us to explore and try new things."

His face softened just a little and he slid his arms around her. "I have nebulous memories of my time on Earth with regard to particular dark proclivities that I rarely shared with just anyone." His whispered voice sent shards of desire zipping through her veins.

"Will you share with me?"

He shook his head, as if coming out of a fog. "I shouldn't."

"But why not?"

"Because I don't want you to go back to being afraid of me. It took me a year to get you to stop being scared silly when it was my night. I don't want to lose ground at this late date."

"You won't lose ground."

He laughed, but it sounded forced. "What we do together is wonderful, not settling."

"Liar."

He broke away and turned his back to her. "Valerie, please don't ask me."

"Why not? I want you to feel as good as I do."

"Because once that line is crossed it would be difficult to go back."

"What line?" She pressed her body to his and whispered, "Tell me."

He sighed again. "I like bondage." He pierced her with a stern gaze and watched to see if his statement had an adverse effect.

"I...I'd be willing to try it." The very word brought visions of spike-studded leather, pain and a tiny bit of fear into her very vivid imagination.

"I appreciate that, babe. I truly do." Dominick grabbed her in a bear hug, pinning her arms to her sides, and buried his face in her neck. "But if you didn't like it—"

"Then I'd tell you. And you wouldn't make me do it anymore."

"But from then on you'd know I'd always want to. I know you. It would change things between us in an adverse way. You'd feel bad or, worse, you'd feel guilty. Please don't make me cross that line."

"Can't we just move over the line a little? Or step on it?"

He laughed. "I appreciate your willingness to try something new, but please allow me to decline."

"Would what you did to me, um, hurt? Like whips and pain?"

His eyes narrowed. He didn't say anything for several long seconds. "No. For me it's about control. I like having all of it. I'd want to tie you down to the bed, hands and feet spread wide. You'd get hot anticipating what I was about to do to you. I might blindfold you next and make you wonder how I'd please you." He slipped behind her and kissed her neck before he nipped the cord of muscle along her shoulder.

"That doesn't sound so bad. What are you really afraid to tell me?"

"I like to penetrate hard and deep when I fuck. I don't want to hurt you."

"You won't hurt me." She sucked in a shuddery breath. "I want to try it, okay? Please."

He wrapped his arms around her torso, squeezing so hard she couldn't breathe in a full breath and asked, "Do you know what a safe word is?"

"Sort of," she squeaked and he released her a little. Johnny had taught her about a word, but after that first night when he'd dressed as a pirate, he'd never tried games again in all this time and Valerie had been relieved. Dominick, on the other hand, was a whole different arena to play in. She wanted to do this with him very much.

"It's a word that we agree on before we start. If you want me to stop at any time for any reason at all, you say the word and I will stop."

"But—"

"No buts, no recriminations. Any reason you want me to stop and I'll stop if you say the word."

"Okay."

"Okay?" The fingers wrapped around her forearms loosened just a bit.

Valerie twisted and stared deeply into his eyes. "My safe word is 'menagerie.' Tie me up, blindfold me and fuck me as hard as you want and if I want you to stop, I'll say menagerie, and you'll stop." Valerie leaned closer and his hands tightened. "But I won't."

His pupils widened to black. "You won't what?"

"I won't say the word." Tilting her head back, she longed for him to touch her.

He kissed her so hard their teeth clacked. He jammed his tongue between her lips with a ferocity of force he'd never used with her before, as if testing her resolve to play the scary bondage game. She was so excited she could barely keep her legs beneath her. His punishing kiss sent pulses of electric desire sizzling between her legs. Arms crossed behind her back, Valerie felt a little thrill when Dominick held her limbs in place and bent her back slightly. Totally vulnerable to his oral assault, Valerie relaxed, ready to let him explore new and exciting sexual practices.

After the brutally arousing kiss, Dominick picked her up, carried her to his bed and deposited her in the middle of it. He turned to a dresser centered against one wall. From the top drawer he pulled out several pieces of colorful fabric. Scarves, perhaps?

Valerie swallowed hard and her pussy gushed in anticipatory arousal of being tied to Dominick's bed.

Turning to face her with the cloth dangling from his fingertips, he said, "I demand complete acquiescence. Do you understand?"

"Yes."

"And you'll do whatever I say without question?"

Valerie gasped as a rush of need barreled through her veins. "Yes," she managed to whisper.

"Take your clothes off."

From her kneeling position, Valerie stood easily in the center of Dominick's bed and stripped as he watched.

Once she'd chucked her clothing over the edge of the footboard, Dominick said, "Now get down on the bed and onto your back."

She slid down as he approached. He plucked her hand from the pillow and tied her wrist to a vertical spindle on his iron headboard. He then bound her ankles to the metal footboard and finished her entrapment using the final scarf on her other wrist.

He glanced down at her nude, very aroused body and rubbed his hands together briskly. "Be right back. Don't move."

Valerie laughed. She closed her eyes and thought about the kind of trust involved in this scenario. She should have been panicked, but instead she could hardly wait to see what he'd do.

He returned with something tucked behind his back, but she couldn't see what he had. She imagined she'd find out soon enough.

"Close your eyes. Keep them closed."

Her lids drifted shut as a smile curved her lips and another ripple of arousal sped down her body.

The mattress gave way beside her hip and she guessed that he'd sat on the bed. She resisted the urge to peek, as the question of what her punishment might be for disobedience had yet to be disclosed.

The barest flutter of his fingertips on her inner ankle above the scarf sent a riot of goose bumps shivering along her leg.

"Am I allowed to speak?"

He cleared his throat. "Yes. But no questions."

No questions? Why were queries all of a sudden the only thing in her mind?

The barest of touches turned into a leg massage as his hands moved up to her knee. His lips pressed a kiss there before they moved further upward. He was getting closer to her center. Her core gushed. She nudged her hips towards his fingers in an effort to connect them with her clit, but he moved his hand just out of reach. A sigh of frustration escaped as her hips relaxed against the sheets.

His mild chuckle accompanied a quick surprise swipe of a single finger across her clit. The hot zap of pleasure was gone in the next moment.

"Please," she whispered, wishing he'd rub her clitoris more.

His fingertips glided from her center to her belly button, circling a lazy path to seemingly nowhere. An edgy sigh of frustration rushed out until, without warning, his warm tongue licked the center of one breast, pebbling the tip. She arched her shoulders off the bed, until the scarves stopped her progress, as a bolt of sharp arousal shot from nipple to clit with his attention.

Dominick stroked a palm to her other breast and cupped her flesh, teasing the other nipple.

Valerie writhed in need, bucking her hips upward, wishing for his tongue to travel south. The mere thought of his mouth between her legs made another wet gush shower her pussy. She was on the verge of climax merely imagining his tongue licking her clit.

"Don't come yet," he commanded.

Had he just read her mind?

"What?"

"No questions," he whispered and kissed the space between her breasts.

"But I want to come."

"And you will, but not yet. Not until I tell you to."

Valerie pushed out a deep breath and began to understand the control aspect of this situation a little more. She was so turned on that if he blew even the tiniest wisp of air on her clit she'd likely explode and unconsciously disobey his command without being able to control herself. Being ordered not to come aroused her to a level she'd never been to before.

Dominick took a nipple between his lips and sucked on her leisurely. His other hand fastened to her other breast and rubbed that sensitive peak in tandem.

Her mind focused on trying not to come, but it became increasingly difficult as he teased and sucked on her nipples. She trembled, trying to ignore the pulsing zaps of arousal as his mouth and fingers worked.

Shifting her hips back and forth, she squirmed, testing the strength of her ankle restraints and tried to think of a way to communicate her unbearable need without forming it into a question.

"Dominick."

His mouth lifted from one nipple with a wet smack. "Yes."

"I want you so much."

"I'm glad."

"I don't think I can last much longer."

"You can. I demand it."

"Dominick. My body isn't responding to your demands."

He chuckled. "I disagree." A finger glanced across her nipple and she jumped at the sensation spiraling to her clit.

"I really want to come."

"Not yet."

She pushed out an exasperated sigh. "When?"

"No questions." He quit the attention to her breasts and removed himself from her. The bed bounced and she knew he'd left it.

"Don't leave me." Valerie's eyes opened to see where he was going.

Dominick hovered over the bed with a stern expression. "Eyes closed."

She sighed and snapped her lids shut again. She heard rustling and the curiosity of what he was doing excited her beyond what she'd ever imagined.

After what seemed like forever she felt him climb back on the bed. She sensed that he was between her legs again and loosened her eyelids, trying to open them the barest sliver to catch a glimpse without being caught.

"Keep your eyes closed."

How was he reading her mind?

Something soft grazed an inner thigh, stroking from her knee to her mound. She opened her mouth to ask what it was, but stopped herself in time. The soft something was brushed over her legs and belly, then each nipple until he finally touched it to her lips and she smiled in recognition. It was a carnation, judging by the wafting scent.

"That feels lovely."

He brushed the flower down between her legs and followed with his mouth. She felt a warning breath of warm air before he licked her clitoris. The overwhelming shot of oral stimulation sent a spasm of desire through her. She was on the rabid edge of a monumental orgasm.

"Ohmigod." Her toes curled trying to keep from releasing. She panted with the effort.

He brushed a kiss on her belly and then two beats later fastened his lips to her mouth. Tangling his tongue inside, she tasted her own musky flavor and pushed her face closer, wanting the connection to last.

He broke the kiss and trailed kisses along her jaw. "I think you're almost ready."

She nodded her head in desperate agreement. "Yes. I'm *so* ready."

Dominick lowered his body onto hers and for the first time she realized he was naked. His erect cock nestled at the apex if her thighs mere inches from her wet and wanting pussy. A shudder ran through her limbs and torso at the thought of imminent sexual intercourse.

Another ripple shook her and he asked, "Are you cold?"

"No. I'm ready."

"Wait for me. I'll tell you when to come."

Valerie pushed out a trembling breath, hoping she'd be able to hold in the orgasmic delight of having his cock buried deeply inside her body. "Right."

Dominick slipped an arm beneath her waist and put his other hand on one hip. He pressed a kiss to her cheek and pierced her to the hilt with his mighty cock until he was fully embedded and tickling her womb.

The seductive power of his shaft filling her to the brink made the difficulty of waiting to climax even more unbearable. With each beat of her pounding heart she risked the sudden fall into oblivion.

With one arm he gripped her waist, the other hand squeezed one thigh as if for leverage and he didn't wait even a second to start pounding his cock in and out of her body with voracious aplomb. Each thrust of his incredibly wide shaft hit her womb and the resulting sharp contact sent a clenching, arousing need spiraling inside. The angle of his thrusting brushed the barest of accidental caresses over her clitoris with every third push.

Delirious with the desire for release, Valerie screamed, "Dominick."

Piercing her so hard she thought she would split from the pleasure, he growled, "Come for me. Now!"

The release she'd been ready to beg for washed across her in a turbulent wave of the most acute pleasure she'd ever experienced. Her slick pussy clamped like a vise on his cock, which still moved in and out with perilously deep thrusts. After the first wave of orgasm had swept by, Valerie took a deep, stuttering breath and heard Dominick say, "Now come for me again."

He groaned, pierced her deeper than she'd thought would ever be possible and showered her core with his release. Barely recovered from the first climax, her body writhed with the beckoning call of another intense orgasm. Valerie fairly shrieked the walls down as pleasure engulfed her senses. The double bang of two sharp climaxes back to back tested her capacity for gratification.

Wrists and ankles all pulled hard at the scarves, testing each of the silk bindings' tensile strength, but the soft cloth held her in place as she panted and came down off the most satisfying sexual experience of her memory.

Dominick, still breathing heavily, kissed her mouth. "That was extraordinary." He buried his face between her neck and shoulder, kissing the sensitive place beneath her ear repeatedly. "I don't recall ever having felt this kind of intensity before."

As her breathing finally returned to normal, she murmured, "It was absolutely indescribable." She tugged at her bonds. "Can I ask questions yet?"

His rich laugher rolled over her. "What do you want to know?"

"When can we do this again?"

Valerie felt a sudden shudder run down his body. "Whenever you want." He pressed another kiss to her lips.

"I love you, Dominick."

Nuzzling her neck, he whispered. "I love you more, babe."

The second time, he blindfolded her so she couldn't peek and added a jar of honey as an additional component of his seduction along with the carnation.

Valerie, immersed in the unexpected satisfaction of sexual experimentation she never expected to take pleasure in, snuggled up to the man she hoped her heart would recognize regardless of their memories of this unusual place in time.

Chapter 17

7 until Return Day

"Why have I been called here? I haven't done anything. Lately." Blue led Valerie to a familiar place, but she still didn't like meeting with the High Committee all alone.

The very first time she'd been called here Mark had accompanied her, but waited outside. After that she'd gone by herself and found she preferred it. Today, she wished Dominick hadn't been at work otherwise she would have dragged him along.

Valerie despised being away from him since their time together had grown so short. In mere days, they'd be permanently separated and she was despondent over the loss.

Stopping briefly in front of the double doors to the High Committee chamber, Valerie tried to remember any little piece of her life before being brought on board this ship. Beyond the fact that she knew she had a life, no details emerged in her mind. She knew she was good with numbers, but didn't recall if that was an important part of her life on Earth.

Dominick only knew he dealt with guns, self-defense and had a bevy of skills befitting a mercenary. Talk about opposites attracting. At least they'd had fun the last few months. Little comfort when she'd found the love of her life only to be separated forever once they left this place and would have no memory of it. Valerie used to long for a speedy return to Earth early on in this unusual journey, but lately she decided she should have been careful at what she wished for.

Blue ushered her through the committee chamber doors to where only Golden waited for her. He was seated alone at the table and Valerie wondered where the other two members were. She hadn't ever seen him without Silver and Bronze poised to whisper in his ears.

"What's going on?" Over her shoulder, Blue closed the chamber doors leaving them alone.

"We brought you here to explain the procedures for your return home to Earth."

Golden stood and led her from the committee chamber to a hidden hallway at the back of the tall room. Following along at a measured distance, a vague recollection of having been here before surfaced in Valerie's memory. A green shaft of light appeared ahead and she remembered exploring this prohibited space with Daisy. Until Dominick had caught them. Approaching the familiar space, she suppressed the urge to shout, "Ah ha!" and mentally rubbed her hands together. Now she'd finally get to see what was in this forbidden hallway.

"All six of us are going back, correct?"

Golden nodded and opened a door to a room she'd never seen in this part of the alien vessel before. "There has been a slight complication. We wanted to discuss it with you privately."

"What complication? How slight?" The spacious white room was well lit, with ambient light seemingly coming from the walls. It looked like her personal vision of mission control on Earth where shuttles and satellites were launched in to space. "What are we doing here?" She didn't mean to sound so impatient. Time away from Dominick made her edgy. She wondered if it would be prudent to ask about finding a way to meet him back on Earth again.

"You have truly fallen in love with one of the men in your group," Golden remarked in a matter-of-fact tone.

Startled that the conversation had strayed into what she'd just been thinking, Valerie crossed her arms ready to do battle. "Am I in more trouble now?"

"No. At least, not trouble which will result in any consequences. However, we would like to offer you the possibility to remember each other once you go back to Earth."

"I thought you said paradoxes would result." Still, hope colored her new exuberant tone.

"They can, but we don't believe this will result if we give you the information. Besides, the likelihood of your meeting is remote at best."

"Okay, tell me what information will help me find him."

Golden pressed his palms together as if in prayer. "Let me explain something to you first. Humans have a unique personification of being while traveling in our vessel. Especially the males."

"Why do you still suck us up into your vortex?"

Golden smirked a little. "Your planet resides near a little-known wormhole exit. This path is the only one our ship can take safely to and from our destination. Unfortunately human capture has become a part of it."

"How long has this been going on?"

"Centuries." Golden looked away.

"After all this time, surely you have better ways through space."

"No. Not really. Our enduring mission is to transport needed medical supplies to our planet's remote and distant colonies across the galaxy. This phenomenon only happens every eighty-one Earth years, however, we endeavor to make right the lives of what humans we accidentally transport on our way back through. Up until very recently, humans were not inhabiting this particular area of Earth."

"So, all the alien abduction stories are true?"

"Not exactly as your media has purported it to be."

"How, exactly?"

"The first occurrence was over 400 years ago and impacted only one human. The number has increased over time. After several hundred years, we finally hit upon a system by which we weren't hurting humans when they fell victim to our gravitational oasis vortex. It was a difficult transition for them initially, but we studied the problem and the environment you lived in was the result of long years of examination and analysis."

"What did you do?" Valerie asked in a near whisper.

Golden pegged her with an intense stare, as if to mesmerize her into listening before he spoke. "First, we allowed the females and males to commingle in the containment tubes. This calmed the male population immeasurably." He paused to take a deep breath and added quietly, "And also by letting the males separate into different personalities and reside this way during the flight. Setting up a process by which they could select an Earth female for sexual gratification purposes while they were on board alleviated all final problems with their captivity."

"I don't understand. What different personalities?"

Golden gestured for her to sit. It was the first time he'd displayed this level of consideration. She sat warily. "Explain the different personalities."

He also seated himself. "The truth is you've only been with one man since you've been on our vessel. He simply has several personalities."

Valerie shook her head. "No. I live with five different men. They are each unique and different, not the same man acting differently." She stood and Golden's eyes widened when she towered above him.

Golden rose from his chair slowly. "Yes. However, on Earth all these men share the same body."

Her mouth fell open. "I don't believe it. They're all too different."

"Yes they are different, and yet they are all the component personalities of one man."

Valerie's brain swirled madly with the shocking information. *All her mates were personalities of the same man?* She swallowed hard before asking, "Which one is it?"

"Dominick, of course, which is why we are even having this conversation. If you'd fallen in love with one of the other personalities then we would have sent you back without the knowledge of a remote possibility of finding each other." He pointed to her chair and they both sat down again.

"We can find each other?" A beacon of hope rose so sharply she almost screamed out loud. Not something Golden and the others were comfortable with, so she tamped down her enthusiasm. "Don't tease me."

"It is not a guarantee, but the possibility exists in certain circumstances. If you come across each other shortly after returning to Earth and get close enough to speak even a single word to each other, then your memories of this place will return temporarily."

"Great. He'll instantly remember he shared me with four other men. I'm sure that will get us off on the right foot."

"Dominick will understand that you were only with his other personalities and not five different men. Merely alter egos of himself."

"Oh yeah." Valerie's skeptical nature came out full force. "How does that work?"

Golden merely smiled tolerantly. "Humans are very complex creatures."

"Really?"

"Yes. This splitting of his mind phenomenon is merely a side-effect of being brought aboard the Chippen. Dominick is the true being of the man. But even you must admit that regardless of where they are, all humans can be different in personality when presented with different circumstances.

"For example, Dominick is dark and dangerous and that's how he lives his day-to-day life.

"However, Hauser is the face that Dominick presents to the world at large because his true self believes it's a better representation for living in your world. He can accomplish more by having a friendlier face to transact business.

"Frasier is the analytical part of his mind dealing with numbers, finances and the general logic of every situation Dominick encounters.

"Johnny is his creative side dealing with resourcefulness, inventiveness and artistic expression when the situation calls for it.

"Mark is his softer side, where things are simple and non-threatening. This is the personality he uses to engage with family and friendships versus his work environment."

Valerie was stunned. "And they're all a part of Dominick?"

The other nodded and folded his hands serenely on the table. "Yes."

"Will it hurt him to have all his personalities put back together?"

"No."

While this information was fairly shocking, she didn't find it hard to swallow. It was, in fact, a huge relief. "And because I foolishly picked a favorite mate against your rules and my better judgment, leading to my supreme guilt-filled existence for the past several months, I'm rewarded with the possibility finding him."

"Precisely."

Galvanized with hope, she asked, "What do I have to do?"

"Nothing. Once back on Earth, only a few minutes will have passed, if any at all. Our goal is to put you back fifteen minutes prior to your abduction. You may have a sense of déjà vu for a few minutes after we drop you off. If and only if you run into Dominick's true self, you must say something so he can hear your voice. The recognition is triggered by the unique sounds of your vocal cords."

"So I won't recognize him?"

"My limited understanding is that he'll seem very familiar to you. If he speaks to you first, he won't recognize you until you speak in return"

Valerie nodded and visualized Dominick. She'd spend the next seven days memorizing his voice.

"Are you ready to go back to resume your life on Earth?"

"I guess. Thanks for the chance to find Dominick."

Golden actually allowed the barest of smiles to form. "Very well. Follow me. We don't have much time left."

"What do you mean? We're leaving now?" She wanted to say good-bye to them. All of them. One last kiss. One last hug. And in Dominick's case, one last enthusiastic intimate bondage encounter. Valerie looked at her watch. "But I still have several days. I wanted to say my farewells."

"That won't be possible, I'm afraid. We feel it best to separate the groups before they realize or it's harder. Trust me." Glancing at his hand-held computer, he made a little noise and jumped up from his chair. He tugged on her arm until she stood up. "We must hurry or you'll miss your window to go back."

Departing from the room, Valerie glanced over her shoulder and calculated her odds of escaping him and finding her way out of the maze of hallways she'd arrived in.

"If you run back, you'll be staying permanently." Valerie hesitated until he added, "And so will they."

Tilting her head, Valerie smirked. "What if I want to stay here with him?"

"You won't be put with Dominick and his group, if you remain." She sighed deeply and turned to follow him.

"Fine." Valerie hastened to keep up as they hurried down the long white corridor to yet another room with a large blue circle centered on the floor of a raised knee-high dais.

"Step onto the gray platform and then into the blue circle in the center and you'll be back before you know it," Golden said.

The lavender-skinned man standing before the panel of lights and buttons looked exasperated. "Ten seconds."

"Did someone tell Dominick he could find me, too?"

"No. Only you. It has to be initiated by you." Golden pushed her towards the blue circle, but she was uncertain and balked.

"…Nine…eight…seven…" Lavender's hand was poised over a large red button on the wall. She noted the snarky irritation in his tone as he counted. This unexpected departure was happening too fast. Would she even remember? *Please remember.*

"Did Dominick already leave for Earth?"

"…Six…five…four…"

"Yes, right before we spoke." Golden pushed her again. "Dominick was as difficult to get on the blue circle as you are."

"…Three…two…"

Valerie stepped both feet on the blue circle as tears erupted from her eyes. She closed her eyes not wanting to see what happened on this ride.

"…One…mark."

The last thought in her mind, the last visual memory she tightly embraced, was of her only true love. *Dominick.*

Chapter 18

Valerie jogged through the park and realized she'd apparently traveled half the path in a complete daydreaming fog. She glanced at her sports watch and realized almost thirty minutes had gone by. Looking at the terrain in her vicinity, she searched the area to get her bearings.

The scent of fresh-mown grass assaulted her as if she hadn't smelled it in a long time and took her back to her childhood and the humid heat of a lazy summer day.

She couldn't remember what she'd just been thinking before being distracted by the fragrance of the outdoors. Something about space or stars perhaps. She couldn't quite grasp the nebulous strands of memory in her mind. Perhaps the strenuous exercise was making her brain soft.

Rounding the trail hill with the elevation that led into the trees on the next incline, Valerie was troubled by her lack of recollection of the past half an hour. It seemed like she was forgetting something. Something big. Her methodic steps slowed to barely a trot. *Was she forgetting something?*

The crunch of the gravel beneath her feet sounding like someone eating Grape-Nuts was overpowered by a loud, engine-revving noise coming from the street that ran alongside the park. She hated jogging along this portion of the path.

Valerie looked towards what sounded like two vehicles racing, but could only see trees. In another hundred yards or so she'd be able to see part of the road.

The racers would probably have zoomed by before she made it, but the sound of grinding metal on metal startled her into a faster trot. The looky-look in her longed to see the accident and view for herself the carnage. It was sick, but she didn't know anyone who could resist the lure of possible bloodshed on the road. The muscles in her thighs protested the sudden burst of energy needed to push her all the way up the small hill to overlook the road.

The sharp bang startled her and she stopped dead in her tracks for a moment before walking the rest of the way. Was that a gunshot or a backfire? Cresting the hill, she widened her gaze and looked down the short incline at the section of street revealed between leafy trees. A large black motorcycle was being chased by a sleek silver one. The rider on the silver bike held a long black weapon. A cross between a rifle and a handgun, he leveled it at the black motorcycle.

The word Uzi pistol came to mind from she knew not where, but that same place told her it was an accurate label for the weapon in the silver rider's hand. The rider of the black motorcycle hugged the frame of his bike. She didn't know how he could even see the road because he was slumped in his seat so low.

The gun she'd miraculously identified as an Uzi pistol fired another volley of rounds and hit the black motorcycle's back tire, popping it. The black rider immediately lurched to the left, lost control of his bike and slid sideways into the ditch twenty yards from her perch at the top of the incline next to the road.

The silver rider continued on speeding by into the moderately heavy traffic and disappeared around the curve of the highway.

Valerie had never possessed a courageous bone in her body, and part of her wanted to run as far away as possible. Instead, she scrambled down the incline towards the black biker, who had slid to a stop in the grassy area beside the road and was now trapped beneath his motorcycle. Her intention was to help him, although her intrigue level was spiking too.

The scent of burned rubber from his blown tire permeated the surrounding air. He wasn't moving. Valerie approached and almost stumbled over a gun at her feet. The Glock 17 nine-millimeter autoloader had the safety off and it was ready to fire. She shook her head. Where did she know the specifics of the gun from? She knew it was factual and reached for the pistol before prudence could caution her about picking up strange guns from probable criminals in a dispute.

Weapon in hand, pointed at the ground for safety, she took another step towards the motorcycle and its trapped rider. Under normal circumstances, Valerie would never approach a stranger or even speak to him. She was compelled to do so for some unfathomable reason.

"What the fuck do you think you're doing?" The black rider struggled to lift his heavy bike off his leg one-handed as a grimace shaped his face. He twisted his body towards her when he failed to secure his freedom and she saw a sliver of his face through the visor of his helmet more clearly. Vivid arctic-blue eyes bored a hole through her. He *did* seem very familiar.

His voice penetrated her and made her mind swirl in dizzy recognition. Where did she know him from?

"I...you...I..." Valerie stopped and took a deep breath. Panicking was not going to help. "I was getting your gun." Fingers closing over the grip, it was funny how comfortable the large gun felt in her hand.

"I never let anyone touch my weapon. Bring it here." The cadence of his sultry deep tone washed over her in warm waves of recognition.

Valerie hesitated. She lifted the gun closer and pointed it away from him, checking the balance and weight like a pro. Flipping the release button, she popped the ammunition magazine out, studied the bullets loaded, full clip. Like she'd used it before. Like she'd spent months practicing. Like the voice emanating from the man at her feet seemed so familiar because he was the one who had taught her how to shoot.

But how was that possible?

The fragment of a dream wafted past her memory and she said, "You told me that I was the exception to your rule. I've touched your weapon plenty of times." The words came out of her before she even knew what she was saying.

He narrowed his lids as if processing her explanation, but didn't argue, shockingly enough.

What? Did she *know* him?

A flood of images swelled in her brain. She remembered everything. The abduction by the Others. The gauntlet arena to choose a group of mates. The alien mating ceremony that joined her to five men for three years. Her forbidden favorite mate. The nightmares, the target practice, the resolution.

The rushed explanation of Golden on her way back to Earth about how to find him. Her soul mate.

Dominick.

The name echoed in her mind and brought forth the words "forbidden pleasure." Why would he be forbidden? One look at his body told her why the word pleasure came to mind. He dripped pure sex appeal, even trapped and struggling as he was beneath his motorcycle.

"Do I know you, sweetheart?" His deep voice caressed an inner dark, illicitly hidden place within her core.

Gazing into faded artic-blue eyes, she suddenly remembered why. A treasure trove of sexual positions and long nights of lovemaking with this man flooded her mind. She cocked her head to one side and said, "Menagerie."

He blinked as if coming awake and pulled his helmet off two-handed. Dominick. They locked gazes. God, he looked amazing. His hair, long and shaggy, brushed his jacket collar and his eyes were blue instead of brown, but it was Dominick. She'd found him..

"Babe," he uttered as she took another step closer

The silver biker strolled into the space as if in slow motion from across the clearing and got off a quick shot at Dominick still trapped beneath his motorcycle with the auto-repeater.

The bullet tore a hole in his jeans, hitting Dominick in the leg, and he grunted once.

Without thinking it through, and certain the silver biker was about to kill her love, Valerie leveled the pistol she held at the silver biker, aimed center mass and squeezed the trigger. She hit her target in the stomach and raised her other hand to steady the big gun and its large recoil.

The silver biker lifted the muzzle of the gun away from Dominick, aimed it in her direction in the next heartbeat and instantly took another shot.

Dominick howled as if in agony and tried to shove the motorcycle off his injured leg. Valerie squeezed off three more rounds in quick succession into the chest of the silver biker before she noticed the one shot her opponent had fired at her had in fact hit her in the chest. She tried to take a breath and failed. She fell to her knees, trying to get any air inside her lungs. And failed. The pain overwhelmed her when she took another attempt at a first breath.

Dominick crawled on his elbows out from underneath the bike, dragging both legs behind him. One injured from the accident and the other one shot by the Silver biker.

She thought she heard one of Dominick's bones snap in his zeal to crawl towards her as she fell forward, face-first into the crunchy leaves on the park floor. Every small breath stabbed like a thousand daggers of pain in her chest.

"Don't you even think about dying, Valerie Jean. We have lots to talk about."

Valerie turned her head away from the loamy ground to see him crawl the rest of the way towards her. She coughed while trying to speak. A rattle sounded in her chest, adding more excruciating pain to her breathing process, so she decided to remain quiet.

He lurched closer slinging an arm around her shoulders. His lips caressed her temple and he whispered, "I love you, babe. Please hang on. I'm calling for backup."

She blinked and nodded slightly. It was the only communication she could manage without fainting from the pain. He stroked her hair and kissed her face again.

Dominick pulled a cellular phone off his belt and thumbed a number one-handed. "I'm at Patrick Avenue and West 53rd Street. I need an ambulance immediately. Connect me to central law enforcement. I need to report in…"

He kept talking into the cell phone, but Valerie couldn't hear him anymore. Watching his beautiful lips move and the concern in his eyes, she fought to stay conscious, but lost the battle soon enough. She slid perilously into an inky darkness with the seductive scent of the man she loved lingering with the earthy scent of fallen leaves.

Chapter 19

"Valerie Jean." The insistent male voice wouldn't shut up or stop calling her name. And though the low tone of his voice was strangely engaging, he used her middle name in conjunction with it. She hated it when her middle name was used, as it often signaled someone's discontent. Likely her mother. Was she in trouble for something?

How did the man with the sexy voice know her middle name?

"Valerie Jean, wake up. I mean it." A tickle of memory assaulted her with the notion that the man's voice was hauntingly familiar. Did she know that voice? Regardless, she decided quickly that she wanted to sleep more than she wanted to learn his identity. Probably why she was always alone. And the logic her mother would apply to explain her lack of grandchildren at the next family gathering.

Valerie mumbled, "No. I want to sleep." She pushed out a deep sigh and snuggled into the bed to rest again.

"Valerie? Are you awake? Did you just say no to me?" The sudden loud rustling sound nearby didn't help her get back to sleep. She *so* wanted to sleep for a week. Her whole body hurt. In fact, her hair ached.

"Yes. I said no. Let me sleep." The weary twinge in her chest made her want to nestle down in the warm bed and slumber the day away. Eyes closed, she lifted her head and added, "And stop calling me Valerie Jean. I hate it when you use my real name."

"Babe, you scared me." A large warm hand gripped then squeezed her shoulder.

Valerie opened her eyes. Dominick loomed over the bed she rested in. It was a hospital bed.

"Where am I?" She tried to sit up before realizing that in doing so the pain banging in her head would make her want to throw up. She put a hand to her forehead to help keep her brain behind her skull and then the other over her mouth to stop anything trying to exit.

"You're at St. Vincent's Hospital."

She closed her eyes and tried to remember. Slipping the hand from her mouth she asked, "Why am I here again?"

"Because you decided to catch a bullet with your chest. You're lucky it only cracked a rib instead of puncturing your lung. You scared the shit out of me, you know?"

The memories of the gun battle in the park assaulted her mind. She'd fired a gun, at a person. "Is that other biker with the silver helmet dead? Did I kill her?"

"No. She's alive."

"Who is she?"

"Her name is Regina. She's an irate, vengeful drug dealer, among other things. My unfortunate association with a rival group set this all off. I'm sorry you were injured as a part of it."

Valerie relaxed a notch. "I'm just glad no one ended up dead."

Dominick leaned in and tenderly kissed her lips. "Me, too."

"Are you hurt?" Valerie studied Dominick through squinted eyes, checking over his superb body for injuries.

"I'm banged up a little, but nothing's broken."

"I thought you got shot."

"Only a flesh wound. I'm fine."

A stranger breezed into her hospital room. "Time's up."

Dominick straightened and turned towards the new visitor. "I need another minute, Kyle. She just woke up."

"Sorry, but my ass is already headed for the sling for letting you visit her at all. Let's go."

Dominick brushed a finger lovingly along her jaw before drawing his hand away and backed up a step as if to depart. Valerie painfully shifted her gaze to the new visitor. It was a police officer, if the badge clipped to his belt was any indication.

"You're the police?" At the stranger's nod, she asked. "What's going on?"

Dominick edged around the foot of her bed to meet the man halfway. Kyle pulled handcuffs out and Dominick put his hands behind his back. "I made a deal. Kyle let me wait until you woke before he arrested me."

"Arrested you? For what?"

Dominick sighed. "Drug trafficking, illegal possession of automatic weapons with intent to distribute, instigating a vehicle chase within the city limits, attempted murder, and I believe there is even a charge for criminal trespass."

Kyle snapped the second cuff in place and said, "You have the right to remain silent."

As Kyle continued reading him his rights, Valerie pierced Dominick with a disheartened stare. "You're a criminal?"

He winked. "I'm innocent, babe. Trust me."

"Valerie? What's going on here?" Her mother and father stood in the door of her hospital room. They'd arrived in time to see the love of her life about to be hauled away in handcuffs for a multitude of illegal acts.

"Do you understand these rights as I have explained them?"

"I'll be back as soon as I make bail, Valerie."

"You most certainly will not." Valerie's mother took a step inside the room. "You will stay away from my daughter or we'll get a restraining order."

Valerie, unable to take her eyes off Dominick, shook her head slightly as a tear slipped down her cheek. "Dominick, I—"

"Come on. Time to go," Kyle interrupted as he muscled Dominick towards the door—or, at least, he attempted to move him in that direction.

Dominick stopped, pierced her with a determined look and said, "Don't forget me, babe. I will return."

Valerie nodded. She believed him, but a wave of dizziness swept across her conscious. Her head pounded. She swayed in the bed as her mother hurried to her side and pushed the call button for assistance.

Kyle pushed Dominick through the open door of her room. Her last image of Dominick was his achingly handsome face etched with concern as he was led away in handcuffs.

She pondered the miraculous irony of finding Dominick only to have him ripped from her because he wasn't in security, as he had been while they were with the Others in space, but rather a criminal with similar skills.

Glancing at her mother's displeased expression, Valerie further imagined her parents would never accept a criminal into the family fold no matter how much she loved him.

* * * *

Valerie woke the next evening to another pounding headache. Her mother, perched close as if relentlessly guarding her from any further unwanted visitors, snored softly in the chair beside the hospital bed.

Her thoughts immediately strayed to Dominick.

She'd been surprised at her mother's dislike of Dominick the day before. Up until now, she'd assumed any man with a pulse and a job, not necessarily in that order, qualified as a contender for her hand in marriage. Although, career criminal likely wasn't considered a viable occupation in the quest for a husband even for someone as desperate for grandchildren as her mother.

The morning after Dominick had been led away in handcuffs, a large gruff federal officer had arrived in her hospital room. He'd explained that Valerie wasn't going to be considered complicit in any charges related to the shooting in the park and also informed her of Dominick's status as an undercover drug enforcement agent. Thankfully, he wasn't actually a criminal.

Valerie's mother was still not impressed. Even with the knowledge of his true profession, she told Valerie not to pursue Dominick. "He's too dangerous. He almost got you killed."

"No, he didn't, Mother."

When Dominick had called her room last night to check up on her, Valerie's mother had answered. She'd made perfectly it clear that Dominick was wasting his time if he expected a further relationship. She blamed him for getting Valerie shot and wouldn't allow him to even speak to her on the phone.

Valerie had spent three years learning Dominick's eccentricities and now she was slowly losing them. Already her memories of the 'trip with the Others' had faded like decades-old wallpaper from her mind and were quickly replaced with the reality of her life on Earth.

Heaving a sigh, Valerie glanced at her mother and wondered if she'd faint or disown her if she ever found out about all the decadent things she and Dominick had done in the name of getting enough of each other to last forever. *Things she already missed and longed for.*

Of course, that was before she'd known there was even a remote possibility that a life with Dominick was possible here on Earth.

Dominick. Simply uttering his name in the privacy of her mind gave her goose bumps and made her anxious in all the intimate places that he had expert knowledge of how to relieve.

As if she'd conjured him from her desire filled and needful libido, Dominick appeared in the doorway of her room like a midnight phantom come to do wicked things. He didn't enter, but instead sent a pointed stare at her mother before refocusing his salacious gaze back on her. Valerie grinned in spite of the throbbing in her brain. The anxious nub between her legs also pulsed in the same rhythm as the pain in her head.

The unlikely vision of grabbing Dominick and forcing him to relieve the ache in her clit was punctuated by her mother's sudden snort.

Her mother's eyes opened halfway. Valerie didn't move. Didn't breathe. Hoping that her mother would just drop back off to sleep again, she purposely didn't look at her, as if to stare was to awaken the protective mother bear instincts to full potential. No such luck.

A second snort louder than the first echoed in the room. After an exaggerated blink, and as if she sensed danger for her child, Valerie's mother turned her head towards the door. Narrowing her focus on Dominick, she frowned and straightened like starch applied to a ruler.

Her mother stood quickly, and spoke as she walked. "I told you that Valerie didn't want to see you." Her amplified whisper, louder than any megaphone, echoed across the room.

"Mother!" Valerie hissed in an over-loud whisper of her own, not wanting Dominick to disappear.

Her mother halted in mid-step and shot a stern look over one shoulder. Twisting back to Dominick, she said through clenched teeth, "Now see what you've done. You woke her."

Dominick advanced into the room and the hand that had been behind his back snaked forward with a bunch of flowers clutched in his fist. He veered away from her trajectory and pointedly ignored her mother's harrumphing sound of disbelief at being thwarted.

"Hi, babe." He strolled along the side of her bed and leaned one hip on the edge. "How are you feeling?"

The utterly delectable masculine scent of him enveloped her and she could have sworn that her mouth watered in anticipation that he might kiss her. He always kissed her. She'd come to expect the sensual greeting like Pavlov's dog waiting for a treat once the bell had rung.

"My head hurts a little," she whispered.

Dominick pointedly ignored Valerie's mother and leaned over to kiss her on the lips ever so gently. Valerie sighed in utter contentment.

"You have to leave this instant." Valerie's mother regained her senses and stalked to the opposite side of the bed wearing an incredulous expression. Her mother was so rarely hindered, the disbelief across her face was almost comical.

Dominick's gaze never left her face. "Sorry it took me so long to get back."

"I didn't think you'd be back." Valerie didn't look at her mother when she spoke, but hoped that he understood.

"Oh, babe. It will take a lot more than one angry, reproachful mother to keep me away."

"Listen, Mr. Whatever-your-name-is, my daughter doesn't need *your* kind of man in her life. As I stated before—"

"Leave him alone, Mona," Valerie's father said from the hospital door. "Come along."

"I will not!" Her mother huffed and stared daggers as if her burning gaze would sway him. "We agreed that he was not the right kind of man for her."

"No. You made a snap judgment. Now, either come out on your own and leave them alone to talk or I swear I'll come in there, sling you over my shoulder and carry you out."

"Oh, really?" Her mother's anger was palpable. She turned to Valerie as if for a final order of reprieve.

"Go on with Dad, I'll be fine."

Uncertainty colored her mother's expression until Dominick straightened to his full height and spoke. "I love your daughter and I've never said that to another woman in my life. No one will ever love her the way I do. Please understand my determination."

"Mona," her father called from the door in the stern voice he saved for the rare occasions when he was angry. "Let's go. Now."

Her mother twisted away, sniffed deeply and without saying another word, exited the room.

Valerie mouthed a thank-you to her father, who nodded and winked once as he escorted her mother away.

Dominick leaned down and captured her lips in a scorching French kiss the second her parents were out of sight. A warm rush of long-denied passion blazed a path across her lips. She moaned and he stopped. "You okay, babe?"

Valerie grabbed his face and pressed her mouth to his again. Slipping her tongue between his lips for a long-awaited taste, she moaned as he tangled leisurely around the confines of her mouth as if to assure himself it was truly her.

She slid her arms around his neck to pull him closer, but he broke the kiss and inserted the flowers between them.

"These are for you." His sexy desire-filled voice made her clit throb with desire.

Valerie buried her face in the soft blossoms, and inhaled the delectable fragrance of carnations displayed in a multitude of different shades.

"Carnations. Good choice. My new favorite flower is the carnation."

"I'm glad you remembered."

She nodded, but frowned quickly. "The memories are fading really fast."

"Me, too. Which is why I'm here so late tonight. I couldn't remember the first time we kissed, so I had to come in and make a new memory." He placed the flowers on the nightstand. Cupping her head, he pressed a kiss to her temple. "I love you, Valerie. Please tell me you feel the same way."

"I'm sorry about yesterday," she said to avoid responding. "My head hurt so bad I couldn't think."

"Shh. Don't worry." He smiled. "I had to take care of some work stuff, but now I'm free for a few weeks."

She tilted her gaze to meet his. "A few weeks?"

"I had lots of vacation saved up. I'm taking some."

"What are you going to do?"

"I'm going to get married."

"What?"

He traced his thumb across her bottom lip. "Will you marry me, babe?"

Valerie knew her eyes were as wide open as possible. "But you don't even know me. Not really."

"I disagree." His grin was infectious. "I'd say that we know each other completely, deeply. Intimately."

"But not on Earth." Valerie flashed to the memories of her existence before unexpected space travel. She led a very quiet, lonely life. Certainly not one filled with guns, criminals, motorcycles or sexy undercover men. Not to mention her love life was a non-existent entity.

"So?" He brought her hand to his lips. "What difference does that make?"

"It's a huge difference."

"No. It's not. Why are you balking?"

Valerie expelled a long sigh. "There were things I did in that extended dream-like existence that I've never done here."

His eyebrows went straight up. "Like what?"

"Like," she paused and glanced at the door. "Allowing you to tie me up and blindfold me before you tortured me senseless with unseen tactile stimulation until I climaxed harder than I thought physically possible. Twice."

He laughed. "Well, that experience was new and different for me also. But so what, we'll just make new memories here."

Valerie got to the heart of the problem she wrestled with and whispered, "What if I don't measure up to all the other women you've had before?"

"Not possible." He grabbed one hand, kissed her fingers gently and added, "Babe. Contrary to your belief of what my sexual proclivities included here on Earth, I've never done that sort of thing with anyone else."

Her mouth fell open. "I don't believe it."

Dominick laughed and shrugged. "It's true. I've never shared those particular desires with anyone before. Only you."

"Well then, why did you share them with me?"

"As I recall, you goaded me into it."

Valerie's cheeks heated in memory. She *had* practically coerced him into the mild bondage games they'd played. She was afraid to admit she wanted more. Did he?

"Right. Well, like I said, I wanted to measure up."

"And instead you set the bar." He kissed her knuckles. "I won't lie to you. Now that we've crossed that line, I'll want to continue. Will that be a problem?"

Valerie lifted her shoulders, but with it came a relieved grin. "I don't know exactly what I want, but I have to admit that I'd miss that particular activity."

"You want me." He leaned in and kissed the tender spot on her neck beneath her jaw.

Time to change the subject before she lost her head and let him talk her into ruining the hospital corners. "I was told you're in law enforcement. Sorry that I thought you were a criminal yesterday."

"Technically, I *was* a criminal yesterday." He grinned engagingly. "It's all a part of the undercover work that I do."

She glanced at his gold hoop earring. "Right. Well, I'm an accounting analyst for the very stodgy law firm of Barrington, Wells and Hartford. Under rigidly conservative in the dictionary, I believe they're pictured."

"And?"

"And with your gun-toting undercover work, I simply mean that we live in different worlds. Regardless of our time in the dreamworld of space, I'm not sure if we fit together in this one."

"How will you know if you don't give us a chance?"

She shrugged. The motion of moving her shoulders made a spike-like pain thrust into her head. She put a hand to her forehead to keep her brain from trying to exit.

"All you have to do is tell me that you don't love me and you'll never see me again."

Valerie lifted her gaze to meet his. A tear slipped out before she could stop it. "You know I can't lie to you, Dominick. Just smelling you overwhelms my senses to the point that I can't think straight. I do love you." Another tear slid down her face.

"Then what's the holdup?" He wiped her tears away with gentle strokes of his thumb.

"How can you still love me after you shared me with four other men?"

"Because all of those men were me."

"That's what the Others told me right before they sent me on my merry way, but I just can't believe it. I saw you as five different personalities. Each of you looked completely different. Golden told me that because I picked your true personality that they'd give us a chance to find each other. Still, you must think I'm a whore to be willing and eager to service so many men, whatever the reason." A sharp sniff escaped to accompany the persistent runnels of moisture from her eyes. She was weak from pain and hated the tears which wouldn't stop in her fragile condition.

"Babe. It wasn't like that. I don't remember that time as sharing you with four other guys. Those men were all me and on some level I knew it even when we were there. Just as I know that you loved me and took care of me. All of me. In every possible mood and temperament and personality and not a bunch of strange guys. I wasn't even able to hide my darkest side from you. The fact that you loved my dark side best of all is why we're even here together."

Valerie's mouth opened to argue, but he stopped her with a soft kiss and whispered, "I'll tell you what. At least spend time with me here on Earth before you make up your mind."

"Okay." Valerie nodded, but the movement made her head ache worse.

"Sorry your head hurts, babe."

Valerie narrowed her eyes. "How sorry are you?"

"What do you mean?"

"I mean, are you sorry enough to help me get rid of it?"

"Of course."

She glanced over his shoulder at the open door to assure that they were alone. "I need."

His brows furrowed in confusion. "You need what?"

"Sex." Whispering the word made heat sting her cheeks. "I ache like you can't even believe."

"Don't you think we should wait—"

Valerie grabbed his hand and pressed it to her breast. "No. I don't think we should wait a moment longer."

As a barrier, the thin brushed cotton of the hospital gown was no match for his warm palm. The heat seared one nipple and it hardened beneath the fabric. She moaned, but he snatched his hand away as if he'd been scalded. Dominick stood, quickly abandoned her bedside and headed for the exit. She almost screamed in frustration until he swooshed her door closed and promptly locked it.

The feral grin shaping his lips when he turned back almost made her come.

"You should know by now that there isn't anything I wouldn't do for you, babe. Think your hospital bed is sturdy enough to hold both of us?"

Valerie shifted to the left and flipped her covers to one side to make room for him. "Guess we're about to find out."

Dominick climbed gingerly onto the bed and pulled her hospital gown all the way to her neck one-handed. His gaze lingered on the white gauze bandage marking the place where the bullet had pierced her flesh.

She covered it with her hand. "It's ugly now, but it'll heal and the scar will eventually fade."

He sighed. "It's not ugly, but I see this injury and I want to shoot Regina all over again. I wasn't prepared to let her murder me after my cover was blown, but I took particular exception to her taking aim at you once I'd escaped as far as the park. Once she recovers she'll go to prison for the rest of her life. I'll see to it."

"Shh. She's gone and we don't ever have to worry about her again. Make love to me. Help me forget. Make my head stop hurting."

Dominick settled onto the narrow bed. "Close your eyes." Once her eyes were shut, he stroked her breasts and thumbed her nipples until they peaked and then sucked on one tip until she moaned in pleasure.

One hand trailed down the center of her body until he dipped to stroke her clit and she fairly burst with an intense bolt of frenzied arousal. Still stroking her clitoris, he slid his fingers inside her slick pussy, pumping in and out several times.

Heart pounding wildly in her chest, and with an unbelievably rapid climb in arousal geared to her imminent a very desired orgasm, Valerie sucked in a sudden breath, and plummeted over the edge of a blinding climax in record time.

She stiffened and moaned deeply, trying to keep her vocal appreciation to a minimum.

"God, you're sexy when you come," he murmured a few minutes later.

Valerie opened her eyes slowly. "Do you think the nurses' station heard me?"

"We'll know in the next minute or so if they start beating on the door. How do you feel?"

"I can't believe it, but my headache isn't as bad."

"Good to know." He brushed his lips across her cheek and nuzzled her neck. "I do love you, Valerie."

"So why don't you unzip your pants and give me what I really want?"

He kissed her lips instead. "Because I forgot my handcuffs and blindfold."

"Are you kidding?"

"Yes. I prefer to use soft silky scarves to bind you. Unless you want to be cuffed?"

"Well, I don't want to take any possible sexual aids off the table."

He laughed out loud. "No problem, but I'll look around for a specialized set that won't chafe your lovely wrists."

"You don't think that once we completely forget about our time in space that we'll wake up one day and wonder why we're together, do you?"

"No. What we feel for each other is way deep inside and embedded permanently in our hearts and souls."

"Poetic. Makes me think of Johnny."

"Ah. My rarely used creative side."

Valerie thought about the other personalities and Mark popped into her mind. "So, do you wear a nipple ring?"

He chuckled. "Not anymore. I did once or twice in the past for an undercover assignment."

"Too bad. I liked it."

"Are you going to ditch me because I'm not the merciless bad boy you think you've come to know?"

"I think I need some time to adjust to you being one person and not five."

"I've been many personalities. I'm happy to resurrect the nipple ring if you liked it, but it's a real pain in the ass at airports."

"Do you remember what Hauser told me regarding why he didn't like to screw skinny women?

He laughed. "Yes."

"Prove it. Tell me."

"Because I don't like picking bones out of my dick the next day."

Valerie giggled. "I thought that was the funniest thing I'd ever heard."

"Yeah, that's me, a laugh a minute."

"What about Frasier? He seems like the most different of your personalities compared to the others."

He ducked his head. "In addition to all my merciless bad boy traits, I'm pretty good with numbers."

"Oh yeah? What's one-hundred and eighty-eight times three?"

His gaze shifted from her face and he paused for only a second before responding with, "Five-hundred and sixty four."

"Is that right? Wow. My shy little accountant's heart just went pitty pat."

A dark grin spread over his mouth. "What can I tell you, babe. I'm a multifaceted guy. Do you have any other questions?"

"Is there anything you regret?"

His brows furrowed. "I regret what happened at the park."

"No. I mean about what happened in space."

Dominick crossed his arms and tilted his head to one side. "Is there something I need to apologize for?"

Valerie sighed. "No. I meant of all the times we were together. Is there anything that you regret."

"I wish we'd been able to come back together. I wish you hadn't gotten shot and I wish I was certain that you would agree to spend the rest of your life with me."

"What you said to my mother about me being the only woman you've ever said 'I love you' to, is that true?"

"Um. Hmm. Yes."

Valerie glared at him, trying to ascertain the truth.

He rolled his eyes to the ceiling. "Okay, fine. I told Lisa Batterton that I loved her, but I was only trying to get her to give me a home-made chocolate chip cookie, and I was in the second grade. I don't think it should count against me."

Valerie grinned. "I love you, Dominick. I really do."

He leaned in close. "The second you're released from this hospital, we're on a plane to Las Vegas to get married."

She put a hand on his shoulder. "What if I want a big church wedding?"

He released a deep sigh. "Then a big church wedding is okay by me. You'll see that we belong together, babe."

Valerie smiled and hugged him tight.

"I told my mom that I'd met the perfect girl. She can't wait to meet you."

"Looks like I'm getting the better end of the deal."

"What do you mean?"

"My mother-in-law will be much more accepting of our relationship than yours."

Dominick's infectious grin made the corners of her mouth lift. "What?" she asked.

Pulling her close, he whispered, "I'm definitely getting the better end of the deal, babe."

Before she could respond he cupped her face and kissed her mouth tenderly. "Big extravagant wedding or quickie Vegas wedding?"

"What?"

"You just agreed that my mom would be your mother-in-law. That means you're marrying me. So your next choice is big or quick."

"What if I want huge, long and slow?"

"The honeymoon is a whole separate issue, babe. Let's finalize the wedding plans before we decide that."

She laughed, pleased that he could read her mind.

"Fine. Let's head for Vegas. And after we do the quick wedding, then I get the huge, long and slow honeymoon, right?"

"It's like you read my mind, babe."

MENAGERIE

THE END

WWW.LARASANTIAGO.COM

ABOUT THE AUTHOR

Lara Santiago is the bestselling author of over twelve books. She's an Ecataromance award winner, a 2007 Passionate Plume finalist for *The Lawman's Wife*, and has garnered a coveted four and half stars from Romantic Times Book Reviews for her novel, *The Blonde Bomb Tech*.

From her futuristic novels to her contemporary romantic suspense, she's known for her independent heroines and those compelling alpha males we all adore.

After turning in her twelfth manuscript, she came to the realization that this writing gig might just work out after all. She continues to dream up stories, keeping no less than ten story ideas circulating at any given time.

Please visit Lara at
www.larasantiago.com

Siren Publishing, Inc.
www.SirenPublishing.com

Printed in the United States
133973LV00004B/45/P